BLAZE

SATAN'S FURY MC- MEMPHIS CHAPTER

L. WILDER

DEDICATION

To all the sexy bikers who give us something to fantasize about.

Editor: Lisa Cullinan

Proofreader- Rose Holub @RoseReads

Proofreader- Sue Banner

Teasers & Banners: Gel Ytayz at Tempting Illustrations

Personal Assistant: Natalie Weston PA

Catch up with the entire Satan's Fury MC Series today!

All books are FREE with Kindle Unlimited!

❦ Created with Vellum

PROLOGUE

*M*emphis, Tennessee had never been your typical city. While the melody of jazz music played down on Beale Street, tourists visited Graceland, and society folks had a drink at the Peabody, deep within the city, there were infamous gangs and rival MCs fighting to take control. Countless conflicts often ended with death and destruction, but when it was all said and done, there was always one that stood above the rest —Satan's Fury MC. With blood, sweat, and tears, they'd claimed the territory. In doing so, the club had made quite a name for itself and was considered the most notorious MC in the Southeast. The mere rumble of their motorcycles roaring by would bring a sense of fear to anyone who heard it, for there wasn't a single soul who didn't know the bedlam they could cause when they came toe to toe with an adversary. Over the years, these bloody confrontations had become legendary in the city where the King of Rock and Roll had once lived.

I'd been a member for almost ten years—patched in

just after my twenty-first birthday. From day one, I learned that even though we'd won many battles, the war to keep our territory secure was far from over. Every day there was a certain amount of bullshit to deal with: a fight to be had or a trigger to be pulled. It was just our way of life. For us, the club wasn't just a group of guys who put on second-rate cuts, pretending to be some kind of hotshot on a crotch-rocket. We were family through and through, and there wasn't one of us who wouldn't take a bullet for a brother. We believed what we had was worth dying for, and when someone put our family in jeopardy, we didn't think twice about taking them down—just like the night when we'd discovered that one of our runners had been skimming from the top.

I'd been asleep for hours when Murphy, our sergeant-at-arms, called my burner. I quickly answered, "Yeah?"

"Need you to get over to the warehouse. Runt's on his way to pick up Johnny and bring him over there so Gus can have a word with him."

Gus was the kind of president who stayed on top of things, and when it came to his club, nothing got by him —*nothing*. "At this hour, I'm guessing he's not wanting to talk about tonight's Cubs game?"

"Fuck no. That asshole came up short on this week's payout."

"How short?"

"Just over three grand."

"You're fucking kidding me."

Three grand wasn't even a drop in the bucket where our drug distribution was concerned. In a week's time, we pulled in ten times that amount, but that wasn't the point. Under no circumstances did anyone ever steal from the club—*period*. As I pulled myself out of the bed, Murphy grumbled, "No joke, brother. Now, get your ass over to the warehouse. We'll meet you there."

"I'm on my way."

It was one of those hot, sultry summer nights in July, and even though it was well after midnight, the air was thick with humidity. The wind could do little to keep the sweat from beading across my forehead as I parked behind the warehouse. I headed over to Runt's SUV and watched as he hauled Johnny out of the back, dragging his feet across the gravel as he took him inside.

Runt motioned his head towards the truck as he ordered, "Get Terry out of the back."

Finding the other man cowering down on the floorboard with a pillowcase on his head, I reached in and grabbed him, following Runt inside. We dumped them both in the center of the warehouse as we gathered around, watching Runt remove Johnny's blindfold. When Johnny finally got a good look at the man who'd kidnapped him, his eyes grew wide with terror. Hell, I couldn't blame him for being scared shitless. One look at Runt, and any man would be shaking in his fucking boots. He was our club's enforcer, and at six foot seven and three hundred and forty pounds of muscle, he was the biggest, most intimidating brother in the club. He had a knack for turning a man, big or small, into a pathetic, groveling mass of flesh, and this poor bastard didn't stand a chance —nor did his sidekick, Terry, who was sitting beside him.

When I yanked the pillowcase off of his head, Terry lost it. "Please, man. I didn't have nothing to do with this shit!"

"Um-hmm," I scoffed. We all knew he didn't have

3

anything to do with his buddy's mishandling of funds, but we brought him along for the show, knowing he'd spread the word about everything that was about to take place. *I* wasn't about to let him know that, so with a condescending tone, I told him, "Whatever you say, Terry."

"I mean it, man. I got no idea what he did, but I give you my word. I'm clean, man. I wasn't no part of his bull-shit." He looked over to Johnny and shouted, "Tell 'em, J. Tell 'em I didn't have nothing to do with this shit."

He didn't say a word. He couldn't. He knew he'd fucked up, and there were consequences to be had—deadly consequences. The second Johnny saw Gus walking in his direction, he nearly lost his shit. The blood drained from his face, and the vein in his neck started pulsing out of control. He knew what was coming. He was well aware that our president had a reputation for dishing out some pretty grim retributions, especially for those who tried to double-cross the club like he had done, so it came as no surprise when the motherfucker started to completely freak out. Like a wild animal, he used every ounce of strength he had to try and break free from Runt's grasp, but it was no use. He was no match for our enforcer, and he ended up with his face planted on the hard, concrete floor. As Gus approached him, Johnny started to beg, "I'm sorry, man. I'll get your money back. I promise. Just let me make a phone call and I promise I'll get it back."

Gus crossed his arms, causing his muscles to bulge as they rippled down from his shoulder to his forearm. His fierce appearance was intimidating, to say the least, as he looked at him with disgust. "It's a little late for all that, don't ya think, Johnny boy?"

"I was gonna pay you back, Gus. I swear it. My girl just had a baby, and with all the doctor bills, I got behind." There was something in his voice that made me believe him when he said, "I wouldn't have taken it, but the baby needed some food, man ... She'd been crying all goddamned night, and it was fucking with my head. The money was sitting right there ... I know it was stupid. I know that, and I'm sorry. Just give me a chance, and I'll get your money back."

"So, you're telling me you stole for your kid?"

"Yeah. I didn't have a choice, man."

With a shake of his head, Gus looked to Runt and said, "Pull him up."

Runt gave Johnny a quick tug, and once he was up on his knees, Gus reached for his arm and pushed up his shirt sleeve, revealing countless track marks. Gus growled, "You're a real piece of shit, asshole. Blaming your kid when you've been using my money to buy fucking drugs."

Suddenly, panic crossed his face. "Those are from a long time ago. I haven't used in months."

Murphy shook his head and grumbled, "Only one thing worse than a thief, and that's a fucking liar."

Hoping that he could persuade Gus to give him a break, Johnny immediately started pleading, "Come on, Gus. I've been working for you for a long time, man. I've helped make you a lot of money, and I just fucked up this one time. You gotta give me another chance."

Gus sighed as he looked over to Johnny and said, "My old man was a farmer. He had over five hundred acres of land and the best stock of horses any man could own. We had us a couple of field hands, and one of them was a good man ... had himself a daughter about my age, and he worked real hard to make a decent life for his wife and kid. But back then, life was tough and he fell on hard times. One night my father found him stealing feed out of one of our barns. Now, at the time, I didn't think much of it. I mean ... what's the big deal about borrowing a little feed, but then, I was just a kid. What the hell did I know?" He reached in his pocket and took out his pack of cigarettes. As he lit one up, he continued, "My father was one of the richest men around with pockets filled with cash. Losing a little straw and grain wasn't gonna hurt nothing, so let me ask ya ... What do you think he should've done about this guy taking feed from his barn?"

Johnny's voice trembled as he answered, "I think he should've given him another chance."

"I can see where you might think that, but like my father explained it to me—it wasn't the first time he'd stolen from my old man. It was just the first time he'd actually been caught."

"Not me, man! This was the first time ... the only time —I swear it!"

"You and I both know that's not true." Gus pulled his gun from its holster and aimed it at his head. "A few dollars here. A few dollars there. That shit adds up, Johnny, but I'll set your mind at ease. I'll see to it that your stripper girlfriend and daughter are taken care of."

And with that, Gus pulled the trigger. When the bullet pierced through his head, blood spewing in all directions, Terry dropped to his knees in horror. He brought his hands up to his head and squalled, "Oh, *shit*. Oh, *fuck*. You fucking killed him."

When he noticed Gus walking towards him, his mouth

clamped shut and the room filled with a deafening silence. Gus slowly knelt down beside him and placed his hand on his shoulder. With a stern voice, he told him, "You don't fuck with the Fury, kid. You'd do good to remember that."

He nodded. "Yes, sir. I got it."

"Good." As he stood up, Gus looked over to Runt and ordered, "Get his ass out of here."

Runt nodded, and as he loaded him up in the SUV, Murphy turned to me and asked, "You good with cleaning this shit up?"

"Yeah. I'll take care of it."

Gus patted me on the back and said, "Go home, brother. I'll get a couple of prospects over here to take care of this."

"You sure? I can—"

He shook his head. "Go home, Blaze. We've got the run tomorrow. I'll need you at your best."

"Understood." I lifted my chin, and then started walking out of the warehouse to head towards my bike. My neighbor was sitting with my son, Kevin, and I was eager to get back to make sure he was okay. "I'll see you at the club first thing in the morning."

Before I exited, Gus yelled, "Be sure to tell Kevin I'm expecting to see that class project he's been working on."

"You got it."

Life as a member of Satan's Fury wasn't always butter-flies and fucking rainbows, but there'd never been a time when I'd regretted becoming a member. My brothers were always there when I needed them. After my ol' lady died in a car crash, they stood right by my side, helping me carry the weight of my grief. I was just getting back on my feet when I found out our son, Kevin, was diagnosed with leukemia, and if it hadn't been for the club, there was no doubt that I would have given up hope. As always, they never let me down, and their support helped us both get through one of the toughest times in my life. I owed them so much, and through them I learned that having family isn't just important—it's fucking everything.

BLAZE

*I*t was my favorite time of day: long before anyone else was awake and the sun was just starting to filter through the blinds. I was laying in my bed listening to nothing but the sounds of my own breathing. Kevin was still sleeping soundly in his room, so I had just a few brief moments to myself where I could begin to prepare myself for the day ahead; one that not only included getting Kevin up and ready for school, but also another big run with the guys. I just wanted to lay there and enjoy the silence for a little while longer, but my alarm went off for the second time, letting me know that my moment of peace was over. I pulled the covers back and got out of bed, rubbing the sleep out of my eyes as I headed to the bathroom for a shower. Once I was done, I got dressed and went into the kitchen to make Kevin some breakfast. Just as I was about to pour myself a cup of coffee, there was a light tap at my back door. Seconds later, I heard the rattle of keys as they unlocked the door, and my mother stepped inside.

"Morning."

"Sorry, I'm late. Your father had one of his spells last night, and I wanted to make sure he was okay before I left."

"Why didn't you call me?" I asked as I offered her a cup of coffee.

"I didn't see the point in bothering you. Besides, after he had a breathing treatment, he was fine."

My father had COPD, a lung disease that obstructed airflow to, well ... the lungs, and he was on a shitload of medication that was supposed to help him breathe. Unfortunately, he refused to give up smoking, so he was only getting worse. "He wouldn't have to do so many breathing treatments if he'd just stop smoking."

"I'm well aware of that, Sawyer," she grumbled, "but your father has a mind of his own."

She was right. He'd always been one to do things his way and wouldn't listen to anyone, especially my mother. It was one of the reasons I was glad they lived close by. After I fixed my coffee, I turned back to her and said, "I don't know why he has to be so damned stubborn."

"You're one to talk," she said in a huff. "Leaving home at all hours of the night, doing who knows what and leaving Kevin with strangers. It's just not right."

"Angie isn't a stranger. She's been living next door to us for six years, Mom. She's a teller at the bank, and she goes to your church. I think it's safe to say that she can be trusted to stay with Kevin for a couple of hours."

"Yes, well ... That doesn't make it right," she chided.

"Are you done? Cause I need to wake Kevin up."

"He's still asleep? We need to leave in twenty minutes!"

"Yeah, but I'll get him up and going," I yelled to her as I

started down the hall. I opened his door and walked over to the bed. "Hey, buddy. You need to get up."

His shaggy blond hair fell over his eyes as he rolled over and groaned, "*Ah, man. Do I have to?*"

I sat down on the edge of the bed and ran my hand roughly over his back. "Yep. You know how your grandmother gets upset when you're late."

"She's taking me to school again?" he whined.

"I told you last night that I had a run today."

He sat up in the bed and his blue eyes grew intense. "When will you be back?"

"Sometime late tonight."

"So, you'll be back in time for my game tomorrow?" he asked sounding hopeful.

"Absolutely. I wouldn't miss it, bud. You know that."

"Good, because coach said he was gonna put me in as quarterback," my little man's voice boasted with pride.

Kevin had wanted to play ball since he was old enough to walk, but that got put on hold when we found out he had leukemia. After losing his mother at such an early age, it was a hard pill to swallow, but he got through it—we both did. Since he'd been in remission, Kevin was bound and determined to make up for lost time, and when he asked to play peewee football, there was no way I could tell him no. I smiled as I stood up and said, "Of course, you are. You've got the best arm on the team. Now, move it, kid, or you're gonna be late for school. I'll have your breakfast ready in two minutes."

"Okay." Just as I was about to walk out of the room, Kevin called, "Hey, Dad?"

"Yeah?"

"Be careful today."

"Always."

Once I'd given Kevin his breakfast, I made my way over to the clubhouse to meet up with the guys. Thankfully, it didn't take me long to get there. It was just a few miles from the house, on the south side of the city. When I pulled up, the guys were done loading up and were standing around their old pickup trucks, and like me, none of them were wearing their cuts. Since we had joined up with our other club chapters and created a new pipeline, we would be carrying a load that contained shipments from five of our fellow chapters. We didn't want to draw any unwanted attention as we transported our load to Louisiana, so we had to get creative. Thinking no one would suspect a few farmers, Gus rigged up a couple of his dad's old horse trailers with hidden compartments under the floor, making it possible for us to hide all the artillery beneath the horses. While it took a little extra work, these runs had been a profitable venture between our clubs, and there were worse things in the world than hauling horses down south.

As soon as I parked my bike, I noticed Riggs, one of my younger brothers in the club, standing beside the trailer in a pair of faded jeans and a plain-white t-shirt. The ladies often called him tall, dark and handsome, but I didn't see it. To me, Riggs was just a smooth-talking pain in the ass. We'd both grown a habit of giving each other a hard time, so I wasn't surprised when I noticed the shit-eating grin on his face. "Well, good morning, sunshine. I'm glad to see you finally made it."

"Fuck off, Riggs. I'm twenty minutes early." Technically, I really was early, but some of the guys had it in their heads that everyone should arrive thirty minutes before the declared time. They thought it made them seem more eager or invested in the club. I thought it was a bunch of bullshit. If you want me somewhere at seven-thirty, then just say *seven-thirty*. It's not that fucking difficult. I got off my bike and started towards the others. "Unlike you, I've got responsibilities."

"Hey, *I've got responsibilities!*" he replied sounding defensive.

"Taking your flavor of the week home doesn't count."

"That hurts, man."

"Um-hmm," I grumbled. "Where's Gauge? I figured by now he'd be sitting on go."

"He went to track down Murph. It shouldn't be much longer."

I ran my hand over my beard and sighed, wishing I'd taken the time to have one more cup of coffee before I left the house. I knew the guys were starting to get anxious when I heard Runt growl, "Fuck, if I know, but he needs to hurry his ass up. I'm ready to get on the road."

Just as the words came out of his mouth, the back door flew open, and Gus came barreling out the door with Gauge and Murphy following behind him. He headed over to the trailers to give them the once-over, making sure they were loaded to his liking. When he got to the second trailer, he shouted, "Runt!"

An uneasy look crossed his face as Runt walked over to Gus. "Yeah?"

"Secure that second latch," he ordered before turning his attention to us. "Just got off the phone with Cotton. I told him we were right on schedule. Let's keep it that way."

Cotton was the president of the Fury chapter up in

13

Washington. He and his brothers were responsible for getting the pipeline underway, and there was no way in hell we could let them down. Knowing how important it was, we answered, "Understood."

Runt eased into the trailer, and once he'd locked the hidden latch, Gus gave his nod of approval. "Looks good. You guys are ready to roll."

"You heard what the man said." Murphy motioned his hand forward, "Let's move it!"

In a matter of seconds, we were on the road and driving towards Louisiana. Thankfully, we got down to Baton Rouge without any complications. When we pulled up to the old, dilapidated warehouse, Riggs jabbed me in the side with his elbow and said, "We're here."

"I see that, smart one." I scowled. "Now, move your ass."

As soon as we got out of the truck, Murphy went over to talk to Ronin, our distributor. We'd done well when we'd chosen Murph as our sergeant-at-arms. Not only was he a fucking badass who could handle any adversary, he was levelheaded and knew how to work the business side of the club. Murphy was respected by some of the most notorious criminals in the South. Once he and Ronin finished discussing the plan for distribution, Ronin's guys came over to help us unload. Riggs held the trailer door open while I led the two mares over to the side of the warehouse. With the horses out of the way, Murphy released the hidden compartment, and we started to unload. Ronin motioned us over to the backside of the barge and shouted, "Over here, guys."

He opened the hatch at the bottom of the grain container, and we stashed our crates in the space hidden beneath it, which would be completely concealed once it was filled. At this point, we'd all broken out in a sweat. As we headed back to the truck, Riggs wiped his brow as he complained, "It's hotter'n blue blazes out here."

"It's this fucking humidity," Lowball grumbled. He'd patched in a few months back, and over the past year, he'd proven himself to be a real asset to the club. Yeah, Lowball looked like the rest of our motley crew, every bit rough around the edges, but he was actually really fucking smart and had helped me a lot at the garage. He ran his fingers through his dark hair and said, "Makes me thirsty for a cold beer."

"You ain't lying. I could use a twelve-pack right about now," Riggs agreed.

As I started towards the side of the warehouse, I turned to him and called out, "Quit your bitchin', and help me get these horses back on the trailer so we can get the hell out of here."

Before we headed out, Murph went over to Ronin and shook his hand, "You know the routine. Keep Gus posted on the load."

From the dock, the barge would carry everything down the Mississippi River, and once it reached the final port down by the Gulf, it was up to Ronin to see that everything was delivered to our buyers. The club had been working with him for as long as I'd been a member, and time after time, he'd proven himself loyal to the brothers. Ronin nodded and said, "You know I will."

"Thanks, brother."

We'd been lucky today. We hadn't run into any cops or had to deal with any assholes who thought they had what it took to steal our load. Those made for long, drawn-out days that often ended with several guys having bullets in their heads. I'd say it was a pretty good day. After Murphy jumped in his truck, he put in a call to Gus, letting him know that we'd secured the load. Once he was done, we followed him back out on the road and started towards home, only stopping once to fuel up and to get a bite to eat. By the time we finally pulled through the gate at the clubhouse, it was well after dark, and we were all exhausted. After being cooped up in a cage for over twelve hours, we were all ready to stretch our legs and grab a beer.

As soon as we stepped into the clubhouse, I could feel myself start to relax. Something about that building just did it for me. I'd always liked the fact that it was once an old train depot that the club had bought and renovated. It took some work, but they created over thirty rooms, which included a full kitchen, a bar, and our conference room. It was pretty quiet when we got to the bar. Most of the guys had already gone home for the night or were off in their rooms having a run with one of the hang-arounds, which suited me fine. All I wanted was to suck down a cold one and get home to a hot shower and my bed. Riggs and I had just sat down when Murphy came over to us. He grabbed a beer and blew out a breath, "Damn. It's been a long one."

He'd just gotten the words out of his mouth when, Sadie, one of the hang-arounds, slipped up behind him. "Hey there, handsome. Did you have a good trip?"

"Um-hmm," he mumbled, obviously uninterested in pursuing anything with her.

She didn't take the hint and plopped herself down on

the stool across from him. "It's been pretty slow here tonight."

With his dark, shaggy hair and blue eyes, he had that James Dean look going for him, and the girls couldn't get enough of it. They all wanted to get their claws into him, but Murphy wasn't having it. He had his rules, and he wasn't breaking 'em—not for any chick. Ignoring Sadie altogether, he took a slug off his beer and turned to me. "You working at the garage tomorrow?"

"Yeah. Why?"

"I was thinking I'd bring the truck in for a tune up. It was riding a little rough today."

"Bring it on in. I'll take care of it."

"Thanks, brother." He stood up and took his beer off the counter. "I'll see you in the morning."

When she realized he was leaving, Sadie looked up at him with a pout. "You're leaving?"

"It's been a long day, doll."

Her lips curled into a seductive smile as she purred, "I could help you end it on a good note."

I could see the wheels turning in his head as he considered her offer, and seconds later he responded, "Let's see what you've got."

With that, she followed him down the hall. "That chick's never gonna learn," Riggs said while he shook his head.

"Nope." It was gonna take one hell of a woman to make him want more than a quick lay. After I finished off my beer, I stood up and said, "I better get to the house. If I know Kevin, he's up waiting for me."

"I'm sure he is." Riggs chuckled. "Tell him I said hello."

"Will do."

As I headed for the door, Riggs called out, "I'll see you at the garage in the morning."

The sun had gone down hours ago when I walked out to the parking lot and hopped on my Harley. As soon as I turned the key and the engine roared to life, the sound alone made the tension of the day start to subside. It was just me, my bike, and the road winding out before me in the night air as I pulled out onto the highway. Memphis was always a beautiful city, especially after dark when she was all lit up. I loved passing by the Arkansas Bridge and the Pyramid. As I pushed the throttle forward, it was as if I was the only man on earth; with the wind whipping around me, I couldn't think of any better therapy. By the time I made it home, my mind was cleared, and I was ready to say goodnight to my son and call it a day.

KENADEE

*W*hen I was growing up, my father had it set in his mind that I was going to do great things in this world. I wasn't exactly sure where he got that grand notion, especially since we lived in a small, no-name town on the outskirts of Fayette County where nobody did anything all that spectacular. I had no idea how a girl like me could make a mark on the world. I was tall and lanky with knobby knees and wild, unruly hair. I could barely ride my bike around the block without having some kind of accident. I tried to convince him that he was wrong about me, but he wouldn't listen. Instead, he'd simply say, *"People who are crazy enough to believe that they can achieve something great are the ones who usually do."* I let his words sink in and decided that he was right. I'd always wanted to be a nurse, and I was going to be the best damn nurse I could possibly be. With his words pushing me forward, I set off to college determined to get my degree. Several years later, I found myself working as a nurse at Regional Hospital in Memphis.

I had no idea that I'd signed up to work in a battlefield. I don't know why I was so surprised. I was in Memphis after all. Like all big cities, she had her fair share of gangs and criminals. It often seemed like they were the ones running the streets, and there was little the police could do to stop them. Gunshot victims, young and old, were constantly streaming into our trauma center, and it was my job to keep them from bleeding to death until the doctors arrived. The things I saw were often disheartening, and more times than not made me downright angry, but there was still a part of me that wanted to believe that I could make a difference. But with each life lost, each child who died in our ER, I started to have my doubts. The only thing that kept me going were the people I worked with. I wasn't sure if I was being naïve, but their spirit and positive attitudes gave me hope for a better tomorrow, and I'd made friendships that would last a lifetime, especially with Robyn.

We were polar opposites in every way. Where I was straight-laced and followed all the rules, she was footloose and fancy free, doing whatever she pleased, whenever she pleased. Since she was a blonde bombshell with a mouth like a sailor and a figure that made men drool, no one ever questioned her. With her crazy antics, I never knew what to expect. She made life interesting, and I couldn't have been more pleased when she suggested that we move in together. Living in the city wasn't exactly cheap, so it was great to have someone to share the expenses with. After a few weeks of looking, we'd found a cute, little apartment that was just a few miles away from the hospital. I loved it, and needless to say, living with Robyn was never boring.

We'd been working nonstop, and it had become one of

our routines to pick up some dinner on our way home from work. Normally, we'd just hit up a drive-thru and grab something quick before we headed home, but apparently, Robyn had grown tired of fast food. "Why don't we call an order in to Daisy Mae's? I'm craving a burger and fries, and not one of those that takes five days to digest."

"Daisy Mae's sounds amazing. Do you think they'll have it ready by the time we get there?"

"If not, we can wait for it. It's not like we have anything to do tonight."

"Okay. I'll give them a call."

"Awesome," she answered excitedly. "I want the usual and … oh, get us an order of those fried green tomatoes, too."

"You got it."

I placed our order, then I went over to the nurses' station to grab my things. After we said our goodbyes, we went downstairs to my car. When we got to the diner, I wasn't surprised to see that it was crowded. Daisy Mae's was known for their amazing burgers and shakes, and it was a hotspot for not only tourists but the locals as well. I parked the car next to a long line of motorcycles, and as I opened the door, I turned to Robyn and said, "It might be a minute. They look pretty busy."

"Yeah, but they're always busy." Then, she reached for the door handle. "I'll go with you."

We got out of the car and headed towards the diner. As soon as we stepped inside, my stomach started to growl. With an exaggerated expression, Robyn turned to me and said, "Oh my God! It smells so freaking good in here! I can almost taste their French fries right now."

"Me, too. I'm starving. I haven't eaten since breakfast."

When I noticed the pies sitting on the counter, I suggested, "Maybe we should've ordered dessert, too. *Gah!* Look at that blueberry pie."

"I'll tell her to add it." Robyn went over to the register and told the waitress that we were there to pick up an order. Seconds later she returned and said, "I added some pie, but our order's still gonna be a minute. You want to grab a seat while we wait?"

"Sure."

I took a quick look around the diner, and as I searched for a place to sit, my attention was drawn to the men sitting at the front counter. And then my eyes landed on *him*. At first, all I could see was his back, but he still drew my attention. There was something about the way he positioned himself on that stool, the width of his shoulders, and all that black clothing. *Then, he turned around.* At that moment I swore the earth stood still, and I suddenly found it difficult to breathe, like all the air had been pulled from my lungs. I tried to turn away, but couldn't. For whatever reason, I was drawn to this guy, and as I fought the urge to step towards him, I heard Robyn say, "Holy cow. Check out that guy at the counter. He's freakin' hot."

We'd both crossed paths with plenty of bikers before, but never once had I seen one who'd looked like him. With just one glance, my traitorous body was feeling things that it had no business feeling, especially for a man who represented everything that I despised. He wasn't just *any* biker. Along with the others at the counter, he was wearing a Satan's Fury cut, which clearly warned everyone around that he was a member of the most notorious motorcycle club in the country. There wasn't a person in the entire city who didn't know how dangerous these guys could be—that they'd killed the very men who'd come through my ER. It should've been enough to make me look away, but it wasn't—not even close, and I cursed myself for it.

Without taking my eyes off him, I replied, "Yeah, he's hot, but—"

"No buts about it, Dee. That man is *fine!*"

She was right. One look at this badass biker and any woman would swoon, even if he was a vicious killer. With his dirty blond hair and rippling muscles, he was good looking—*extremely good looking*, and as I stood there staring at him, I imagined what it would feel like to have the arms of such a strong and dangerous man like him wrapped around me. The very thought had me spellbound, and while I knew it was wrong—very, very wrong —I couldn't stop myself. My heart pounded. My knees trembled. And just when I feared I might do something I would probably regret, he turned and looked right at me. As soon as those gorgeous blue eyes met mine, the entire room grew still. While it was just a moment's glance, it was enough to leave a lasting impression long after he'd turned his attention back to the men next to him. I could still feel the heat of his stare on my skin, making my entire body hum with an unexpected thrill of desire. *Damn.*

I was still trying to gather my composure when Robyn nudged me with her elbow. "Watch this."

To my horror, Robyn turned and started walking towards the group of men. With a warning tone, I hissed, "Robyn! *Wait!*"

Ignoring me, she kept going. Seconds later, she walked

up to a biker who was sitting beside the man who'd caught my eye. I watched with dread as she tapped him on the shoulder, and when the dark-haired, burly brute turned to look at her, she gave him one of her sexy little smiles. "Hey there, good lookin'. I saw you sitting over here, and I just had to come over and ask … Have you and I met somewhere before?"

With one of his eyebrows arched, his dark eyes slowly roamed over her small frame, and I suddenly became jealous of how good she looked in her scrubs. Where mine hung on me like a paper sack and had dancing sheep all over them, hers were bright magenta and fit snuggly over her perfect curves. Apparently, the big, bad biker was pretty smitten with her because he replied, "Can't say that we have, darlin' … cause there's no way in hell I'd ever forget a woman as beautiful as you."

"Well, aren't you the sweetest thing, and so handsome, too," her voice purred, and I rolled my eyes. "You got a name, good-looking?"

I shouldn't have been surprised by Robyn's behavior. She'd always been a big flirt, but this guy looked like he wanted to devour her, making me worry that she'd picked the wrong man to tangle with. I was about to intervene when the waitress called out to me, "Hey, Hun. Your order is ready."

Well, Craptastic. I went over to the register, paid our bill, and thanked the pretty, young waitress.

"No problem." She smiled. "I hope you enjoy it."

I glanced back over at Robyn, and she was still carrying on with her new biker friend. Knowing I couldn't leave without her, I started walking in her direction, but it was simply too crowded to get over there with my hands full of our food.

"Robyn!" I called out to her, but she couldn't hear me. Feeling a little flustered, I finally turned back to the waitress and asked, "Could you do me a tiny favor?"

"I can try." She smiled. "Whatcha need?"

"Can you let my friend know that I'm taking our food out to the car?" I pleaded.

"Sure thing."

"Thanks."

As I started towards the door, I looked over at Robyn one last time. Damn. She was laying it on thick, laughing and tossing her long blonde hair, and I doubted that she'd even care that I was leaving. Just as I was about to reach for the door, I started to lose my grip on the bag of food. I tried to adjust my hold, but it wasn't working. I was about to drop everything, when I heard a man's voice behind me, "Need a hand?"

I turned to see who'd offered to help me, and my breath caught in my throat when I saw that it was *him*—the hot biker. Before I could forge a response, he lifted the bag right out of my arms. I was a little startled by his actions, so it took me a moment before I mumbled, "Um … thank you. I guess."

"No problem." He was standing just inches away, and I found myself feeling overly nervous. I couldn't tell if I was in fear for my life or if I was simply so attracted to him that I didn't know what to do with myself—or maybe it was both. "Where you headed with all this?"

Trying not to sound like a complete nutcase, I told him, "Just out to my car. I'm parked right out front."

He nodded, and then, with my bag of food in tow, he

headed out the front door. I wasn't sure this whole thing was a good idea, but with Robyn acting like a wench in heat, I really didn't have a choice. Following him outside, I showed him to my car. "It's right over here."

"I'm right behind ya."

We walked over to my car, and I nervously unlocked the door and placed our drinks in the cup holders. When I turned back around to face him, I quickly realized that he was even more gorgeous up close, and again, I found it difficult to speak. "Thank you for your help."

A playful look flashed across his face as he said, "Well, I might've had an ulterior motive."

"Oh? What's that?"

"Walking a beautiful woman to her car." He smirked.

His comment surprised me, and I found myself blushing. "Well, either way, I still really appreciate it."

"Not a problem." As I put the bag in the car, I heard him ask, "So, you from around here?"

I had no idea why he even asked. We came from completely different worlds, but a part of me liked the fact that a man who lived such an exhilarating life would want to know anything about me. "Kind of. I grew up about an hour from here in a small town you've probably never heard of."

His voice was deep and demanding, but *oh, so very sexy,* and it sent shivers down my spine as he said, "Try me."

Seeing that devious look on his face there was no way I could refuse. "LaGrange. It's out in—"

"In Fayette County. Yeah, I know it well." He crossed his muscular arms and leaned against my car. "It's got all those historical antebellum homes."

"Yeah, that's right. I'm impressed you knew that."

"There's not much I don't know."

His playful smirk had my heart hammering in my chest like it never had before, and I found myself smiling ear to ear. "Is that right?"

"Um-hmm." He took a quick glance down at my scrubs and asked, "So, you're a nurse?"

"Yes. I work over at Regional." As I looked down at his leather vest, I found myself wondering what he did when he wasn't riding his bike. "And you? What do you do?"

"Nothing as cool as saving lives."

"Well now. Let's not get carried away. I'm more like the middle man. I stabilize, take blood pressure, and put in IV's. I wouldn't say that I've actually saved any lives … unless you count the time I did the Heimlich maneuver on a guy who was choking on his cough drop." I giggled.

"Oh, yeah. I'd definitely count that." His entire body shook as he laughed. Damn. He was handsome. With his muscles and tattoos, I should've found him menacing, but he wasn't—not in the least. In fact, he seemed quite the opposite, and even though I knew it was the last thing I should be doing, I enjoyed talking to him. To make matters worse, I wanted to know everything about the dangerous biker. I was walking a fine line, and I didn't even care. "I work down at the club's garage."

"You know, there's some people who would say that our jobs have a lot in common. You clean carburetors and replace batteries. I change bed pans and administer medications. We do what we do to keep the world running."

"Yeah. If you say so," he scoffed. He motioned his head towards the diner "Is that your friend back there?"

As I looked back through the diner's window, I could

see Robyn talking to the guy at the counter. I nodded. "Yeah. That's my roommate, Robyn."

"I think she might be interested in my brother, Runt."

"Yeah. Maybe just a little bit." I laughed. "She has a bit of a thing for tall, dark, and dangerous."

My heart nearly jumped out of my chest when his eyes quickly skirted over me, checking me out. "What about you. You got a thing for tall, dark, and dangerous?"

"I wouldn't say that." I smiled.

"No?" he pushed.

"For one thing, I don't really have time to date, and ... I don't really have a type, especially not one that includes *tall, dark, and dangerous.*"

"So, you're not seeing anyone?"

"No. I'm not seeing anyone."

A strange look crossed his face as he gave me a quick nod. "Good to know."

"Well? What about you? Is it just you and your Harley, or do you have a special lady in your life?"

He tilted his head to the side as he asked, "What makes you think I've got a Harley?"

"Don't all serious bikers ride a Harley?"

"If they're not, I feel sorry for 'em." He smiled. "And I'm not dating anyone at the moment."

When a large group of people came out of the diner, he glanced over his shoulder and said, "I guess I better get back in there."

"Okay. It was really nice talking to you."

"Yeah, it was." As he started towards the diner, he looked over to me and said, "You know, your girl is still inside. You want me to send her out for ya?"

"Oh, yeah. That would be great."

He nodded, and just before he stepped inside the diner, he looked back over to me. "It isn't exactly safe out here. Do us both a favor and get inside your car and lock your doors."

"Okay." I smiled and gave him a quick wave as I got in my car, locking the doors behind me. I watched as he headed inside the diner, and I found myself wondering if I would ever see this biker again—I really hoped I would.

BLAZE

$\mathcal{I}$t had been a long time since a woman had turned my head, but when she walked into the diner, I couldn't take my eyes off her. She was one good looking woman with long, dark hair and coal-black eyes. It wasn't simply because she was beautiful. No. It was so much more than that. There was light inside of her, one that shined deep within her. As a man filled with darkness, I found myself drawn to it. I hadn't realized just how long I'd been hungry for it until I saw her. Now, I would use any excuse to get close to it. When I noticed her struggling with her bag of takeout, I took my chance. I went over and reached for her food, lifting it out of her hands just before she dropped it on the floor. I followed her out to her car, and as we started talking, I found myself more intrigued than ever. I couldn't get enough of her, and with every piece of information she shared, I only became hungry for more. She simply captivated me, and I didn't want our conversation to end. Unfortunately, I didn't have a choice. She was ready to leave and her friend was

still inside the diner. Without thinking of the consequences, I volunteered to send her out. After I took one
more lingering look, I went back inside and sent the
blonde bombshell on her way.

As soon as she walked out the door, Runt turned to me
and started bitching, "What the fuck was that?"

"Her friend was out there waiting for her." I couldn't
blame him for being pissed. There was no doubt that the
hot, little number was into him, and I'd ruined his chance
of hooking up with her.

"So what? She could've kept waiting," he growled.

"Come on, Runt." Murphy chuckled. "It's not like you
didn't get her number. You'll still get your chance."

"Maybe … if Blaze doesn't fuck that up, too." He
looked over at me and shook his head. "Fucking
cock-block."

Thankfully, Cyrus came over and distracted him by
asking, "You guys need anything else?"

"I couldn't eat another bite, brother."

Murphy turned and looked at the crowd of folks
behind us. "Looks like another busy night."

"You ain't kidding, brother." Cyrus chuckled as he said,
"I need a beer and foot rub."

"If you're looking for volunteers, you're barking up the
wrong fucking tree, brother."

While it sucked to hear that he was having a rough
day, it was good to see that the restaurant was doing so
well. Having a big crowd meant that money was changing
hands—lots of money—and that was always a good thing,
especially for the club. We'd been using Daisy Mae's to
cycle funds for years, and we were lucky enough to have
Cyrus and his sister, Louise, to keep things going. We all

knew they argued like cats and dogs, but whether they liked to admit it or not, they made a good team. Cyrus was one hell of a cook and his sister was great at running numbers; with the two of them running the show, they'd made quite a name for our little diner. He gave me a go to hell look as he said, "I'd rather have a finger in my ass than have your hands on my damn feet, asshole."

"I guess it depends on whose finger was in your ass." Runt snickered.

"Alright, I've had enough of this shit," Murphy complained as he stood up.

"Where you running off to?"

"Got an early one tomorrow," he told us as he tossed a twenty on the counter. "Since it's a new dealer, Gus wants me with T-Bone and Lowball when they pick up that shipment in Arkansas."

"You gonna be back in time to help me pull the engine out of that Chevy tomorrow afternoon?" I asked.

"Planning on it." As he started for the door, he looked over to Runt and said, "Don't forget to call that nurse. You wait too long, and she might come to her senses about you."

"Keep talking smack, wise-ass, and see what it gets ya," Runt barked.

Murphy shook his head and smiled as he walked out the front door. Once he was gone, Cyrus asked, "Did y'all hear what happened with the Southeast Rogue Riders?"

"Yeah, somebody smoked their clubhouse and their strip club last night," Riggs answered as he emptied his glass of tea.

"What the fuck?" I barked.

"Yep. Somebody leveled the motherfuckers." Cyrus

started clearing the dirty dishes from the table as he continued, "Nothing left but a pile of rubble and ash."

"What the hell? Any idea who was behind it?"

"Not a clue."

"That doesn't make any sense. Who'd want to fuck with them?" Runt asked.

"Beats the hell out of me, but I gotta say … I don't have a good feeling about it." A concerned look crossed Cyrus's face as he said, "Maybe I'm wrong, but where's there's smoke, there's fire. We need to keep our eyes and ears open."

"Agreed. Does Gus know about all this?"

"Yeah. You know him. He's the first to know everything."

I looked down at my watch, and when I saw how late it had gotten, I reached for my wallet. After I tossed my money down on the counter, I stood up and said, "I gotta get to the house. Let me know if you hear anything else about the Rogues."

"Will do, brother."

After I left the diner, I went home and crashed, and from the time I got up the next morning, I'd been set on go. If I wasn't busting my ass in the garage, I was helping Mom out with something at the house or tossing the football with Kevin. By the time Friday rolled around, I was exhausted, so when Riggs and Runt asked me to head down to Beale Street with them, I turned them down. I had no desire to spend the night out with those two, especially since Kevin had a game the next day. Knowing we'd have to be up early, I ordered us a couple of pizzas and pulled up some movie he'd been wanting to watch. We'd only been watching it for an hour when I fell asleep in the recliner. The next morning, I woke up to the sound of Kevin yelling from the kitchen. "Hey, Dad! Have you seen my cleats?"

As I rubbed the sleep from my eyes, I shouted, "They're on the back porch! Your grandmother cleaned them up for you."

"What about my socks?"

"In the laundry room," and before he could ask, I added, "and your mouth guard is in the cup by the sink."

"I already got it."

I glanced over at the clock and groaned when I noticed that it was only eight. "Dude, what are you doing? You've got four hours until the game."

He came into the living room and looked at me with a scowl. "Last night you said we had to leave early, because you had to help Gammy with something."

Remembering that I'd promised to help fix her leaky sink, I grumbled, "Oh, yeah. I forgot about that."

"She called while you were still asleep and said she's making us pancakes for breakfast. I told her that I couldn't eat a big breakfast before a game, but she wouldn't listen."

"You gotta eat something. Might as well be pancakes."

"Dad! I'm supposed to eat protein, not a bunch of carbs." He fussed.

"Damn, son. Do you hear yourself? You don't sound like an eight-year-old kid."

"I'm nine," he argued.

"No. You're eight. You won't be nine for another month," I told him as I got up from the recliner and started towards my bedroom. Even though I still worried that his cancer would come back, I could see that he was growing stronger, more confident, with each day that passed, and I couldn't have been prouder. "Go get the rest of your stuff. I'll be ready in twenty minutes."

After I showered and got dressed, we went over to my folks' place for breakfast. While I fixed the sink, Kevin told my folks all about his week at school. Apparently, he had a speech coming up in a few days, and he'd decided to talk about the largest dogs on the planet, Mastiffs. I had no idea why, but he'd always had a thing for these giant dogs. He'd asked for an English Mastiff several times over the years, but knowing how hard it would be to have a pet that size, I always refused. Since his birthday was just around the corner, I had a feeling that the conversation would be coming up again. Once we were done at the folks' place, we headed over to the football field. When we got there, Kevin's team was already warming up.

"Crap. We're late," he huffed.

I looked down at my watch and cursed under my breath when I saw that we were fifteen minutes early. Just like my brothers, these jerk-offs didn't know how to tell fucking time. "Don't worry about it, sport. You have plenty of time to warm up."

"If you say so," he groaned as he took off for the field.

"Good luck!"

"Thanks, Dad!"

I made my way up to the bleachers and found a place to sit right at the fifty-yard line. Since there were only third and fourth grade kids playing, there wasn't much of a crowd. My folks weren't going to be able to make it, so I figured I would be sitting alone, until I saw Riggs, Runt, and Murphy heading up the steps. The game was just about to start when they plopped down beside me, and I couldn't help but notice that Riggs and Runt looked like shit. With a knowing smile, I asked, "Long night?"

"Yeah, but we had one hell of a time." Riggs chuckled. "Didn't we Runt?"

"Um hmm." He was looking a little rough around the edges as he grumbled, "Would've been better if you hadn't bought so many fucking drinks for her friend."

"How was I supposed to know she couldn't handle her liquor?"

"The chick was practically green when you got that last round."

"Green or not, she still looked hot as fuck in that miniskirt and those boots," Riggs smirked. "You got yourself a real stunner, brother."

"You ain't lying." Runt snickered.

"You two care to tell me who you're talking about?" I asked.

"The chick from the other night at Daisy's." When I looked at him with confusion, Riggs added, "You remember ... the hot, fucking nurse who was practically crawling in Runt's lap."

"Oh, yeah." I thought back to the beautiful brunette who had caught my eye, and when I thought about her being out with Riggs and Runt, my blood ran hot. For reasons I didn't understand, I had to fight the urge to reach for my brother's throat. "I remember."

His eyebrows furrowed. "You alright?"

"I'm fine." I lied as I ran my hand over my beard. "Just wanted to know who the fuck you were talking about."

"If you say so." Riggs shrugged. "You should've come out with us. You missed out on *a real good time*."

Dreading the answer, I asked, "What kind of good time?"

Riggs had always been one to exaggerate, so I knew to take it with a grain of salt as he explained, "Runt called up Robyn. You know ... *the hot, fucking nurse...*"

"*Yeah, I got it. The hot, fucking nurse,*" I snapped.

He gave me a strange look as he continued, "Anyway, he called and asked if she wanted to meet up. Since she was already out with some of her friends, we decided to meet up at Silky Sullivans."

I asked, "What happened after that?"

"Nothing much, I guess. We sat out on the patio and had a few drinks."

"*A lot of drinks.*" Runt snickered.

"Okay. Yes, we had a lot of drinks."

"And?" I pushed.

He shrugged. "When the bar started shutting down, they invited us back to their place."

"So, you *hooked up?*" I asked, biting back my anger.

With his eyebrow cocked high, he shrugged. "You know I'm not one to *kiss and tell*, brother."

"The fuck you're not," I spat.

"What's crawled up your ass?" Riggs asked.

"I already told you. Nothing."

"Well, I'm not buying it. You're obviously ticked about something. Maybe if you'd gone out with us last night, you would've gotten you some action and wouldn't be in such a bad mood."

"I feel ya. All I got were blue balls last night," Runt grumbled. "When we got back to Robyn's place, her roommate was home. I might've stayed until Robyn sobered up or something, but that roommate of hers wasn't having it. She just stood there, giving me the stink eye until I left."

"Hold up. I thought Robyn's roommate was out with you and Riggs."

Like it was no big deal, Riggs said, "Yeah. She was for a little while, but she went home early. She had to work or something."

"So, who exactly did you hook up with last night?"

"One of the chicks Robyn was out with last night. They were having a bachelorette party or something, and there was a whole slew of them."

Before he could respond, Murphy motioned out to the field and said, "Hey, Blaze. The coach is putting Kevin in."

And just like that, my attention was drawn to the game, and as I watched Kevin make one great play after the next, I got to thinking. For years, it had been just the two of us, and I was good with that. We both were. We had my folks and the club, and that's all we really needed —or so I thought. While our encounter was brief, there was something about the chick from the diner that made me wonder if my life was missing something. It was a thought that caught me by surprise. I hadn't realized what an impression she'd made on me until today, when Riggs had me thinking he'd hooked up with her. Just the thought of him touching her had me on edge, and I hadn't felt like that about anyone in years. I liked the feeling. I liked it a lot.

*M*y bad night turned into an even worse morning when I woke up to the sounds of Robyn getting sick in the bathroom. It was partly my fault. I should've never left her alone at that bachelorette party. When I'd agreed to tag along, I thought it would be a quiet night, especially since we were all older and those wild college nights of partying were over. Unfortunately for me, a quiet night was not what they had in mind. They were all about having the night of their lives, and when Robyn mentioned that the hot biker she'd met was coming to meet us, and he was bringing some friends along, the girls couldn't have been more intrigued. I was, too, for that matter. I found myself watching the door, curious to see if the man who'd brought butterflies to my stomach would come walking into the bar. I hadn't seen him since that night at the diner, and I found myself wishing that I would get another chance to talk to him. Sadly, my hopes were quickly dashed when the door opened, and Runt walked in with a different guy entirely

—one that wasn't nearly as handsome and far less charming. I tried to make the best of it, but I just wanted the night to end. When I'd had enough of the loud music and the obnoxious flirting, I left, telling the girls I had to work the following morning.

When I heard Robyn vomiting again, I asked, "You okay in there?"

"No," she groaned. "I feel like a semi-truck ran over my head and a cat shit in my mouth."

As I pulled myself out of bed, I told her, "Thanks for the *oh, so vivid description*, jerk-face. I could've done without that."

When I walked into the bathroom, her head was down in the toilet bowl, making her words echo as she said, "I think I may be dying. *Seriously*. You need to check my pulse."

"Stop being so dramatic." I fussed as I tried to ignore the horrid smell that had filled the room. "Get your head out of the toilet and go get in bed. I'll bring you some water and Tylenol."

"No. I can't move," she whined. "The room is still spinning, and I hurt *everywhere*."

"Well, it might do you good to remember this moment," I told her as I reached for her arm and helped her up on her feet. "You're not as young as you used to be."

"I could do without a lecture from you right now. *Just saying*."

"You know I'm right. *Just saying*. Now, go get in the bed!" Once we were in the hallway, I let her go and as I headed towards the kitchen, I asked, "Why did you drink so much?"

"I wasn't thinking."

"No. You weren't." I grabbed her water and Tylenol, and when I returned, I found her sprawled out on the hallway floor with her arm covering her eyes. *"Really?"*

"I'm dying, Dee," she cried.

I reached down and helped her back up to her feet, then I led her over to her bed. Once she was settled, I continued, "You really worried me last night."

"Why? I was fine."

"Obviously, you weren't. Runt had to carry you to your room, Robyn," I snapped. I was beyond furious when that asshole showed up at our door with my best friend passed out in his arms. He just came strolling in our apartment like it was no big deal. I followed him down the hallway into Robyn's room, and it was all I could do not to kick him right in the balls when he started to kick off his boots. Thankfully, he stopped when he noticed me standing at the door, eventually taking the hint that it was time for him to leave. "There's no telling what could've happened if I wasn't here."

"Wait … Runt brought me home?" she asked, sounding confused.

"Oh, dear lord. You mean you don't remember?"

She winced as she replied, "Um … Not exactly."

"Do you have any idea what could've happened…" I stopped myself midsentence and sighed. As much as I loved Robyn, it wasn't my job to keep her in line. With a wave of my hand, I turned to leave. "Never mind. Just get some sleep."

"Wait." Robyn pouted. *"Please don't go."*

"Oh, come on. Don't go and get all pitiful on me." I sat down on the edge of her bed and asked, "Why don't you tell me about last night? Did you have fun?"

"Yeah, I really did," she answered with a half-smile.

"So, you like this guy?"

"Umm … He's hot and all that, but he's a little intense. And we have absolutely nothing in common. *Like nothing at all.*"

"So, are you going to see him again?"

"I don't know. Maybe, but like you said … I'm not as young as I used to be. It's probably time I start settling down."

"You settling down? Let's not get carried away." I teased. "Besides, you still have plenty of time to find your Mr. Right."

"With the way I feel right now, I don't care if I ever find him." She rolled on her side to face me and asked, "Do you really have to work today?"

I shrugged. "No. I just said that so I could leave without looking like a lame-ass."

"Good. I don't want to be here alone … especially since I'm on my *death bed* and all."

"Give it a rest. You're not going to die. You've just got a hangover." I stood up and started towards the door. "I'm going to get you some crackers and ginger ale. Maybe that will help settle your stomach."

"Thank you, sweetie," she mumbled. "You know, you're too good to me."

"I know. I keep telling myself that." I teased.

We spent the entire weekend bumming around, watching TV and eating comfort food as Robyn recuperated from her night out. It was nice to have some time to just chill out, to catch up on laundry, and spend time relaxing at home. By the time Monday rolled around, I thought we'd be prepared for anything, but I was wrong.

It was the Monday of all Mondays, and with the amount of crazy people coming into the hospital, I started to wonder if it was a full moon. My latest patients had come in with their six-month-old daughter who had a high fever. She'd been crying for hours, and the parents were frantic. While I couldn't blame them for being upset, they were taking their frustrations out on me.

"Where the hell is the doctor?" the guy asked as I checked the baby's oxygen level.

"He should be here shortly."

"We've been waiting for over three goddamn hours." He was young, maybe twenty-one and he was skinny with dark circles under his eyes, making him look like he hadn't slept in days. The girl next to him didn't look like she was in much better condition, but she was at least trying to keep herself under control. "How long does it fucking take to check on a baby?"

"Sir, I know you are worried about your daughter, but you need to try to calm down. We're doing the best that we can," I explained.

"She's my niece, not my daughter, and your best isn't good enough!"

"Your niece?"

The blonde woman turned to me and said, "I'm Kate Dillon. Lacie is my daughter. Her father was killed a few weeks ago, and Terry has been helping out. He watches Lacie at night while I'm at work."

"I'm sorry to hear that about Lacie's dad."

"It's okay. He was a total deadbeat." She looked over at her brother as she said, "I'm sorry that he's being such an asshole. He's just worried about the baby."

"I wouldn't have to be such an asshole if these fucking

doctors would just do their damn jobs, and Johnny wasn't a deadbeat, Kate. He tried to do right by you and the baby, and he got himself killed for it. That wasn't his fault!" he roared.

"Sir, there are young children— "

"I don't give a fuck." When he waved his arm in the air, I thought I saw several track marks, but I couldn't be sure.

"Terry. That's enough. Seriously. She's doing the best she can." Kate ran her hand over Lacie's head and sighed. "Besides, she's finally stopped crying. If you keep shouting like that, you're going to upset her."

"Well, on a positive note, her oxygen level is good," I told them.

"What about her fever?" Terry asked. "And her blood pressure?"

"Well, those are both a little concerning. I'm sure the doctor will want some blood work drawn to see what is going on."

"Can't you go on and get that started?"

"Not without the doctor's orders."

"What a load of bullshit!" Terry complained.

Just then, Dr. Daniel Tate stepped into the room. He was one of the younger, more attractive doctors who worked at the hospital, and he was often the topic of idle gossip with the nurses. Not only was he easy on the eyes, I found him to be friendly and easy to talk to. I caught him up to speed with Lacie's symptoms and waited as he gave her a thorough examination. Once he was done, he looked over to Kate and said, "It looks like she has an ear infection. I'll call her in a round of antibiotics, and she should be fine in a couple of days. Take her in to see her pediatrician next week if she doesn't feel better."

"Thank you, doctor." Kate smiled as she held her daughter close to her chest. "I was so scared it was something serious, especially with all her crying."

"Ear infections can be very painful. Be sure to give her infant Tylenol every four hours for the fever and for the pain."

"Yes. Of course."

"Alright." Daniel gave me a quick smile and said, "That should do it, Kenadee."

"Okay. Thanks, Dr. Tate."

Even though I was a little concerned that he didn't call for bloodwork, I didn't say anything, assuming he knew better than I did. I waited for him to write the information in the file, and once he was done, I took the chart over to the desk to start the discharge paperwork. I was just finishing up when Robyn came over to me. "If you don't get me some coffee or some chocolate, I'm going to throat punch someone."

"I see you're having a bad day, too."

"A bad day doesn't even begin to describe it," she complained. "Please tell me this day is almost over."

"Um … it's nine o'clock."

"Shit."

"Yeah." I chuckled. "It's gonna be a long one, but we'll get through it."

"Hey, I overheard Daniel talking." She leaned forward as she whispered, "The word is he's planning to ask one of the nurses out."

"Yeah, I know." I'd heard the same rumors myself, and I wasn't surprised by them in the least. "You should go out with him. He's a really nice guy, and he's so good looking."

"Me? Why would I go out with him when he's been talking about asking you out?"

"What?"

"You heard me. He's going to ask *you* out."

"*No way.* You've got to be kidding me"

"Nope. I heard him talking to Dr. Sheridan this morning, and he was definitely talking about you."

I glanced back over at Daniel and found him staring in my direction. When our eyes met, he smiled at me with a big, goofy grin, and I immediately wanted to duck in a corner and hide. I quickly turned to her and gasped, "Oh, shit."

"I don't see what the big deal is. You said yourself he's a nice guy, and he's hot and…"

I simply didn't want to talk about him a moment longer, so I pleaded, "Can we not talk about this right now?"

She was right. He was nice and handsome, but when I was around him, I just didn't feel a spark—none whatsoever—especially not like the ones I'd felt that night when I came face to face with the mysterious biker. With him, there was a sense of mystery, danger and intrigue that should've made me run for the hills, but I'd found myself longing for it—longing for him. I knew Daniel was a safer bet, and I should give him a chance, but I needed to know if the feelings I had for the biker were just in my head or if they were something more.

BLAZE

*W*hen Gus started the garage, he knew it would be an ideal way to launder money. With parts and remodels, cash would exchange hands easily on a daily basis. As the garage had grown bigger, those sums of money had also increased, which had helped immensely, especially since we'd established the pipeline. Cars and bikes were moving in and out of the garage faster than I could count. There were times when I found it hard to keep up, but just when I was at my wits end, one of the brothers would come through and help get us caught up. It was one of the great things about having so many brothers who knew their way around an engine. After one of the busiest weeks we've had in months, Alex Avery, one of our best customers, came in with a huge order. He had three Chevy pickup trucks that he wanted remodeled, and, as usual, he was crystal clear in how and when he wanted them done. Even with the quick turn-around, we could handle the job, but I'd have to make a run to Conway, Arkansas, to get the right parts. I'd need to get a custom-made grille and a couple of wide vintage bumpers for the '57 Chevy 3100, and while I was there, I'd also need to grab new headlights for the '69 Chevy C10 and a rear fender for the '63 Chevy C10. I didn't like the idea of being on the road on a Saturday, especially when Kevin had a football game, but I didn't have a choice.

Before I headed home, I stopped by the clubhouse to see Gus. When I got there, I found him in his office with Moose. The tension in the room was palpable, and from the look on Gus's face, it was clear that he was pissed about something. "Is everything alright?"

"Not sure just yet," Moose answered as he leaned back in his seat. His dark eyes grew intense as he said, "We've been hearing talk about another MC trying to move into town, but nothing has been confirmed yet."

"I've heard enough," Gus protested. "If these mother-fuckers even think of stepping foot on my territory, I'll wipe them out. Every last one of them"

"We don't even know if it's an MC or just another fucking gang, Gus," Moose grumbled. Even though he was built like a brick shit-house and towered over most of the guys in the club, Moose was our voice of reason, and as our VP, he tended to remain calm in all situations, thinking things through before he acted. Gus was just the opposite. He was a man who acted first and never once asked for forgiveness—because he didn't have to. I'd never seen him wrong about anything. Gus's gut instincts were spot on. "We've just gotta be patient here."

"Fuck that." Gus slammed his fist down on his desk. "You heard what happened to the Rogues last week. I'll be damned if these motherfuckers hit us, too."

"No one has confirmed that it was foul play, Gus,"

Moose tried to assure him. "Just give Riggs some time to look into it."

Riggs was our tech guy. If there was something to be found, he'd find it. When Gus heard his name, it set his mind at ease and the tension in his face softened as he leaned back in his chair. "Let me know as soon as he hears something."

"You know I will," Moose assured him.

It might not have been the best idea, but I said, "While he's looking, you could have the prospects on patrol. They can keep a look out and make sure nobody's fucking around. Better to be safe than sorry."

"Not a bad idea." Gus nodded. "Was there something you needed?"

"Just letting you know that I'm heading up to Conway in the morning. I've gotta grab some parts for the shop. We've got a big order that came in today."

"Good to hear," Gus replied. "Who you taking with you?"

"I was thinking about taking Riggs until I heard y'all needed him. I guess I'll just head up there myself."

"Nah. Don't want you going alone. Take Murph or Shadow with you," Gus ordered.

I groaned at the sound of Shadow's name. He was a good guy, but he wasn't exactly the best travel companion. He was a man who liked to keep to himself, only speaking when spoken to, and I couldn't imagine being stuck in the truck with him for six hours. Hoping for a way out, I said, "I'm sure Shadow's got better ways to spend his time."

Gus gave me a knowing look as he said, "Well, then get with Murphy or Gunner. Just make sure you take one of them with you."

"You got it, Prez." I smirked as I headed for the door.

I left his office and headed to find Murphy. Once I made arrangements with him to leave first thing in the morning, I headed home to Kevin. I needed to break the news to him that I wouldn't be able to make it to his game the following day. When I walked in the house, I found him sitting on the sofa watching TV. He didn't even look up as I strolled over to sit down next to him. "Where's your grandmother?"

"Laundry room."

"How was school?"

His focus was still on the television screen. "Fine."

"How'd you do on that math test?"

With a slight shrug, he said, "I did alright."

"What's that supposed to mean?"

"I made a B plus," he answered flatly.

"Well, that's good."

"Um-hmm."

I was growing tired of competing with *SpongeBob*, so I reached for the remote and turned off the TV. "I need to talk to you about something."

"Okay. What is it?"

"I'm not going to be able to make it to your game tomorrow."

"Yeah. Already knew that."

"How did you know?"

"Murphy just called to tell me that he was sorry, but he might not make it to my game because he was going with you on a run."

He was trying to hide it, but I could hear the disappointment in his voice as he spoke. "Dang. I was hoping I was gonna get to talk to you first. You've got the late game tomorrow, so I'll try to get back by the last quarter."

"Don't worry about it. It's not a big deal." He turned to look at the blank screen and asked, "Can you turn the TV back on?"

"Come on, bud. Don't give me a hard time about this. You know I have to work."

"I know. I just thought you actually meant it when you promised to be at all my games."

"Damn. You're killing me here." I sighed. "You're right. I screwed this up, but there's nothing I can do about it this time. I give you my word I won't let it happen again."

"Okay."

"And when I get back tomorrow, you and I'll do something special. I'll take you out after your game. We'll go wherever you want to go."

"Anywhere?"

"You name it."

He smiled and said, "You got a deal."

With that, I turned the TV back on. "Good. I'll get the play-by-play from your grandfather."

"You picked a good day to miss. We're playing that team out of Tipton, and they aren't very good."

"Well, I hope you smoke 'em," I told him as I stood up and started towards the laundry room to find his grandmother.

After listening to my mother's thirty-minute guilt trip, I finally worked it out for her to keep Kevin for the night and to take him to his game the following day. I also called my father and made him promise to keep me posted on all the big plays. So, by the time Murphy showed up at my house the following morning, I was feeling better about leaving. We hadn't been riding long when I asked, "Gus tell you there's talk about another MC trying to move into the territory?"

Sounding uninterested, he answered, "Yeah. He mentioned it."

"You think there's anything to it?"

He shrugged. "Wouldn't be the first time somebody tried. Won't be the last."

"So, you aren't worried?"

"I don't worry until there's a reason to worry, Blaze; it's a lot less stressful that way. Besides, Gus worries enough for all of us," he scoffed. "But that doesn't mean I'm not making sure we're prepared for whatever might come our way."

"Yeah. It's only a matter of time before a club with some real manpower comes in and decides they want to be king of the jungle."

"And when they do, they'll be in for one hell of a fight," Murphy barked.

"We'll be ready," I assured him with an arrogant smile on my face. "No way we're giving up our claim."

A couple of hours had passed, so I reached for my phone and called to check on Kevin. After listening to the full rundown from how long he'd slept, to what he was watching on TV, and what he'd had for breakfast, I finally hung up the phone. Seconds later, Murphy looked over to me and asked, "You ever think about getting tied down again? You know, if the *right chick* came along?"

Murphy had always been a bit of a player, moving from one hot number to the next, never spending more than a couple of nights with the same chick, so I was surprised by his question. "I don't know. *Maybe*. Why?"

"I was just thinking about Kevin. Figure it's gotta be hard dealing with a kid on your own."

"It's not that difficult. Kevin's a great kid, and it helps to have my folks."

He ran his hand through his thick hair and added, "Yeah, I know. That's not what I meant."

"Alright. Then, tell me what you meant."

"Nothing." He sighed. "Forget I brought it up."

"Whatever you say, man." I had no idea what was really going on in his head, but there was no doubt something was bothering him. I remembered him telling me that he'd spent a few years in foster care after his mother ran into some trouble with the law. With just the little bit he'd told me, I got the feeling he didn't have the best childhood, so it wasn't surprising that he hadn't found someone he could trust. No one could blame him for that, but if he wanted things to be different, he'd have to find a way to make a change in himself. A few minutes passed, and I glanced back over at him. "I'll tell you something my old man said to me right before I married Kevin's mother. He told me: 'It isn't about finding the right woman. It's about being the right man.'"

He gave me a look that let me know he wasn't buying it, so I went on, "You gotta think about it, brother. A woman with a good head on her shoulders isn't gonna put up with any bullshit. She'll see that you aren't doing right by her, and she'll hit the door running."

"*Damn, brother.* I was just asking if you planned to settle down again," he complained.

"I'll settle down when I can be the kind of man a good woman needs me to be. How about that?"

"Whatever you say, man."

"What about you?"

"Doubt I could ever be the kind of man a good woman needs me to be. Now, a bad girl ... that's a different story." He smirked. "I can make her happy all night long, and me, too, for that matter. For now, that's good enough for me."

He turned his attention to the road ahead, so I knew he was done talking, at least for the time being. We made a quick stop for coffee and a bite to eat before driving over to Lou's Auto in Conway. Thankfully, my guy had all the parts pulled and ready to go when we got there, so it didn't take us long to get everything loaded and strapped down. Once the bill was paid, Murphy and I were back in the truck and headed home. I glanced down at my phone and was feeling pretty good about our time. Kevin wouldn't start playing for another couple hours, so there was still a chance that I could make it to the last quarter. We topped off with gas, and as soon as we were out on the highway, I pressed my foot down on the accelerator.

"Easy there, brother. Last thing we need is to get pulled over by the cops," Murphy warned.

Murphy was probably right about that, so I eased back on the speed a bit. "I know. I'm just ready to get back. Kevin's game starts soon."

His blue eyes shined with warning as he said, "Yeah, but it's better to get back in one piece than not at all."

Murphy tried to distract me with talk about this year's SEC football schedule, and the potential of our new prospects, but neither topic was able to take my mind off that damn clock. Just as we crossed into the next town, my father sent me a text message to let me know that Kevin had just made it onto the field. I glanced over at Murphy. "Games starting."

"He'll do great."

Over the next hour, my dad sent message after message, describing each and every play Kevin made. Things were rocking along, until the messages stopped coming. I tried calling him, but I didn't get an answer. At first, I thought it was his phone. I figured the battery had gone dead or he'd fucked it up somehow, so I tried calling my mom, but she didn't answer hers either. That's when I started to panic. I turned to Murphy and said, "Something's wrong, brother."

"Why? What's going on?"

"Not sure. Just got a bad feeling."

I waited a few more minutes, and then I tried calling my mother's phone again. This time she answered, "Sawyer?"

I could hear the worry in her voice, so I immediately asked, "What's going on?"

"It's Kevin. He's been hurt."

I felt like I'd been hit in the chest with a sledge hammer, and before she could continue, I shouted, "What do you mean, he's been hurt!"

There was a commotion with the phone, and then I heard my father say, "Sawyer, he's going to be okay. It was a bad tackle, and a kid landed on Kevin's elbow the wrong way. It's probably just a bad sprain, but the coach wants us to run him over to Regional to get him checked out."

A feeling of helplessness washed over me as I thought of my son being so far away when he was hurt. "Shit."

"I know this is hard, Son, but everything's going to be okay."

My voice was strained as I said, "I'll get there as soon as I can."

"No reason to get all out of sorts. You know how those ERs can be. We'll be waiting there for hours," he assured me. "We've got Kevin covered. You just get here when you can, and be careful."

As always, my father had a way of calming me down when things got rough. "Thanks, Pop."

"Keep your phone close. I'll call you as soon as I know something," he told me as he hung up the phone.

There was absolutely nothing worse than having your child out of reach when they were hurt or in a bad situation. As I gripped the steering wheel and sped towards the hospital, I had only one thing on my mind—finding the fastest way to my son. We were making good time, flying through one town after another, but just as we were coming into Forest City, we ran into an accident that brought us to a screeching halt. As fate would have it, I wouldn't be getting to my son any time soon.

KENADEE

Over the years, I've learned that you could never truly predict how any given night was going to be in an ER, especially in the city. Some nights were slow, with only a few patients trickling in, while others were pure chaos, where I'd barely had time to take a breath. Some might call me crazy, but personally, I liked the fast-paced shifts that kept me hopping from one station to the next. It made the time pass by faster, and I always felt like I'd accomplished something at the end of my shift. I was having one of those insanely hectic nights when Dan and Janice Mathews came in with their grandson. By the time they made it back to me, I could tell they were feeling pretty anxious about him. I couldn't blame them though. They were forced to sit in a crowded waiting room with a small child while he was in excruciating pain.

After the front nurse got him settled in the room, I walked over to the grandparents to introduce myself. "Hi. I'm Kenadee. I'll be Kevin's nurse while he's here in the ER."

"Hi, Kenadee. I'm Janice, and this is my husband, Dan. Kevin's father is on his way. He's a few hours away, but he'll be here as soon as he can."

The front nurse had already explained their situation, so I said, "That's okay. We'll manage until he gets here, and I see that Kevin's father has given you permission to handle his medical care?"

"Yes. He did that a while back."

"Then, we shouldn't have any problems." I made my way over to Kevin's gurney, and when he looked up at me with his handsome, blue eyes, there was no doubt that he was scared. "Hi Kevin. I have a few questions for you. Is that okay?"

With his elbow safely tucked close to his side, he answered, "Yes, ma'am."

"Good." As I placed a pillow behind his back, I continued, "It says on your chart that you've hurt your elbow. Can you tell me what happened?"

"I was playing football, and this guy tackled me from behind." He extended his good arm to demonstrate as he went on, "I put my hand out to stop my fall, and I heard my arm pop."

"Oh, man. That doesn't sound good."

He grimaced as he added, "And it hurt really bad, too."

"I'm sorry, buddy. We'll get you fixed up soon, and maybe you'll get a cool cast out of the deal. How about that?"

Giving me a half smile, he replied, "That might be cool."

"Alright. Moving on. Do you happen to know if Kevin's allergic to any medications?"

"He's not," Janice answered.

"Okay. Has Kevin had any previous surgeries or major illnesses that we might need to be aware of?"

"I had ALL," Kevin answered for her. "Acute lymphocytic leukemia. I've been in remission for almost three years now."

"That's pushing it a little, Kevin." Dan corrected him. "It's been two years and just under seven months."

"Well, it's pretty close," he argued.

"Not close enough." He turned his attention back to me and said, "Kevin went through chemotherapy, and we were very blessed that it's gone into remission. He goes for regular checkups, and so far, things are looking good."

"Wow. That's pretty impressive. It's takes a tough guy to go through all that."

He gave me a little shrug. "It wasn't so bad."

I pulled my monitor cart over to his bed and told him, "I'm sure you've seen all these before."

"Yeah. You're gonna check my heart to make sure it's pumping right ... and my temperature, and probably my oxygen level. But all of those are fine. It's my elbow that's messed up."

"You're probably right about that, but it's my job to check." I smiled. He was one of those kids who made it difficult to see him as just a patient. His personality lured you in, making you want to get to know him, and his smile was just adorable. "You're a pretty smart kid."

As I took his blood pressure and temperature, I glanced down at his elbow, and when I saw how swollen it was, I had my doubts that it was just a bad sprain. After I wrote down his stats, I asked him, "If you had to rate your pain from one being the least and ten being the worst, what would you rate your pain level right now?"

"I'd say around a seven or eight, I guess."

"Okay. Well, I'm going to need to take a couple of X-rays to see what's going on. The doctor's going to need to know if it's broken."

"Is it gonna hurt?"

My nose crinkled a bit when I answered, "Well, I don't want to lie to you. It might just a little, but I promise to be as careful as I can."

"Okay."

I stepped out of the room, and with the help of one of the orderlies, we rolled the mobile x-ray machine into his room. He helped me position Kevin's arm where I would get the best shots without causing him a great deal of discomfort. After we'd taken several pictures, I pulled them up on the computer screen to be sure that I'd gotten a clear image. As soon as I saw the state of Kevin's elbow, I knew they were going to be in for a long night. I looked over to Kevin and said, "Okay, buddy. We got everything we need."

"That's it?"

"Yep. That's it."

"That wasn't too bad," he said, sounding surprised but then his little eyebrows furrowed when he added, "It hurts a lot though."

"I bet it does." I smiled warmly. "I'm going to get these x-rays and your file over to the doctor right away, and we'll be back after he's looked them over."

"Is it broken?" Dan asked.

As much as I wanted to tell him, I knew I couldn't, so I told him, "It's really best for Dr. Tate to discuss the x-rays with the patients. I'll see if I can go get him now."

"Thank you, Kenadee."

"No problem."

After I left Kevin's room, I sent Cindy in to get his IV started, then went to find Daniel. After he looked over his chart and reviewed the x-rays, he turned to me and said, "We need to see which orthopedic surgeon is on call tonight."

"I already checked. It's Wanscott."

"Well, that's good. He's one of the best." As he closed Kevin's file, he said, "Send these x-rays over to him and see when we can get the surgery scheduled."

"You got it."

I put a call into the head nurse and was relieved to hear that he would be right over. Once he arrived and examined Kevin's x-rays, I led him to Kevin's room. He walked over to the side of the bed and said, "Hey there, Kevin. I'm Dr. Wanscott."

After he shook his hand, he introduced himself to Dan and Janice and explained to them all that he was an orthopedic surgeon. Eager to hear about his grandson, Dan asked, "What do you think about Kevin's elbow?"

"It's a pretty extensive break." He walked over to the computer and pulled up an image of the break. As he pointed to the screen, he said, "You can see here, it's shattered right along the socket. I'd like to take him into surgery and set the break with several pins to secure the loose fragments around the growth plate."

"How long does a surgery like this take?" Dan asked.

"About an hour. Give or take."

"And when would you want to do it?"

"As soon as we can get it scheduled." He glanced down at his watch. "Possibly within the next half hour."

Kevin's voice was filled with panic when he asked, "When's Dad gonna get here?"

"I don't know, sweetheart. He's coming as fast as he can, but you heard what he told your grandfather about that awful wreck."

When Kevin's eyes started to fill with tears, his grandfather walked over to him and said, "Don't worry, kiddo. You're gonna be fine. We've gotten through worse things than this."

"Okay."

"That's my boy." He smiled.

Kevin perked up when he asked, "Will I have a cast?"

"You sure will," Dr. Wanscott answered. "You got a favorite color?"

"Blue."

"Blue it is." Wanscott turned to me and said, "Have him prepped and up to the second floor in twenty."

"You got it."

Just as the good doctor had requested, I had Kevin prepped and on the second floor, but just as the orderly was about to push him into the operating room, I heard someone call out, "Kenadee!"

I looked down the hall and saw one of the nurses waving me down. "Yes?"

"Sawyer Mathews is on his way up. He wants to see his son before he goes into surgery," she shouted.

"My dad's here?" Kevin asked as excitedly as he could, considering his groggy state.

"Yep. Looks like he made it after all." I smiled. I turned to the orderly and said, "Hold on just a second. Kevin's father wants to speak to him before we take him in."

I'd barely gotten the words out of my mouth when I

heard the sound of footsteps barreling down the hall, and as I turned to see who was walking in our direction, I couldn't have been more surprised. It was *him*—the hot biker from Daisy Mae's. Similar to that night, he was wearing his leather cut, with a tight, black t-shirt, faded jeans and black boots, and while he was hot enough to make my ovaries nearly explode on the spot, there was something different about the way he looked. This time he didn't have that friendly smile, or that charming demeanor. This time he looked like a man *possessed*. His brows were drawn together, his blue eyes were narrowed, and his hands were bawled into fists as he charged towards us like a raging bull, revealing another side to the mysterious biker. As he grew closer, my heart started thumping in my chest, and a slight shiver jolted down my spine. Mortified by my reaction, I looked down at Kevin and stuttered, "Uh … Umm … Your dad will be here in just a second."

"Kevin?" the biker called, and my heart literally stopped beating.

I looked up, and he was standing at the side of gurney, looking down at Kevin. His expression had softened, and all I could see was pure love in his eyes.

"Dad! You made it." Kevin was a little loopy, but his eyes still lit up as soon as he saw his father.

Dear Lord. My hot biker was Sawyer Mathews, father of Kevin Mathews. Damn. Sawyer leaned over and kissed Kevin on the forehead. "I'm sorry it took me so long, bud."

"It's okay."

"And don't you worry about this surgery stuff. In a blink of an eye, that doctor will have your elbow all fixed up, and you'll be good as new," Sawyer assured him, and my heart nearly leapt right out of my chest. There was just something about seeing such a strong, tough guy acting so sweet to his child.

Knowing that Dr. Wanscott was on a tight schedule, I said, "I'm sorry, but we really need to get Kevin inside."

Sawyer nodded, but he hadn't yet made eye contact with me. Understandably, his focus was totally on his son. "I'll be here when you get done."

"Okay, Dad."

We wheeled Kevin into the operating room where Dr. Wanscott's staff took over. When I went back out into the hall, I was stunned to see that Sawyer was still standing there. His hands were tucked in his front pockets and he was staring at the floor, lost in his own thoughts. It was easy to see that he was consumed with worry, and suddenly all those feelings of overactive hormones were replaced with something completely different. I walked over to him and said, "Hey. You doing okay?"

He looked up at me, and a surprised expression crossed his face. "It's you."

"It's me." I smiled. "I didn't realize you had a son. He's a pretty great kid."

"Wait. You met Kevin?"

"I was his nurse today." I laughed. "You didn't see me, but I was one of the nurses taking him into the operating room."

"Oh, damn." He quickly glanced down at my name tag. "Sorry about that, Kenadee. I totally missed that."

"It's okay. You were a little preoccupied." I teased him, but quickly added in a little bit more of a professional tone, "Kevin's in good hands, by the way. Dr. Wanscott is one of the best orthopedic surgeons in the city."

"Well, that's good news at least." The tension in his shoulders seemed to ease just a little as he took a deep breath. "So, how long should this thing take?"

"Maybe an hour … and honestly, when you hear the word *surgery*, it makes 'this thing' sound worse than it really is. The doctor just needs Kevin to be asleep, so he can set the break and place the broken fragments where they need to be. He'll use little pins to keep them in place. Once he's done, Kevin will be in recovery for an hour or so," I explained. "That's all there is to it."

He gave me a quick once over and smirked. "You're pretty good at this stuff, aren't ya?"

I shrugged. "Maybe just a little."

"Beautiful *and* smart. It's hard to top that." I could feel the heat of his gaze as his eyes slowly skirted down my body, and by the time those gorgeous blue eyes landed on mine, I was practically panting. "So, you're Kenadee. I've finally got a name for the pretty nurse from the diner."

"I guess you do. And you're Sawyer. I like that name, by the way. It suits you."

"Glad you think so." He smiled as he glanced down at his watch. "I'm a nervous wreck, and it looks like I have some time to kill before Kevin gets back. You know, I may have a heart attack if it takes too long. Why don't you do a guy a favor and help him pass the time by having a cup of coffee with him?"

I wasn't sure it was a good idea, but at that moment, I just didn't have it in me to turn him down. "Um … Yeah, I think I could do that, but I don't have long. My break's only twenty minutes."

"I'll take what I can get."

"The cafeteria is downstairs."

He motioned his hand forward and said, "Lead the way."

He followed me to the elevator, and I took him down to the cafeteria—my heart pounding all the way. My reaction to him was just as strong as it was the other night, if not stronger, and I was struggling to keep myself from looking like a complete idiot. We both ordered a cup of coffee and sat down at a table that left us mostly to ourselves. I could see the guilt in his beautiful eyes as he explained that he was working at the time of Kevin's accident, and the difficulty he had trying to get back. "Where's the guy you were riding with?"

"Murphy? Oh, after he heard they'd taken Kevin into surgery, he took our parts over to the garage, so the guys could get them unloaded."

"Well, that worked out well."

"I guess. Things could've been worse. I don't know what I would've done if my folks weren't here today."

"They were really great with Kevin. It's obvious they're crazy about him."

"They are." The smile he gave could light up a room. "But they spoil him rotten."

"Well, that's what grandparents are for."

"What about you? Are your folks still around?"

"Yes, but I don't see them as much as I'd like to. Now that they're retired, they spend a lot of time traveling, or at my brother's. He has two young kids, so they're all about spending time with them."

His eyebrows rose as he said, "I'm sensing a little jealously there."

"No. Not at all. I want them to enjoy their retirement and see the world. They deserve it after how hard they've worked. I'd just like them to stop by and see me once in a while. Or call and check in to say hi. *Something.* They're over at Luke's every other week, and they'll spend the entire day over there, and they can't even pick up the phone to call me? What is that about?" Realizing how catty I'd just sounded, I paused for a moment, then said, "Okay. I might be a tiny bit jealous, but just a tiny bit."

"It's okay. I get it." He snickered. "Sibling rivalry and all that."

"I don't know about all that." I laughed. "I think it's time to change the subject. Tell me something about yourself that nobody else knows."

A mischievous glimmer flashed through his eyes. "That's kind of personal for a first date, don't ya think?"

"*Not a date*, and if you tell me yours, I'll tell you mine."

"Fine, but no judgements."

"No judgements."

"I've always had this thing about clowns. I'm not exactly afraid of them, but I just don't like them."

I couldn't hide my surprise. "Clowns? Really?"

"Yep. Your turn."

"I can hold my breath for four minutes and twenty seconds." I glanced up at the clock and sighed as I stood up. "Ugh, I've got to get back upstairs, but I'll check in on Kevin and see how things are going."

"I'd appreciate that."

"I really enjoyed talking to you again, *Sawyer*."

"Me, too."

"Kevin is going to be fine, and he's going to love his new cast … for about an hour."

He laughed. "Yeah. You got that right."

When I started to walk away, he called out, "Kenadee?"

"Yeah?"

"When will I see you again?"

"In about half an hour," I answered playfully. "I'll be with Kevin when he comes out of surgery."

"And after that?"

I looked at him standing there with his tousled blond hair, thick, unruly beard, biker clothing, and muscular build, and there was no question that he wasn't like any man I'd ever dated before. Without a doubt, this man was strong and fierce, but there was a kindness, a vulnerability to him that I was drawn to from the moment I first saw him. *That* part of him had me coming back for more. The corners of my mouth curled into a smile as I said, "I guess we'll have to see about that."

And then I turned and walked away.

BLAZE

*T*he doctor called us into Kevin's room and said that the surgery went as expected. After going through all the ins and outs of the procedure, he mentioned that he had a few prescriptions for Kevin and instructed us to call his office to set up some follow-up appointments. We were also informed that as soon as Kevin was fully awake and able, he'd be ready to go home. I couldn't believe my ears. When I first got to the hospital, I was a total wreck, completely consumed with worry and guilt. Watching my son being wheeled into that operating room nearly ripped my heart out. If it hadn't been for Kenadee, I don't know what I would've done. Just having her there at that moment gave me a reprieve from the shit-storm that was going on in my head and kept me from losing my mind. She was so easy to talk to, and it didn't exactly hurt that she was even more beautiful than I remembered. When she left the cafeteria, she told me she'd see me when Kevin came out of surgery, but he'd been out for over forty-five minutes and she was nowhere in sight.

"Dad?" Kevin mumbled.

I hopped up out of my chair and rushed over to the bed. Kevin's eyes were barely open. "Hey, buddy. How ya doing?"

"I'm hungry. Can I have some ribs?" he mumbled.

"You want ribs?"

"Yeah. Fried pickles with ranch."

"Okay."

"He hates pickles," my mother whispered from the corner.

My mother had a bad habit of reminding me of things I already knew. She was just trying to help, so I tried not to let it get under my skin. "I know, Mom. He's still pretty out of it."

"Okay." She held her hands up defensively. "Just making sure you knew."

Shaking my head, I looked back to Kevin. "I can get you some fried pickles, bud. Whatever you want."

"I wanna go to the clubhouse tonight and get the guys to sign my cast."

"That, I'm not so sure about. You're gonna need to get some rest tonight, buddy, but I can run you over there tomorrow. I'm sure all the guys will want to sign it, but you gotta save some room for your friends at school."

"*I don't like none of dem people,*" he answered sounding like the biggest southern hick I'd ever heard.

"Kevin!" my father scolded.

"Yo, Kevin. Why don't you just lay back and get some rest?"

"I ain't gonna sleep ... Nope. I ain't gonna do it."

I had no idea where he was coming up with this shit, but it was only a matter of time before he said something that was going to send my folks into a conniption fit. I leaned over the bed and gave him a firm warning, "Kevin, go to sleep."

"I done told ya. I'm not tired," he said with his eyes closed. "I done broked my elbow. You know, I should *kick dat boy's ass* for breaking my elbow like he did!"

"*Whoa.* Hey, now." The light shimmered in Kenadee's dark brown eyes as she fussed. "Young, handsome boys like you don't talk like that."

"Hey! Nurse Kenadee!" Kevin shouted with a slur. "Dad, look. *It's Kenadee!*"

"I see that." I smiled. "Hello, nurse Kenadee."

"Hi, Sawyer." Then, she turned to my folks and said, "Hi, Janice. Hi, Dan."

My mother replied, "Hi there, sweetheart."

She pushed her monitor cart over to Kevin and said, "And hi to you, too, honey. I need to check to see if your heart is still pumping. Is that alright?"

"Yes, ma'am. I think it's still pumping."

"Well, let's just check to be sure."

I watched as she checked his vitals, and even though I'd seen nurses do it to him a hundred times before, I was completely mesmerized as I observed her with him. Watching them talk and cut up together was absolutely surreal. Kenadee was utterly amazing on all levels. She hadn't just won me over; she'd gotten to the whole Mathews crew. When she was done, she looked down at Kevin's cast and said, "You know, blue is my favorite color."

"It is?"

"Yep. When I broke my arm a couple of years ago, I had a cast just like yours."

"Awesome."

"So, are you about ready to go home?"

"Yes!"

"I thought you might be. We'll need to monitor you for just a bit longer, and if everything looks good after an hour or so, then you should be set to go."

"Okay."

"Would you like something to drink ... or maybe a Popsicle?"

"He was just telling us that he wanted ribs," I told her.

"Umm ... I think it's a little too soon for that." She laughed. "How about some crackers and a Sprite?"

Kevin nodded. "That sounds good. I want some Goldfish."

"You got it, kiddo. I'll be right back."

Once he was able to eat and drink a little without having any problems, and the anesthesia finally wore off, the doctor approved him for discharge. Kenadee brought in all of his paperwork and prescriptions, and once I'd signed everything, we were set to go. My father walked over to her with a warm smile and said, "Thank you, Kenadee. You've been wonderful."

"It's been my pleasure," she answered. "Kevin's a great kid."

I lifted Kevin out of the bed and put him into the wheelchair, then, Kenadee wheeled him out of the room and into the hall. Once we were at the front doors, she turned to us and said, "I'll wait with him while you go get your vehicle."

My dad handed me the keys and said, "It's parked right out front."

"Okay. I'll be right back." I rushed over to my dad's car and pulled it up to the curb. By the time I'd gotten out, she wheeled Kevin over to the passenger door. Stopping her, I said, "That's alright. I'll get him."

As I put him in the backseat and buckled him in, my parents were busy getting themselves inside. Once they were out of the way, she leaned in the window and said, "Take care of that elbow, kiddo."

"I will."

"Bye!" She waved and started to walk away.

I looked at Kevin and said, "Are you good for just a second?"

"Yeah. I'm good."

"Okay. I'll be right back." I rushed over to Kenadee, stopping her before she went through the door and said, "You know, you never did answer my question."

The wind was blowing, making her long, brown hair flutter around her face as she asked, "What question?"

"When am I going to see you again?"

A light blush crossed her face, letting me know I'd caught her off guard. "I don't know. What do you have in mind?"

"Why don't you give me your number? I'll give you a call later and we can figure it out."

"I guess that could work." She reached in her pocket and took out her phone. "What's your number?"

"Hold up. I thought you were giving me yours."

"I will when you give me yours." She smirked. "I'll send you a text."

"Fair enough," I told her before giving her my number.

Seconds later, I felt my phone vibrate in my back pocket, and she said, "I better get going."

Before I could respond, she'd slipped through the door and was gone. Having no choice, I walked over and slid in the seat beside Kevin. He was sitting with his arm propped in his lap, and he was meddling with the tips of his fingers. "You alright?"

"I'm good. It's just my fingers are still numb."

"That'll get better soon," I assured him as I patted him on the leg. "Alright, Pop. I think we're ready to go."

Once he started driving, I reached in my back pocket for my phone, and as soon as I saw the unknown number, I clicked on the message.

KENADEE: *Just so you know, I hate clowns, too.*

AFTER I ADDED her to my contacts, I went through all my other missed messages. My brothers had been calling and texting to see about Kevin, and I'd been too preoccupied to get back to them. Just as I sent them a message, letting them all know that he was doing fine. As we were headed home, I looked over at Kevin and found him staring at me with a concerned look on his face. "Everything alright, bud?"

"I just wanted to say that I was sorry about today."

"Why would you be sorry?"

"I messed up your run, and—"

"Kevin," I told him as I leaned closer to him. "You are

and always will be the most important thing in the world to me. You got that?"

"Yes, sir," he answered.

"And you didn't mess up anything, so get that out of your head."

"So, you aren't mad?"

Shocked by his question, I asked, "Are you still on the loopy juice or something? Why would I be mad at you?"

"I don't know."

"Kevin, I'm not mad at you. Not even the tiniest bit. I was worried sick about you, and I hated that I wasn't there when you were hurt. If anyone should be mad here, it should be you."

He perked up with that, like I'd given him new ammunition. "I was a little sad that you weren't there."

"I can't blame you for that."

"Especially after you promised to be at all my games."

I'd officially opened a can of worms. "You're right."

"And it really hurt when that kid broke my arm," he pushed.

"Um-hmm. I'm sure it did. Must've hurt like hell," I told him as I tried not to smile. He was gonna hit me up big this time. I could feel it.

"It did, and I was really scared when I had to go to the hospital without you."

"Yeah. I'm sure that was pretty tough on you. You might be scarred for life over that one," I teased.

His blue eyes widened as he fussed, "I'm serious, Dad."

"I know you are. So, how can I make it up to you?" I asked.

"I don't know. I'll have to think about it."

I could almost see the wheels turning in his head as he bit his bottom lip. Thankfully, our conversation got interrupted when Dad parked the car and announced, "We're home."

After I helped Kevin out of the car, he went inside and crashed on the sofa. We were all wiped, so my folks said their goodbyes and slipped out. I sat down on my recliner, and in a matter of minutes, we had both dozed off. I had no idea how long I'd been asleep when I heard someone pounding on my back door.

I glanced over at Kevin, and he was still out like a light. With a groan, I pulled myself out of the chair and tried to be quiet as I made my way to the back door. When I opened it, I was surprised to find Gunner standing there with Sadie. "What the hell, Gunner?"

Gunner was in his late thirties and built like a fucking tank. He'd gotten his name in the military. Word was that he was one of the best snipers around, but he was wounded during a raid and never quite the same after that. His voice was low and calm as he said, "Gus sent me over. He's called us all into church."

Knowing he wouldn't call church this time of night unless something was up, I asked, "What's going on?"

Without answering, he looked over to Sadie and said, "He thought she could sit with Kevin while you were gone."

Fuck. At least he'd sent Sadie to watch him. Of all the hang-arounds, she was the most responsible, so Kevin wouldn't be freaked out if he woke up and found her there with him. Having no other choice, I took Sadie inside and showed her his medication. After explaining when he'd need to take it, I followed Gunner out to our bikes. Suddenly my exhaustion was gone, and I could feel the adrenaline pulsing through my veins as I started up the engine and followed Gunner out onto the main road.

By the time we made it to the clubhouse, the brothers were already filing into the main meeting room. When I walked in, Gus was at the head of the table talking with Moose and Runt. The room was oddly quiet as I made my way over to my spot next to Spyder and Riggs, making me even more anxious for Gus to get on with the meeting. I had no idea what the hell was going on, but the tension in the room was building by the second.

Gus finally turned his attention to us and said, "Chaos and Sinners were hit tonight."

"What the fuck?" one of the brothers grumbled.

"Someone set Chaos's club and garage on fire and there was a drive-by shooting at the Sinner's club bar. They might totally be unrelated to the hit on the Rogues, especially since they're smaller clubs, but I'm not taking any chances." He leaned forward, placing the palms of his hands on the table as he growled, "I want to know who the fuck is doing this shit."

"These clubs are out by the docks. There might be a connection there," Gunner suggested.

"Maybe, or it could be a matter of some kind of retaliation that we aren't aware of," Spyder added. "You know how those assholes can be. They're always arguing about something."

"I've already spoken with the presidents of all the clubs involved. There's no feud among the clubs, so that's not what's going on here," Gus clarified.

"Then, somebody's trying to move in," Runt snarled.

"Maybe." Moose motioned over to Riggs. "Tell 'em what you found."

Gus sat back in his chair and crossed his arms as he watched Riggs stand. My brother was all business when he said, "Someone's been trying to fuck with our security cameras at the garage and at the diner."

"You gotta be fucking kidding me." Runt leaned forward and asked, "When?"

"A couple nights ago, and again, last night."

"It'd take someone with some mighty big balls to come fucking around our shit," Runt barked. "Did you see who it was?"

"No. The guy was wearing a hoodie, and I couldn't get a good look at him."

Obviously on edge, Runt snapped, "So, what exactly do you know other than this guy's *wearing a fucking hoodie?*"

"I'd say this guy isn't a professional, otherwise, he wouldn't have to keep coming back, so we still have a chance to catch him and figure out what he's up to," Riggs answered calmly.

"How you plan on catching him?" I asked

"I'd say we could try setting up motion sensors, but with the traffic that comes in and out of the diner and the garage, it's not gonna do us much good."

"We've got the prospects taking shifts, keeping a close eye on things, but everyone needs to be on watch," Moose warned. "We all need to be in on this. If you see or hear anything, *anything at all*, you come to us. Understood?"

After all the brothers agreed in unison, Riggs said, "I'll put a few extra cameras along the street corners and down the alleyways to give us some better angles and see if we can get more of a view of what's going on."

Gus stood with his fists clenched at his sides, and his voice was full of caution as he said, "As of now, consider the club on high alert. I need every one of you at your best. During times like these, one mistake could cost us *everything*."

*I*t's amazing how one person can have such a powerful effect on another person. Of course, that can be a good or a bad thing. Luckily for me, Sawyer seemed to have a very positive effect on me. It didn't matter what kind of mood I was in, he always managed to brighten my day, and I'd find myself smiling like a school-girl with her first crush. He'd send a random text or call at the end of a hectic day, and I'd find myself practically giddy. I knew I wasn't being sensible, that I was teetering on the edge of the unknown, and possibly even something dangerous, but I just couldn't stop myself. With each little morsel he tossed my way, I snatched it up, drawing myself even closer to him. I simply couldn't resist the temptation. I loved looking at him and talking to him. I longed to get to know him better, hoping that I would find that he was truly as nice as I thought he was. Ready or not, I was about to get my chance.

It was late, and we'd been talking on the phone for several minutes when he suggested taking an afternoon ride on his motorcycle. Surprised, I told him, "I've never ridden a motorcycle before."

I could hear the mischief in his voice when he laughed at that. "There's a first time for everything, darlin'."

"But what if I fall off or something?"

"I won't let you fall off, doll. You'll be fine," he assured me.

"What about a helmet and all that?"

"I'll bring Kevin's. You can use his until we get you one of your own."

When he implied that there would be future rides, I felt a flutter of butterflies in my stomach. "I'm game. What time do you want to go?"

"I'll be at your apartment around ten. Just text me the address."

Trying not to sound overly excited, I said, "Okay. I'll do it now."

"And *one more thing*."

"Yes?"

"Since you haven't ridden before, thought I oughta tell ya … wear jeans and boots if you have them. Not sure if you're one that tends to get cold, so you might want to wear long sleeves."

"It's eighty-five degrees outside," I scoffed.

With a slightly condescending tone, he asked, "Have you or have you not ridden a motorcycle before?"

"Umm … *I have not*."

"Wear jeans and boots. I'll leave the shirt up to you."

"Yes, sir," I said sarcastically.

"*Hmm* … I like the sound of that."

"Well, don't get used to it."

"I'll see you in the morning."

"Okay. I'm really looking forward to it. Sleep well," I told him before I hung up the phone.

I lay in the bed for several minutes just staring at the ceiling with a big, goofy grin on my face until I finally dozed off. The next morning, I woke up with that same bubbly feeling, but then it dawned on me that I was going to actually see him in a few hours. And it was just going to be the two of us. Alone. For hours. Oh God, I had no idea what the hell to wear. I jumped out of bed and rushed over to my closet. I was flipping through all my different shirts and jeans, but nothing seemed right. I started tossing things on the floor and onto my bed, hoping that I could find something that would make me look like a hot biker chick. Unfortunately, everything I had just seemed wrong. Feeling frustrated, I huffed, "Damn."

Robyn came to my door and said, "What the hell happened in here?"

"I'm looking for something to wear."

"For what?"

I hadn't told her about Sawyer. I was afraid that she would be upset with me. It's not like I wouldn't deserve it. I'd given her all kinds of crap about Runt, but I'd convinced myself that Sawyer was different. I just wasn't sure she'd see it that way. Knowing I couldn't hide it any longer, I confessed, "I have a date."

She crossed her arms and gave me one of her little smirks. "Is that right? Is this date with the guy you've been talking to all week?"

"How did you know I was talking to someone?"

"Come on, Dee. You've been on cloud nine for days. I figured you'd met someone. I was just waiting for you to tell me about him. So, who is it?" she pushed.

"His name is Sawyer," I started. "He's actually … a friend of Runt's."

I bit my bottom lip as I waited anxiously for my words to sink in. She blinked a couple of times, then asked, "He's a friend of Runt's? You mean he's in that motorcycle club?"

"Yes. I met him that night at Daisy's … and, again, at the hospital when his son broke his arm. We've been talking, and he asked me out."

Her eyes drifted up to the ceiling as she let out a deep breath. Strange noises vibrated through her chest as she mulled over everything I just told her, then she looked back over to me and said, "So, you really like this guy?"

"Yeah, I do."

"And you think you can handle all this biker crap, because there's some pretty heavy stuff that comes with that," she warned.

"I don't know, but I think I'd like to try."

She cocked her eyebrow as she said, "Okay, but you let this guy know, if he does anything shady, I'll put a scalpel to his balls."

I giggled as I told her, "I'll be sure to let him know."

As she walked over to my closet, she asked, "So, where are you going on this date of yours?"

"He's taking me for a ride on his bike. He told me to wear jeans and boots."

"It's eighty-five degrees outside!"

"I know!"

"Okay. We'll make it work," she assured me. "So far, he's only seen you in scrubs, right? Anything would be a step up from that."

"You'd think, but I'm not so sure."

"Have faith, chick. I'll have you fixed up in no time."

As promised, Robyn found me the perfect outfit. I wanted to wear my hair down, but she convinced me to braid it, warning me that the wind would make it a tangled mess. When I gave myself one final check in the mirror, I didn't think I looked half bad. As I started downstairs to meet Sawyer, my nerves were churning inside of me, building with each step, and by the time I made it to the front door, I was practically trembling. After several slow, steady breaths, I forced myself forward, and once I was outside, I found him standing beside his motorcycle. Just as I imagined, he looked sexy as hell, and my heart started to race as I took my first step towards him. As soon as he spotted me, the corners of his mouth curled into the most delicious smile, sending my hormones into complete overload.

"Morning, sunshine."

His voice washed over me, sending a seductive chill down my spine. "Morning."

"You ready to go?"

"Um-hmm."

Sensing my unease, he asked, "Nervous?"

"*Mmm* ... Just a smidge."

"About the bike or about the date?"

I feigned a smile and replied, "A little of both."

Then, he did something I wouldn't have expected in a million years. With one quick swoop, he reached for me, placing his hands on my waist, and pulled me towards him. Before I had time to think, he lowered his mouth to mine and kissed me with an intensity like I'd never known. His lips were soft and warm, and suddenly, I was leaning right into him. It was clear that he was no *Prince*

Charming. There was no white horse. No castle on the hill. He was rough, tough, and sexy as hell—and my God, he could kiss like it was nobody's business. His arms wound tight around me, inching me even closer as his tongue found its way into my mouth. I was holding on by a thread, and just as I was becoming completely lost in his touch, he pulled back, quickly breaking our embrace. His blue eyes danced with lust as they locked on mine. He lifted his hand up to my mouth, gently brushing the pad of his thumb across my bottom lip and asked, "You still feeling nervous?"

Still feeling a bit dazed, I muttered, "Hmm?"

"I'll take that as a no." He chuckled as he reached for my hand and led me over to the bike. He handed me a helmet, and after helping me put it on, he said, "You're all set. Just hop on behind me."

He got on and extended his hand, guiding me as I swung my leg over and eased on behind him. "Now, what?"

"Just put your feet on the pegs and hold on. Leave the rest to me."

"I think I can handle that."

"I thought you could."

He started up the engine, and I held onto his waist as we pulled out onto the road. I'd lived in Memphis for three years, driven down the same roads we were riding on a hundred times, but everything seemed completely different being on the back of his bike. It was like the city was alive, a living, breathing organism, and we were a part of her. The wind was her breath. The different sounds, the music, the horns blowing in the distance were her voice. And the people, diverse in so many ways: rich, poor, dreamers, the homeless, those who sought a future, others who found despair—they were her heart. I'd never felt such a rush as I did nestled up behind him, crossing street after street, and when we finally stopped at our first destination, I was feeling better than ever. As he helped me off the bike, he asked, "Well, what did you think?"

"I loved it." I glanced up at the Pyramid and asked, "So, what are we doing here?"

"I thought we'd go up to the lookout deck and grab a bite to eat," he answered as he took off his helmet and put it on the back of the bike.

"Sounds good to me." Once I removed my helmet and handed it to him, I followed him towards the door. I'd heard several of the nurses talking about how one of the bigger hunting stores had purchased the Pyramid and added several restaurants, places to shop, and the lookout deck, but I hadn't actually gone to see it for myself. As soon as we walked through the door, it was clear that a lot had gone into the renovations. I looked over to Sawyer and said, "Have you been here since they've changed everything?"

"A couple of times. Kevin likes to come look at the fish."

"This is amazing."

"I was hoping you might like it."

We spent an hour or so just walking around looking at things and then he asked, "You ready to go up?"

"Sure." He led me over to the elevator that took us up to the lookout deck. Once we made it up to the top, he reached for my hand and I followed him outside. We stepped out onto the deck, and the view was absolutely incredible. You could see the Mississippi River and all of downtown. "It's beautiful. I can't believe I've never done this before."

He slipped his arm around my waist and said, "Not nearly as beautiful as you."

I rolled my eyes as I said playfully, "Really? I didn't think a stud like you would need to use a cheesy line like that."

"I take offense to that." He chuckled. "I wasn't using some cheesy line. I was simply giving a compliment to a beautiful lady."

"Um-hmm. If you say so." I giggled.

He poked me in the side. "So, you think *I'm a stud*, huh?"

"You picked up on that one, did ya?"

"You're the one who said it." Just then, a surprisingly playful expression crossed his handsome face. "So, you think I'm a stud. I like that. *My beauty thinks I'm a stud.*"

Shaking my head, I started walking towards the door. "Okay, that's enough of that."

"Hey! Where ya going?"

"I'm hungry." Hoping to distract him from the stud comment, I asked, "How about some lunch?"

"Yeah." He smiled and patted his stomach. "This *stud* could go for something to eat."

Trying to bite back a huge grin, I sighed and said, "Move it *stud*. This beauty is withering away. I must eat before I starve."

We were both laughing as we headed into the look-out's restaurant for lunch. We spent the next hour eating and talking while enjoying the beautiful views of the city. It was really nice. I loved talking to him, even when he was teasing me about the stud thing. Once we were done eating, we went back out to the bike. Like before, I saddled up behind him as we rode down Riverside Drive. From there, we went to places I'd never been before. Honestly, I didn't care where we were, I just enjoyed being on the bike with him. I thought about all the men I'd been attracted to before. Sometimes, it was because of their dashing good looks, their charming personality, or simply because of their great sense of humor, but with Sawyer, it was all those things and more—*so much more*. I was shocked at how my attraction to him ran so deep, and as I wrapped my arms around him, inching myself closer, I was in a state of pure bliss.

I'd hoped that feeling could last a bit longer, unfortunately, he pulled up to the curb at my apartment, signaling the end of our date. Once we got off the bike, I smiled up at him and said, "I really had fun today."

"I did, too. Maybe we can go again sometime."

"I'd like that."

I suddenly started to feel nervous. I couldn't help myself. It was the way he was looking at me, like a lion about to pounce. When he reached for me, I took a step back, but I was too late. I was already wrapped in his arms with his mouth pressed against mine. Every single nerve in my body came alive as rough, calloused hands held me against his broad, muscular body. Did he even realize what he was doing to me? My insides felt like they were on fire. *Holy crap*, Sawyer literally had my head spinning. Before I melted into a messy puddle by the curb, I wound my arms around his neck and held on tight, pulling him closer as he deepened the kiss. When his hands started to slowly roam over my body, I knew we were getting carried away. We were standing out in front of my apartment, in broad daylight, pawing each other like horny teenagers, and as much as I was loving every single moment of it, we had to stop. I placed my hands on his shoulders, and with great, *great* hesitation, I took a step back, breaking our connection.

Licking his lips, he flashed a devious smile and asked, "You got plans for tomorrow night?"

BLAZE

Over the last few days, things had been relatively quiet. There hadn't been any sign of our hooded stranger, and no other clubs had been hit. We'd all been doing our part to keep watch, and it seemed to be working—at least I'd hoped it was, especially since I'd made plans to see Kenadee again. I knew the timing was bad, but then again, if I waited for a perfect time, I might never get my chance. When I'd gone to get her, I wasn't sure where I should take her, but the minute I saw Kenadee's outfit, I knew the perfect spot. Every time I looked across the table at her, the same thought crossed my mind: that she was absolutely beautiful. Kenadee was wearing one of those shirts that slipped down around her shoulders with a short, denim skirt and sandals. Her hair was down with soft curls around her face, and when she smiled, everyone else in the room seemed to disappear. I knew better than to sit right beside her. If I had, I wouldn't have been able to keep my hands off of her. I'd even pounded one out in the shower, and I still had a hard-on as I sat there staring at her like an idiot. I just couldn't help myself.

The truth was, I truly liked Kenadee. She was the kind of girl I could see myself building a future with, but damn, I couldn't think about the future for wanting her so much. I needed to knock the edge off, or I was never gonna make it—neither of us were. I could see the way she was looking at me. It was right there in her eyes. There was no doubt she was feeling the same fucking way, and if she licked her lips one more goddamn time, I was gonna take her on the table right then and there. *Fuck*. She was killing me.

She took a drink of her beer, then said, "The music's great. Do you come here often?"

"No." I'd brought her down to Beale Street to one of the small clubs at the end of the row to listen to some jazz music, thinking she'd like the atmosphere. But ever since we'd gotten here, listening to the sultry sound of the music and the sexual energy that was building between us, I was beginning to think it was a mistake. "I haven't been here in over a year."

She leaned forward, revealing just a hint of her cleavage. "Well, the band is incredible."

"I'm glad you like it." I watched as she took another sip of her drink, and I'll be damned if her tongue didn't slip out of her mouth and glide across her lips. I clenched my jaw as I shifted in my seat and asked, "You about ready for another drink?"

She looked down at my full beer and asked, "Why aren't you drinking? Is something wrong with your beer?"

"My beer's fine," I answered. "You ready for another?"

"Maybe in a minute." She gave me one of those looks,

one that was filled with hunger and desire, and my entire body grew tense. Fuck it. I couldn't take it a minute longer. I stood up and reached for her hand, and her eyes widened as I led her out onto the dance floor. "What are you doing?"

Without answering, I put my arm around her small waist and pulled her body close to mine, and for the first time that night, I finally had her right where I wanted her. We slowly swayed to the rhythm of the music, and once she started to relax, she lowered her head to my chest. It was nice, romantic even. I tried to focus on the soulful sound of the music and not think about how good Kenadee smelled or how she felt in my arms, but then she looked up at me with lust-filled eyes and I was done.

I lowered my mouth to hers, and as soon as our lips touched, I knew it was a mistake. I knew I didn't deserve a girl like Kenadee. She was far too good for a man like me, but from the very start, I found myself drawn to her for reasons I honestly couldn't explain. I wanted her, and as she pressed her breasts against my chest, there was no denying that she was feeling the same way. My hands roamed across the curves of her body, and damn, she felt so fucking good. When she inched closer, squirming against me with a whimper, I knew that one kiss would never be enough. Our need for each other was only growing stronger, and even though I wanted her—*God, how I wanted her*, I didn't want to fuck things up by pushing her too fast. I eased away from those sweet lips of hers and let out a deep breath. Looking down at the confused expression on her face, I kind of felt a twinge of guilt. "I need some air, darlin'."

"Umm ... Okay." She followed me towards the door,

and as soon as we were outside, she asked, "Is everything okay?"

"Yeah. I just needed a minute." That was a lie.

"*Sawyer.* There's obviously something on your mind. Just tell me."

She looked up at me with those beautiful brown eyes, and I wasn't sure what to say to her. "I think we've got a good thing here. I really do, but ..."

"But what?"

"But I want you. I want you so bad I can't fucking see straight." I pulled her close and went on, "I know you're one of those good girls, and you'll think it's crude when I say this ... but I want to *fuck you*." I knew it was a risk, but I told her exactly what was on my mind. "I want to fuck you long and hard. I want to make you come ... over and over again. And I don't know how much longer I can wait."

With her dark eyes locked on mine, she bit her bottom lip and considered what I'd said. It took her all but a few brief seconds before she shrugged and said, "Then, don't wait."

I was stunned by her response. "What?"

"I want you, too, Sawyer. More than I ever dreamed possible. You know ... tonight, I don't want to be 'the good girl.'" She arched her eyebrow and said, "Show me what's it's like to break all the rules."

Damn. I wasn't expecting that at all. I reached for her hand and asked, "Your place or mine?"

"Yours."

I nodded and led her over to my truck. We were both silent as I pulled out of the parking lot and onto the main road. Just as I was worried that she might be having doubts, she eased over closer to me, placing her hand on my thigh. Her touch was innocent; mine was not. With my eyes focused on the road ahead, I lowered my hand to her knee and slowly trailed along her inner thigh. As I got closer to the hem of her skirt, her knees fell open, and her breath quickened as the tips of my fingers grazed the lining of her lace panties. My cock throbbed against my zipper knowing she was already wet. Damn. She had me all tangled up, and it was all I could do to not stop the truck and take her right then and there.

She shifted her hips forward and rested her head on my shoulder, closing her eyes as I continued to slowly caress her—tease her, and as I pulled into the driveway, her breath was ragged with need. I parked the truck, and when she followed me into the house, I was thankful that my folks had agreed to keep Kevin for the night. I reached for Kenadee, kissing her as we stumbled into the kitchen. Her fingers dove into my hair as she clung to me—hungry for me.

"Can't stand it a minute longer," I told her as my hand slipped under her

skirt, reaching for her lace panties. With one quick tug, I ripped them from her hips, and her eyebrows furrowed with disapproval. With a smirk, I lifted her up onto the kitchen counter, and her sandals dropped to the floor. "I'll make it up to you."

She gasped when I lowered her shirt just enough to reveal her perfect round breasts, and her frown quickly faded after I dropped my mouth to one of them and began swirling my tongue around her nipple. "Oh God."

I nipped and sucked, relishing the sounds of her little moans and whimpers as I teased her with my tongue and my teeth. Needing more of her, I stood and reached for the hem of my shirt. I didn't miss the spark of desire that flashed through her eyes as I pulled it over my head. "You like what you see?"

"Um-hmm." She purred as she placed the palm of her hand on my chest, her finger traced the line of my tattoo until she looked up at me.

"I like what I see, too, baby," I said as I eased her back on the counter, then lowered my mouth down between her legs before I placed them over my shoulders. She inhaled a deep breath as soon as my beard brushed the inside of both thighs, and my tongue skimmed across her center. From that very moment, I knew I was in trouble. Like the most addictive drug on the planet, one taste of her would never be enough. I teased back and forth in a gentle rhythm against her sensitive flesh, loving the way her body instantly reacted to my touch. "Damn, baby. I don't think I'll ever get enough of you."

Her breath became uneven and hitched as I thrust my finger deep inside her, rubbing against her g-spot slow and steady. When I added a second finger, she tensed around me and goosebumps prickled across her skin. I continued to tease her, staying just inches away from where she wanted me. Her hips lifted up from the counter, begging for me to give her more. I instantly drove my fingers deeper inside her while my mouth clamped around her clit and sucked hard, giving her exactly what she needed.

"Sawyer!" she shouted as her head thrashed back.

"That's right. Come for me, baby."

I continued teasing that spot that was driving her to the edge as I tormented her with my tongue. She whispered my name over and over as she spasmed around my fingers. While she was still in the throes of her release, I quickly pulled my wallet out of my back pocket and grabbed a condom before I dropped my jeans to the floor, kicking them off along with my boots. I rolled the condom on and settled between her legs, pulling her closer to the edge of the counter. *Fuck.* She looked so damn beautiful with her long dark hair flowing around her shoulders and that wanton look in her eyes. Like a moth drawn to a flame, I inched towards her, raking my cock across her center. She was warm and wet, and I ached to be inside her. Clearly feeling the same, she arched her back towards me and moaned while her legs wrapped around my hips to pull me forward.

"You want my cock?"

"Don't tease me, Sawyer." Her lips curled into a wicked smile as she shifted her hips, forcing me inside. I froze. She felt too fucking good. I needed a second to get my act together or I'd be done before I ever got started. I regained my focus, then worked myself in deeper until I'd given her every inch. Relishing the sensation, my tortured growl echoed through the room as I slowly withdrew.

"Fuck, baby. You're so goddamn tight." A slight hiss slipped through her teeth as I drove into her again and again—each time a bit faster and unforgiving.

Her heels dug into my back and she shouted, "Oh God, yes!"

Still buried deep inside her, I slipped my hands under her ass, lifting her from the counter and carried her into my bedroom. I lowered Kenadee down onto the mattress, then took a moment as my eyes roamed over every inch of her gorgeous body. Her chest rose and fell as she tried to steady her breath, each gasp of air sounding more desperate than the last. "Sawyer?"

Hearing my name on her lips drove me wild, and I couldn't wait any longer to be back inside her. Kenadee's smile went right through me when I said, "You're so damn beautiful."

I lowered myself onto the bed, settling between her legs and instantly slammed myself deep inside her. Shifting her hips upward, her tightness gripped firmly around me. I rocked my hips forward, sending an intense heat coursing through my body. I burned for her, every inch of me, and as I drove deeper inside her, I only yearned for more. I could feel her muscles contracting all around me as her second orgasm started to take hold. My body grew rigid as I struggled to hold back my own release, and it only became more difficult when she clamped down around me as her body writhed in pleasure. "Oh my God, Sawyer! *Fuckkkk.*"

I looked down at her sprawled out on my bed in an orgasmic daze and smiled. The good little nurse was a bit of a wildcat, and I liked it. I liked it a lot. But I wasn't done yet. With her body still trembling, I dropped my hands to her hips, and she gasped when I abruptly flipped her onto her knees. With her perfect ass in the air, I fisted my hand in her long hair, giving it a gentle tug, and she cried out in pleasure when I plunged inside her once again. I couldn't imagine a better feeling. Unable to control myself, I slowly drew back and slammed into her again and again, giving her everything I had. She was so damn hot, so tight, like her body was made just for me.

"Fuckkk!" I shouted out as my throbbing cock demanded its release too fucking soon. I wanted to take my time with her, but she was just too fucking tight, felt too fucking good to stop. I continued to drive into her in a feverish rhythm, until at last, she twisted the sheets with her hands and let out a tortured groan. Her body clamped down around me like a vice as my hips collided into hers, and I was done. I recklessly drove into her a few more times then finally came deep inside of her. As I fought to catch my breath, I kept my hands planted on her hips, holding her in place as our heartbeats began to slow.

We were surrounded in darkness as I collapsed beside her and whispered, "Damn, woman. You're quite the wildcat when you want to be."

"*Yeah?*"

"Yeah." With a smile, I teased her. "I kinda think you liked breaking the rules."

"Maybe just a little." A light blush crossed her face as she turned to me and added, "But I'm pretty sure it was because it was you. I don't think it would've been the same with someone else."

"Flattery will get you everywhere." I chuckled as I pulled myself out of bed and went into the bathroom. When I came back out, she was trying to adjust her shirt, so I asked, "You want one of mine?"

"Yes, please."

I opened up my dresser and found her a fresh t-shirt and a pair of sweats. After I handed them over, I went back and grabbed myself a pair as well, and by the time I'd pulled them on, she was already dressed. My clothes swallowed her, and she was doing her best to keep them from falling off. Trying to bite back my smile, I asked, "You hungry?"

She was tugging at the drawstrings when she answered, "Yeah, I could eat something."

"Okay. I think I can scrounge up *something*." She followed me into the kitchen where she found her ripped panties laying on the floor. Her eyes skirted over to me as she bent down and picked them up. "Hey. I told you I'd make it up to you."

"That you did." She giggled. "So, what are you going to fix us to eat?"

I opened the fridge and quickly realized I didn't have many options. "How about a grilled cheese?"

"Sounds good to me." She sat down at the counter, and as I turned on the stove, she said, "So ... your tattoo? Does it have meaning?"

I looked down at my chest and smiled as I explained, "It's basically a Celtic compass," I told her as I started cooking our sandwiches. "A while back I went through some rough times and lost my way. I got the tattoo to remind myself to not let that happen again."

"Was that back when Kevin had leukemia?" Her question caught me off guard, especially since she was right. She must've sensed that I was taken aback, because she quickly said, "I'm sorry. I shouldn't have just blurted that out like that. It's just ... he told me about it at the hospital."

"It's fine. Really." I brought our sandwiches over to the counter, and after I grabbed us a couple of beers out of the fridge, I sat down beside her. "It was pretty rough there for a while, but we got through it."

"Kevin seems like a pretty awesome kid."

"He is. I don't know what I'd do without him." I knew she must be wondering about his mother, so I told her, "His mother was killed in a car accident when he was three, so it's just been the two of us for the past five, almost six, years."

"Oh, wow. I'm really sorry." Concern crossed her face as she said, "The two of you have had some pretty hard hits over the years."

"Yeah, but we got through it"—I smiled and gave her a wink— "and things seem to be looking up these days."

"I'm glad to hear that." She smiled as she took a bite of her sandwich. "Not bad. Not bad at all."

After we finished our sandwiches, we talked for a little longer and then, Kenadee reminded me that she had to work the next morning. Reluctantly, we both got dressed and headed out to my bike. I'd enjoyed my night with her, like really fucking enjoyed it, and as she leaned her head into my back and slipped her arms around my waist, I could tell she did, too. When we pulled up to her apartment, I was disappointed that our night had to end so soon. She eased off the bike, and as soon as she took off her helmet, I could see that nervous look in her eyes had returned. So fucking cute. I placed my hands on Kenadee's hips, pulling her close as I pressed my mouth against hers for one last kiss, and as soon as our lips touched, I could feel that familiar hunger building inside of me. I wanted her to know the effect she was having on me as the kiss quickly became heated. By the time I finally pulled back, we were practically breathless.

I shook my head as I looked down at her and said, "Damn, woman. You do things to me that I can't begin to explain."

Her lips curled into a sexy smile. "I feel the same way, but I kind of like it."

"Yeah. I like it, too. I like it, *a lot*." I gave her a quick kiss just below her ear, then said, "It's getting late. You better get inside before I change my mind about letting you go."

"Okay. I'll talk to you soon."

"Goodnight, wildcat. I'll call you."

I hadn't meant to lie to Kenadee and had every intention of calling her, as she was definitely on my mind, but between the garage and the club, I was overloaded. With everything that was going on, I couldn't get a free minute to myself. By the time I finally made it home, I was so exhausted that I fell asleep before I had a chance to call her. The next day, I had to take Kevin to his doctor's appointment, and by the time we were done, I had to get over to the garage.

The guys and I spent the rest of the afternoon working on an engine breakdown that had to be completed by morning. We were just finishing up, when Murphy came over and said, "Gus just called us into church."

I grabbed a rag, and as I was wiping my hands off, I said, "I gotta get Kevin. I'll be over in a minute."

"I'll see ya there."

Lowball and Crow had gone to the back, so I motioned to them as I shouted, "We gotta close up. Gus has called us in."

They both nodded, and I went to pick up Kevin. When we got to the clubhouse, all the brothers were filing in, one by one. We'd all heard the talk about the shit that was going on around us with different street gangs being hit, and it was putting us all on edge. I couldn't help but wonder if something else was going on. When I ran into Runt, I asked, "Something happen?"

"Fuck man. It's about to get real around here."

I had no idea what the hell he meant as I followed him into church. The others were already taking their seats around the table, and Gus was standing up front with Riggs and Moose. As I looked around at my brothers, I leaned back in my chair and inhaled a deep breath. Then, it happened. I suddenly caught a faint scent of her on my clothes, and the room stood still. It was only for a minute, but it was enough to make a lasting impression. Once everyone was settled, Gus sat down and looked around the room, taking his time to study each and every one of us. He leaned forward, placing his elbows on the table and intertwining his fingers like he was about to pray.

His voice was low and threatening as he said, "There's a war coming, boys. I can feel it. I don't know when. I don't know who. But it's going to be big, and I'm afraid that some of you sitting at this table right now aren't going to survive the hit."

We all knew Gus's instincts were always right, so I wasn't surprised when Runt asked, "You want to tell us what the fuck you're talking about?"

Moose turned to him and answered, "Gus has it in his head that someone's trying to take over the territory. They're wiping out the entire south side."

"That's easier said than done," Gunner scoffed.

"Agreed," Moose replied. "We all know it's not just MCs that are getting hit. Several gangs have been completely wiped out. Killed every last one of them. All on the south side, by the river—like us."

I looked over at Gus and asked, "So, it's got you thinking they'll be coming after us?"

"Absolutely."

"Any idea who these motherfuckers are?"

Gus turned to his left. "Riggs?"

Riggs leaned forward as he looked at us and said, "We all know that crystal meth is back. It's stronger, more addictive than it's ever been, and it's not your typical buyers getting this shit. Everyone wants a piece of it, so we know the demand is there."

"Yeah. We've known this, Riggs. What are you getting at?" Cyrus asked.

"I'm getting there," he told him. "This shit is coming from somewhere. It's just a matter of figuring out who. I hacked into the DEA files, and they're on the hunt for these motherfuckers, too. They don't have much. They just know it's coming from outside the city limits."

Lowball shook his head as he said, "That doesn't tell us a fucking thing."

"Here's the way I see it. If I'm right, and the same people who are trying to stake claim on the south side are dealing the meth"—he paused and shook his head—"it only makes sense that they'd set up their distribution ring right here. They'd use the barges to take their shit down the Mississippi River and continue their distribution from there—a lot like we've done with the pipeline. Hell, I'd do the same fucking thing."

"You've only got bits and pieces right now, and you can't even be sure you've got the facts straight, brother!" Murphy spat.

"You're right," Riggs answered. "But you gotta admit, it all fits."

"He's right," I agreed. "It makes sense."

"So, these guys are knocking everybody off, so they can get access to the river without any interference?" Runt asked.

"Looks that way. They're basically just working their way up the food chain," Riggs answered.

"What about this guy who was fucking with the cameras?" I asked.

Gus snarled as he said, "I think he's one of ours who's turned on us."

"What makes you think that?" Gunner asked sounding dumbfounded.

"Just feel it. You find him, and he'll lead you to others. *Guarantee it.*" Gus stood up as he made his final order. "I'm calling a lockdown. Get your families together and get them over to the club. I know there are things that need to be handled. Make it happen. You have twenty-four hours to get everything in order."

KENADEE

*I*t had been days since I'd heard from Sawyer. I was trying my best not to let it get to me, but the fact was, it did. I liked him, and after the night we shared and the things he'd said, it hurt that he didn't feel the same. I assumed that he'd changed his mind. We came from two totally different worlds, and I couldn't say that I totally disagreed. While I knew very little about his club and what they were involved in, I'd heard the rumors. I knew they had a reputation. On the other hand, my life was simple, boring even, and I had little to offer a man like Sawyer. It was easy to see why he'd lose interest in me so quickly. Having no other choice, I tried to convince myself that I needed to move on. Thankfully, I'd been working lots of overtime at the hospital, and I'd been too busy to dwell on the fact that it had been almost a week, and I still hadn't heard from him.

I was just about to finish discharging one of my patients when Robyn rushed over to me and asked, "Is it time for your break?"

I looked down at my watch and then said, "Yeah, but I need to finish this up first."

"Make it quick. I need coffee ASAP."

"Give me two minutes," I told her as I went over to the nurses' station. Once I was done, I went back over to her and said, "Ready when you are."

I followed her down to the cafeteria, and as soon as we got our coffee and a bite to eat, we sat down at one of the tables. "This morning has been a killer, dude."

"You're telling me, and I've got two more days of it."

She gave me a slight grimace as she asked, "Still no word from him?"

"Nope. Not a peep."

"I don't see why you don't send him a message just to—"

"No," I cut her off. "He'll think I'm desperate or something."

"Girl, times have changed. It's not like that anymore. You just send him a quick message to get the conversation going. Trust me."

Hope started stirring in the pit of my stomach as I reached for my phone.

"Are you sure about this?"

"Absolutely."

I took a deep breath as I pulled up his last message.

ME: *Hey. I hope you're having a good day. I've been thinking about you.*

As soon as I sent it, I instantly regretted it. Robyn looked down at my screen and smiled. "Perfect. I bet he responds in no time."

She was right. He responded alright.

SAWYER: *Hey. Sorry I haven't called. Got a lot going on. Bad timing.*

THAT WAS IT. That was all I got. I took my phone and put it back in my pocket, trying my best not to lose it in the middle of the hospital cafeteria. Seeing the look of disappointment on my face, Robyn asked, "What did he say?"

"Nothing." I stood up, and as I turned to leave, I told her, "I need to get back to work."

She got up and chased after me. "If he didn't kiss your ass, then he's a complete idiot, Kenadee! You're an amazing catch."

"Apparently, he didn't think so." As we got on the elevator, I grumbled, "*Apparently*, it's bad timing or some bullshit like that."

"Well, screw him. You're the bomb.com, girl. He doesn't know what he's missing." She nudged me with her elbow. "It's his loss."

I wanted to believe what she was saying was true, that it was his loss, but I couldn't help but feel like I was missing out on something pretty great, too. With a heavy heart, I made my way back to the nurses' station and grabbed the next patient file. When I read the name *Kate Dillion*, it looked familiar, but it didn't register until I pulled back the curtain and saw the young blonde holding a crying baby in her arms. "Back again so soon?"

"Something's wrong with her," Kate replied with panic in her voice. "Her fever is really high, and it's like she can't catch her breath."

I rolled my cart over to the gurney and started checking her stats, and Kate was right. The baby's fever was high, and her oxygen level was low—too low. Worried that she might have RSV, I told her, "I'll be right back."

I called Dr. Sheridan into the room, so he could make a diagnosis. After looking her over, he turned to Kate and said, "I need to run some tests. It shouldn't take long."

With a worried look on her face, she nodded and said, "Okay. Whatever you need to do."

I followed him out into the hallway after he ordered a round of bloodwork, and while we were waiting for the results, he prescribed her an IV of fluids and a breathing treatment. Just as I was getting her taken care of, all hell broke loose in the ER. Over the scanners, we heard that there was a shooting at one of the restaurants downtown, but the dispatcher's voice was jumbled, and I couldn't make out what he'd said. Seconds later, I could hear the sounds of ambulances approaching the back door, and in a blink of an eye, paramedics were charging inside with one gunshot victim after the next. Sadly, it wasn't exactly anything new. Over the last few weeks, it was like we'd entered some kind of war zone with all the gunshot victims who had been coming into the trauma center, but unlike today, most of them were DOA.

I rushed over to Charlie, one of the paramedics I worked with on a daily basis, and asked, "What do we got?"

His shirt was covered in blood, and his voice was

strained as he answered, "Female in her late forties. Critical gunshot wound to the left side flank. Blood pressure sixty-two over forty. Heart rate forty-six."

As I pushed back the curtain, he and his driver wheeled her into the room. Several orderlies and nurses came in to help us move her over to the gurney, and as soon as we had her settled, I moved to the head of the gurney to check her airway. As I looked down at her, covered in blood, clothes cut away, and shattered glass all around her, she asked, "Where's my daughter?"

"It's okay, ma'am." Charlie placed his hand on her shoulder as he said, "She's right in the next room over. She's going to be fine."

She managed to nod, and then, we got to work. While we were busy stabilizing her, I could hear the commotion outside the room. It was a madhouse as the other doctors and nurses rushed around helping the other incoming patients. Curious to know what went down, I turned to Charlie and asked, "What happened this time?"

"A drive by at Daisy Mae's."

I'd been working at the hospital a long time, seen and heard a lot of things, but hearing that a place like Daisy Mae's had been hit by a drive-by shooting in broad daylight took me by surprise. "You've got to be kidding me!"

"Damnedest thing." He started towards the door. "Makes you wonder what they'll do next."

The next few hours were a complete blur as I moved from one patient to the next, and just as the adrenaline started to wear off, it was over. All of the patients had either been sent off to surgery, admitted to their own room, or discharged with minor injuries. Every muscle in my body ached as I sat at the nurses' station and tried to catch my breath. It wasn't until that very moment when I remembered Kate and her daughter, Lacie. With everything that had been going on, I'd totally forgotten to go back and check on them. I got up and rushed over to the room, and when I walked in, I found Kate with her head propped against the wall, and Lacie sound asleep in her arms.

"Hey. How are you two doing?"

"Not so good. One of the nurses just came in and said that Lacie has RSV."

Remembering her high fever and low oxygen level, I wasn't all that surprised by the test results. "Are they admitting her?"

"Yes." She sounded terrified as she said, "They're about to take us to her room."

"Don't worry. They'll take great care of her."

I was about to slip out, when her brother came barreling into the room. "Kate?"

"Terry! Where have you been? I've been calling you for hours."

His face and clothes were covered with dark smudges, and there were rips and tears in his jeans. His hand was tucked protectively at his armpit as he grumbled, "I already told you. I had something I had to take care of."

"Are you okay? It looks like you've been in an accident or something."

"I'm fine." His beady, little eyes skirted over to me, and I knew he was lying when he said, "Wrecked my bike is all."

"I told you that thing was dangerous," she scolded. "I don't know why you ever bought it."

As I listened to the banter back and forth, I became more and more uncomfortable. I just wanted to get away from them both, so I made up the excuse, "I better get back to work. I hope Lacie gets to feeling better."

"Thank you," Kate replied. "I hope she does, too."

When I walked out, Robyn was waiting for me at the front desk and immediately pointed at the clock, letting me know that our shift was finally over. Relieved, I grabbed my things and followed her out to the car. On our way home, I asked, "Are we stopping for takeout or calling something in for delivery?"

"Actually, neither for me." She shrugged innocently. "I have a date tonight."

"A date? With who?"

"I'd rather not say. I don't want to jinx it."

"Jinx it? Seriously?"

"Don't worry. I'll tell you all about him once I see how things are gonna work out."

"I'm going to hold you to that."

With a smirk, she replied, "I know you will."

When we got back to the apartment, she rushed off to take a shower, and a half an hour later she came out looking like a million bucks in her skinny jeans and black halter top. She stood in front of me as she asked, "How do I look?"

"Incredible, as always."

"Thanks. I better get going. I don't want to be late." As she started for the door, I noticed that she was carrying a small duffle bag, so I asked, "What's that for?"

With a coy, little smirk, she replied, "Oh, you know. In case things turn interesting during dinner."

"Okay." I rolled my eyes and said, "Have fun and be careful."

"Will do. I'll call you if I'm going to be late."

As soon as she was gone, I changed into my pajamas, made myself a bowl of cereal, and plopped down on the sofa. Hoping to just relax and watch TV, I reached for the remote and started flipping through the channels. Just when I thought I'd found the perfect movie, there was a knock at my door. I assumed Robyn must've forgotten something, but when I got up and opened it, I was shocked to see that it was one of the guys from the club. I'd met him the night of the bachelorette party, but it took me a minute to remember his name.

"Uh … Hey. Riggs, right?"

"Yeah. That's right."

I glanced around, looking for any sign of the others. "You looking for Robyn or something?"

"No." With a serious tone, he replied, "Actually, I came here looking for you."

"Me? Why?"

"Something's come up, and I need you to come with me."

I'd only met Riggs the one time, and while he'd seemed like a fairly decent guy, I knew nothing about him. I certainly didn't know him well enough to just leave with him without a really good reason. Feeling a little wary, I took a step back as I asked, "And why would I do that?"

"I can't explain that now, Kenadee. I just need you to get your shit and come with me."

Startled by his tone, I reached for the door and slammed it shut. Unfortunately, he stuck his boot in the doorway and prevented it from latching. "You've got two seconds to move your fucking foot, or I'm going to call the police!"

"Look, I'm not trying to scare you, Kenadee. You've gotta listen to me," he pleaded. "I'm here about Blaze."

I'd never heard that name before, so I asked, "Who's Blaze?"

"It's Sawyer."

"Sawyer?" I leaned forward, peeking through the crack of the door, and asked, "What are you talking about?"

"He's hurt, Kenadee. He needs your help."

When I saw the worried look in his eyes, there was no denying that he was telling the truth. When I thought about him being hurt, hurt bad enough for one of his brothers to come ask for my help, every muscle in my body fell limp. "Oh God."

He eased the door open as he said, "Look, I know this comes as a shock and all that, but he's in pretty bad shape and—"

"If he's hurt so bad, why doesn't he just go to the hospital?"

"There's no time to explain, Kenadee, but I wouldn't have come here if I had some other choice." I could hear the desperation in his voice as he pleaded, "I need you to come with me before it's too late."

"But …"

"You've gotta trust me here. Just go change. We don't have much time."

I stood there staring at him for a moment, and I found myself thinking back on the time I'd spent with Sawyer— that first night at the diner, our ride on the bike, being in his arms as we danced at the bar, and the way he'd made me feel when we'd made love. Maybe I was just being hopeful, but I'd felt a connection with him, a connection beyond anything I'd ever felt before, and I couldn't turn my back on him, even if he'd already turned his on me. Even though I had no idea what I was getting myself into, I looked up at him and said, "Okay."

He waited as I went to my room and changed. Once I was done, a thought crossed my mind, and as I came back out to the living room, I asked, "What about Robyn? I need to tell her—"

"I'll take care of Robyn. Let's go."

For some crazy reason, I trusted him and followed him out the door, locking it behind me. Once we were downstairs, we ran over to his truck. I was a nervous wreck and couldn't even think straight as I watched him climb in next to me and start the engine. My hands were trembling as we pulled away from my apartment, and as we drove further away, an uneasy feeling washed over me. I couldn't help but wonder why Sawyer hadn't just gone to the hospital if he was hurt—why he needed me to help him. It just didn't make sense, but then again, lately nothing about him seemed to make sense. I hoped seeing him might give me some of the answers I'd been looking for.

Riggs pulled up to a large metal gate, and after he gave a quick hand signal to one of the guards, he drove around to the back of the building, parking next to a row of motorcycles.

As we got out of the truck, I asked, "Where are we?"

"The clubhouse." I looked up at the old cobblestone building, and even in the dark, I could still see that it was massive, taking up almost a full block. There was very little light coming from the windows, giving the walkway an ominous feel as I followed him towards a back door. "Keep your head low and talk to no one."

Suddenly feeling even more anxious, I replied, "Um ... *Okay.*"

As soon as he opened the large wooden door, I could hear men's voices in the distance, but Riggs moved too quickly for me to see where they were coming from. His boots thumped against the concrete floors as he led me down a long, corridor, and I had to hurry to keep up with him. I glanced around as we passed one room after another, only catching small glimpses here and there when he suddenly stopped at the end of the hall. My stomach twisted into a knot as he placed a hand on the doorknob.

Before he opened it, he said, "Don't freak out."

"Oh my God. You did not just say that, Riggs!" I scolded. "You do not tell a woman not to freak out, *especially when you don't want her to freak out* ... Oh, just forget it. Just open the damn door."

He shrugged as he eased the door open, and my mouth dropped in complete and utter shock. I stood there frozen in disbelief as I stared at the make-shift hospital room. I couldn't believe my eyes. I'd seen crazy things in my life but standing there watching a man frantically try to perform surgery in the middle of a biker clubhouse was a new one for me. I was trained for situations like this, but it was hard to take it all in. I finally turned to Riggs and asked, "Who's he?"

"That's Mack. The club's doc. He's kind of got his hands full right now."

"I see that."

He motioned me forward. "Sawyer's over here in one of the side rooms."

I nodded as he led me over to a side door in the corner, and just before we entered, I noticed two gurneys off to the side with blood stained sheets covering them. I'd been in enough morgues to know a dead body when I saw one, so I turned to Riggs and asked, "Who is that?"

"No one. Just keep walking." He motioned for me to go inside, then followed behind me. When I found Sawyer lying on a gurney, the first thing I noticed was the blood. *Damn.* It was everywhere—his skin, his clothes, the sheets, even the walls. As I stepped closer, I noticed a large piece of metal protruding from his chest and a seeping laceration on his lower thigh. I looked over to Riggs and asked, "Oh my God! What happened?"

Sawyer's eyes shot open, and when he saw me standing there, a strange expression washed over him. After several seconds, he turned to Riggs and asked, "What the hell is she doing here?"

Stunned by his reaction, I muttered, "Um ..."

Riggs tried to stay calm as he said, "Easy there, brother."

"Answer the goddamn question, Riggs!" he snarled, like a mad dog. "Why the fuck did you bring her here?"

"I really don't need this shit, not after the day I've had," I snapped. As I turned to leave, I said, "Have a nice life, Sawyer, and good luck with that big chunk of metal that's stuck in your chest."

BLAZE

*W*hen Gus called for the lockdown, I didn't have much time to get things in order. I knew the routine. Take care of the family, then tend to the garage. Once I had Kevin and my folks packed, I brought them over to the clubhouse and made sure they were settled in. They'd been there enough to know their way around, so I knew they'd be okay while I took care of things at the garage. Since we'd be shut down indefinitely, I needed to close out all the orders we'd completed over the past week. I'd also have to make arrangements for the two orders we weren't able to finish, but we had plenty of connections. It didn't take long to get everything covered, especially with Murphy there to give me a hand. After we had everything sorted, we started locking everything down, securing every window and door from front to back. I'd just closed the final pulldown gate, when I heard a strange click, one that made the hairs on the back of my neck stand tall—like someone had just walked across my fucking grave. Knowing something was about to go down,

I took a step back, and an explosion sent Murphy and I sailing backwards, with debris and fire coming right towards us.

When my brothers got us back to the med room, I quickly realized it wasn't just the garage that had been hit. I couldn't believe my fucking ears when Moose told us about the diner. A fucking drive-by in the middle of the day when we had surveillance at every corner just didn't make fucking sense, but as I watched Mack work frantically to save Runt's life, I couldn't help but accept it. Since I wasn't as bad off as the others, I was taken to a room off to myself to wait until Mack could get to me. They'd given me some painkillers and I was doing alright until Riggs brought Kenadee here. As soon as I saw her beautiful face standing there in the corner, I saw red, and when I realized that the man I trusted most was responsible for her being there, I wanted to ring his fucking neck. "What the fuck were you thinking bringing her here?"

"I thought she could help."

"We don't need her help!"

Riggs glanced out in the hall as he said, "I think you might be wrong there, brother. We've already lost Runt and Lowball. I'd say we need her help more than you think."

"We lost Runt and Lowball?"

"Yeah, Mack did what he could, man." Riggs leaned towards me as he said, "But Runt was DOA, and Lowball was just too far gone. There was nothing he could do, and it's fucking with his head. He's doing what he can to save Gauge now, but it's touch and go. Then, there's you, and we've got Murphy in the other room. He's not too bad off

... just a couple of burns on his hand, a few cuts and bruises, but it's still too fucking much for Mack to handle on his own. We *need her help*, brother."

I looked over to Kenadee standing in the corner with an angry scowl as she listened to our conversation, and I could only imagine what she must be thinking. I knew she'd seen shit like this before. Hell, she'd been working in the trauma center for years, but this was different. In here, her life was on the line. I had no way of knowing what these motherfuckers were going to pull next, none of us did, and looking at Kenadee made my stomach twist into knots. While I didn't know exactly *what*, I knew in my gut she meant *something* to me, and I'd never forgive myself if something happened to her. "And if she gets hurt in all this?"

"I won't let that happen. You've got my word," he promised.

"Give us a minute."

He nodded and walked out of the room, closing the door behind him. After several seconds passed, she finally looked over to me. She was trying to hide it, but I could see the hurt in her eyes as she said, "So, I guess you were right about it being bad timing."

Damn.

She had me by the balls, so I had no other choice but to come clean. "I fucked up. I should've called a hundred times, but too many things were going on ... and I wasn't sure how all this was going to play out."

"What is *all this* exactly?" she pushed.

I knew she would have questions, questions that I couldn't answer, but I'd have to find a way to set her mind at ease. I grimaced as I replied, "Can't really talk about it."

She rolled her eyes. "I seem to be getting a lot of that."

"I'm sorry about earlier. It's not that I …"

"Don't. I get it," she told me as she walked over and started to examine my wound. Fuck. She looked just as beautiful as I remembered. I could smell a hint of her perfume, and it was fucking with my head. As she glanced down at the gash in my thigh, she asked, "Should I even bother asking how this happened?"

"An explosion at the garage." She sighed as she turned her attention back to my chest, and when she started pressing down on the wound, I groaned, "Damn, woman."

"Yeah. It looks pretty bad."

"Hurts like a bitch," I groaned

She quickly withdrew her hand. "I'm not sure I can do this. It's in there pretty deep. You've lost a lot of blood, and there might be muscle damage and—"

"Just do what you gotta do, Kenadee. I trust you."

"I don't think you get what I'm saying," she argued. "I'm not a doctor, Sawyer. I just don't have the experience to handle this kind of thing."

She was starting to freak out, so I shouted, "Riggs!"

When he stuck his head through the door, I said, "I know he's got his hands full, but see if Mack can tell her what to do about this shit."

"I'll see what I can do." He motioned for her to follow. "Come with me, Kenadee."

With a groan, she followed him out of the room, and twenty minutes later, they both returned with their hands full of medical supplies. Kenadee put on a brave face as she came over to me with what looked to be an IV. "I'm going to give you something to put you out. It won't be like general anesthesia that you'd get at the hospital. It's pretty strong, so I won't be—"

Knowing it's what Mack had given her, I urged her on, "It's fine. Just do it."

"Oh, okay."

I felt her hands trembling just as she was about to prick me. "Kenadee?"

"Yeah?"

"You remember that morning when I took you on your first ride on the bike and how nervous you were?"

She started to smile. "I do."

"And, when I kissed you … do you remember how you forgot about how nervous you were?"

She started to smile. "Um-hmm."

"Well, I'd kiss you now, but …"

"Thanks, but I think I can manage," she told me as she quickly inserted the needle into my vein. "See. I managed just fine."

"There's my *wildcat*." I smiled.

Riggs peered over her shoulder and said, "Good job. Now, if you can just get that big piece of shrapnel out of his chest without letting him bleed to death or causing him permanent damage, we'll be set."

"Gee thanks, Riggs." She shook her head. "Maybe it would be best if you just *stopped talking*."

"Yeah. I can do that."

"Thank you." Kenadee looked down at me and said, "Are you sure about this?"

The pain meds doc had given me were wearing off, and my entire body was on fire. At that point, I was desperate for it to stop, so I replied, "Absolutely."

She took a needle and as she stuck it into my IV, she

said, "Okay. Here goes nothing. I'm going to give you this shot, and in a few minutes …"

Within seconds, my eyelids grew heavy, and it became difficult to understand what she was saying. And then, everything went dark.

I had no idea how long I'd been out when I started to come back around, but it took me some time to pull my wits back together. The room was spinning, and my head throbbed like I'd been hit by a fucking truck. I tried to open my eyes, but everything was blurry. I heard someone calling out my name, over and over. I wanted to respond, but my mouth felt like it was stuffed with cotton. Eventually, the haze started to clear, and I was able to force myself to wake up. It seemed like it had only been a few seconds, but when I opened my eyes, I found Kenadee hovering over me with tears in her eyes. "Sawyer! Thank God."

I swallowed, and my voice was low as I replied, "Hey."

She ran her palm across my forehead, and as she moved it down to my cheek, I found myself leaning into the coolness of her hand. As she wiped the tears from her face, she looked at me and said, "I can't believe you're finally awake."

My throat burned as I told her, "Hey … don't cry. I'm alright."

"Don't try to talk. Try to take a sip of this," she ordered as she offered me a drink of water. "I'll let Mack know you're awake."

I nodded and watched as she slipped out the door, and a short time later, Mack came in. He looked like death warmed over as he walked over to me and asked, "How ya feeling, brother?"

"Been better." Knowing they were probably wondering how I was doing, I asked, "My folks know I'm alright?"

"They do. I just had words with Dan." I winced when he started to peel back my bandage, and as he examined my wound, he announced, "Looks like your girl did a damn good job. Don't know what we would've done without her tonight."

"And Murph and Gauge?"

"We'll talk about them later. For now, you focus on getting some rest." With that, he left the room and turned out the light. It wasn't a good sign that he wouldn't tell me how my brothers were doing, which didn't exactly make it easy for me to rest. Every time I'd start to doze off, my mind would go back to them, and I'd find myself wondering if they were okay. A couple of hours later, I was relieved to see that Kenadee had finally returned. She eased over to the side of my bed and asked, "You doing okay?"

"Getting there."

"That's good. 'Cause for a while there, you had me scared half to death."

"Why's that?"

"You were out for a long time." Her voice trembled with concern. "I was worried you might not wake up."

I looked down at the bandage on my chest. "But I did, and from what Doc said, you did alright."

"You got lucky. It wasn't as deep as I thought." She sighed. "There's still a high risk of infection. This isn't exactly the most sanitary place I've ever been."

"Kenadee, I'm gonna be fine."

She shook her head. "You're not out of the woods yet.

"But thanks to you I'm getting there."

"How can you be so calm about all this? You could've died tonight. And your friend ... the one who was shot at the diner, he's hanging by a thread in there. And Murphy ... even though they aren't as bad as I first thought, his burns need to be seen by a specialist," she argued. "I just don't understand. You should be in a hospital, *a real hospital*, and so should they."

I understood why she would question the club's decision to bypass the hospital, especially when things were as bad as they were, but we'd learned from experience, that it was too much of a risk to put our trust in people we didn't know. The last thing we needed was for people knowing our business—like the club's connection to the diner or the fact we'd just lost two of our brothers. We'd managed to stay off the cops radar by keeping all aspects of our lives guarded, protecting ourselves from any outsiders. An attack like we'd just experienced at the garage and Daisy's would definitely send up red flags, and that was the last thing we needed when a war was about to erupt. It was simple. In our world, trust was not easily given. "We didn't have a choice."

"But why?" she pushed.

"I've already told you. It's club business, and you don't talk about club business. Period."

"That's bullshit, and you know it," she snapped. "I put my neck on the line for you and those men out there! With one slight infection, all that hard work will go up in flames. It's just not right."

I was still trying to clear my head from all the drugs, and with her pushing so hard, I let my guard down. "Like you, people at hospitals ask questions."

"So?"

"Questions lead to more questions, and then we have a problem. It's best not to have a problem. That's why we have Mack. With him, we have less problems."

Her eyes narrowed as she glared at me with anger. "Seriously? That's all you're going to tell me?"

"That's all I can tell you, and even that's too much."

"Well, that's just not enough," she huffed.

"I get that you're upset, babe, but—"

"Oh, no," she snapped. "Don't you *babe* me, Sawyer Mathews! This whole thing is way over the top. Unexplained drive-by shootings, explosions, a clubhouse with an in-house doctor, and God knows what else, and I ask one question. *One question.* Babe—my ass!"

It seemed like such a simple thing to her, but it was far from it. The brothers kept club business under wraps for a reason. It kept the people we cared about safe, and whether they liked it or not, it was something we needed for their protection. I looked up at her and noticed the dark circles under her eyes. "Have you gotten any sleep?"

"Don't try to change the subject."

"Answer the damn question."

"No. If you must know. I haven't." She inhaled a deep breath. "But I have the next few days off, so I can sleep late."

Damn. They hadn't told her. When she found out, it was going to send her for another fucking loop. "*Kenadee.*"

"I know. I'll go home soon. I just couldn't leave until I knew you were okay," she replied innocently.

"*Kenadee.*"

"What?"

I tried to keep my voice calm and steady as I told her, "You can't go home."

"What are you talking about?"

"The club's on lockdown. No one can leave … Not now. It's not safe," I tried to explain.

"You can't make me stay here, Sawyer." She didn't even sound mad. It was like she actually believed what she was saying. "I get that all of you are worried about all this gunfire and mayhem, but I'm not involved in any of that. There's no reason for me to stay."

"You're not leaving."

Her cheeks flushed red with anger. "Yes, I am."

"Kenadee, there's no way in hell that I'm letting you walk out that goddamn door when those men … the same men who've already killed two of my brothers and left two more fighting for their lives are still out there. Not a chance in hell I'm gonna let that happen. So, you might as well get that thought out of your pretty little head."

"And who the hell are you to tell me what I'm going to do?"

"In this clubhouse, you're mine, and I'm damn well gonna take care of what's mine."

"I'm not some kind of plaything, Sawyer," she chided. "I can't take any more of this right now. I'm too tired to think straight. I need to get out of here."

She turned, and when she started for the door, she face planted right into Gus's chest. When she looked up at him, he smiled at her and said, "And where you running off to so fast, darlin'?"

KENADEE

*M*y head was practically spinning as I stood there staring at the stranger's face. Once I'd realized that Sawyer was going to be okay, every ounce of adrenaline that was racing through my body had vanished, leaving me completely drained and unable to think. After all the things I'd seen and heard, I knew there were questions that needed to be asked, but Sawyer had made it clear that I wasn't going to get the answers that I wanted. I was beyond frustrated, angry even, and when I ran into the older man with the burly beard and bulging muscles, I wasn't in the mood to meet another one of Sawyer's brothers. I just wanted to get the hell out of that room. I needed a moment to take a breath and collect myself before I said something I might regret. Unfortunately, that wasn't going to happen, because the big, burly man I'd just run into wasn't just another brother. He was head honcho of the entire club. Damn.

After Sawyer introduced me to Gus, I feigned a smile and extended my hand. "It's nice to meet you, Gus."

"Mighty nice to meet you, too, Kenadee. I've heard a lot about you." He smiled. "I wanted to thank you for all that you did to help our boys last night. Mack said you were really something."

I glanced over to Sawyer, remembering how vastly different he'd looked the night before, and once again, my mind was bombarded with questions. While I wasn't necessarily in love with him, I did care about him, and it did something to me to think that he could've died last night. I wanted to know who had caused that explosion at the garage. I wanted to know who was behind the drive-by shooting at the diner, and why there were so many secrets with the club. None of it made any sense, and as I turned back to Gus, the leader of all these strong, loyal men, I could tell just by looking at him that he had all the answers. There was something about him, maybe his strong, confident stance or that fierceness in his stare that let me know there was no way in hell he'd ever share those answers with me. As far as the club was concerned, I would stay there left in the dark forever, and there was nothing I could do about it.

Angered by the whole situation, I crossed my arms and said, "I did what I had to do. I still think they all would've been better off at a hospital." I shrugged. Before he had a chance to respond, I glanced back over at Sawyer with an angry scowl. "So, Sawyer just informed me that I'm not allowed to leave the clubhouse. Is that true?"

"He did?"

"Yes. *He did*, and considering all I've done to help, I don't think it's asking too much for you to let me go home. I'm not going to say anything about all this.

Besides, it's not like anyone would actually believe me anyway," I scoffed.

"Come with me," he ordered with a blank expression.

Feeling a little uneasy about his tone, I asked, "Um … do I have a choice?"

"No." Without another word, he walked out of the room, and I followed him through a side door that I'd never seen before. It led into a long, interior hall, and when he came up to the third door, he stopped and opened it, motioning for me to go inside. "Sit."

I was feeling like I'd been summoned to the principal's office as I walked into the small room and was surprised to find that it looked quite different from the med-room. It reminded me of a quant, little hotel room with a mid-sized bed with a fluffy, gray down comforter and a small desk in the corner. There was a flat-screen TV mounted on the wall and a small bathroom to the side. I was a little shocked as I sat down on the edge of the bed. Feeling guilty about my behavior back in the med-room, I looked over to Gus and said, "I'm sorry if I seemed rude back there. I'm not usually like this. I'm just really tired and confused. I have a hard time when I don't know what's going on."

His eyebrows furrowed, and I suddenly got the feeling it was time for me to stop talking. "I get that all this is a lot to take in, especially when you're just thrown into it on a night like last night."

"Um-hmm," was all I could manage to respond.

"The thing is … you got yourself tied to Blaze. It might not have been something either of you planned, but it happened, and seeing that he's a brother of this club, that means you're also tied to Fury. Now, take a second to let that soak in."

He crossed his arms as he leaned against the desk and watched as his words crushed me like a ten-ton weight. As I sat there thinking about what he'd said, I found myself wanting to argue with him. I'd only known Blaze a few weeks, so we weren't actually a couple. I didn't see how it was possible that I'd gotten myself tied to him or the club. Just as I was about to tell him that, he started to shake his head.

"Before you try to tell me I'm wrong, I want you to think about something. Last night, when Riggs came for you, you could've told him to fuck off, but you didn't. You heard that Sawyer was hurt ... *a man you'd like to think you don't care that much about, but we both know you do.* You heard he was hurt and that was all it took ... and you didn't just help him, you helped Mack with Gunner, and then you did what you could with Murphy. Kenadee, whether you want to admit it or not, you are right in the center of Fury."

I sighed as I dropped my head into the palms of my hands. "Damn."

"We needed you last night, and you did everything you could to help our boys. That shit goes a long way in this club. The brothers will always be grateful for what you've done."

I nodded.

"But, here's the deal." His voice grew stern as he continued, "There are bad men out there who are trying to kill us, Kenadee. They've been watching us for weeks. Honestly, I don't know what they've seen and what they haven't. I don't know if they saw Blaze with you. I don't know if they saw the two of you at your apartment. You can leave here if you choose and take your chances, but I can't promise you that you won't end up like Runt and Lowball, dead under a white sheet. No way I can know what's gonna happen ... or you can stay here where the men are grateful for what you've done for their brothers, and they'll put their lives on the line to protect you. That much I do know. I'll see to it."

"Can I ask you something?"

His eyes narrowed as he replied, "Yes, but that doesn't mean I'll answer."

"If these men might have been watching my apartment, what about my roommate Robyn? She's still there, and she has no idea about any of this."

"We've got her covered. Got a prospect watching her. If anything comes up, he'll bring her here," he explained as he walked over to the door and opened it. "What's it gonna be, Ms. Brooks? You staying or going?"

"Has anyone ever told you that you're a very persuasive man?" I smiled.

"A time or two." He chuckled.

"I don't have any clothes or anything to take a shower with ... or even a tooth brush."

With a knowing smile, he replied. "I'll get one of the girls to take care of it."

"Okay."

Before he closed the door, he said, "Start your shower. I'll have your things to you in a minute."

As soon as he closed the door, I sat on the edge of the bed, frozen in dismay. I wanted to convince myself that I'd just agreed to stay at the clubhouse because there was a chance my life was in danger, but truthfully, as I sat there listening to Gus talk, I found myself actually wanting to stay for other reasons—reasons I couldn't even begin to explain. Hoping that it was just the fatigue and that I hadn't gone completely mad, I got up and went into the bathroom. Just as I'd turned on the hot water, there was a knock at my door. When I went to answer it, there was a young woman standing in the hall with her arms full of clothes.

"Hi! I'm Sadie."

She walked right past me and into my room, then dropped the bags of clothes and towels onto my bed. "Uh… Hi."

"Gus told me to bring these things over for you. He said you and I were about the same size, but you might be a little thicker around the middle than me … but it's all good. I think these will fit you just fine." She peeked into one of the bags as she rambled on, "I brought shampoo and conditioner, soap, a hairdryer, a toothbrush, towels, and umm… I can't remember what's all in here. If I missed anything, just let me know. We've got plenty of stuff in the stock room."

I nodded. "Okay. I appreciate it."

"So, you're Kenadee, right?"

She was young, maybe twenty-one with pretty, red hair and freckles, reminding me of Isla Fisher with her bright smile and youthful demeanor. I smiled at her and replied, "Yes. That's right."

"I heard some of the guys talking about you last night at the bar. They said you were Blaze's new girl." I could tell that she was fishing when she added, "I didn't realize he was seeing anyone."

Something told me this was a conversation that I

didn't need to have, especially with someone I didn't know or trust, so I told her, "I better get to my shower before the water gets cold."

"Oh, yeah, of course." She started towards the door and just before she left, she turned back to me and said, "If you need anything, just let me know."

"I will. Thanks, Sadie."

Relieved that she was gone, I grabbed everything I'd need for my shower and went to the bathroom. As I started to undress, I glanced up at the mirror and gasped when I saw my reflection. My hair was all over my head, there were blood stains all over my clothes and face, and the heavy, dark circles under my eyes made me look like I was at least ten years older.

"Shit. I look like I'd been to hell and back," I grumbled to myself as I tossed my dirty clothes onto the floor and stepped into the shower. Thankfully, as soon as the hot water hit my shoulders, I forgot about my horrid appearance and let the tension start to ease from my body. I started to think back over everything, and I was hit with an epiphany. I'd spent the last few years trying to do what I could to save the world and make it a better place, while the men of Fury and the people they were associated with were out there destroying it. I didn't know how I'd gotten myself caught up in their world, but I knew when the coast was clear, I'd have to get the hell out of there before it was too late—otherwise, everything I'd worked for would've been in vain.

After I got out of the shower, I went through all the clothes that Sadie had brought and managed to find something to put on. Once I was dressed, I crawled into bed, and the minute my head hit the pillow, my exhaustion took over and I fell fast asleep. I had no idea how long I'd been sleeping, but it hadn't been long enough when I heard a light tap at my door. I was so tired that I just rolled over, trying to ignore it, but when I heard it a second time, I forced myself out of bed. I eased the door open, and nearly had a coronary when I found Sawyer standing there. "Sawyer. What are you doing here?"

He was wearing a pair of low-hanging sleep pants that showed off his well-defined V and a pair of white socks with nothing else. A bandage was covering most of the left side of his chest, leaving the rest of his gorgeous, muscular torso bare. There was sweat beading across his brow. "I came to check on you."

"But, you should be in bed!" I fussed.

He glanced over at my bed, and as he slowly started to hobble towards it, he replied, "Okay. If you say so."

I watched with surprise as he slowly started to lay down in *my bed*, propping the pillows behind his head as he made himself right at home. Once he was settled, I asked, "Are you comfortable?"

"Yep. This is good." He grinned.

"What in the world were you thinking, Sawyer? You just got out of surgery. You could've pulled your stitches out by getting up too soon."

I could tell by his blank stare that he didn't like my reaction. "I just told you. I was *checking on you*."

I inhaled a deep breath and tried to lose my mothering tone and asked, "And why exactly are you *checking on me?*"

If I hadn't known Sawyer was a bad ass biker, with rippling muscles and know-it-all attitude, I'd say the man was pouting when he said, "It's been a while since you left. I figured you would've been by to at least check

Murphy's bandages, so I thought I better come check on you."

"Yeah. I guess I slept a little longer than I meant to. I should probably get over to the med-room and see how Murphy is doing," I goaded him.

"No. You don't have to do that." He took the bait. "He's alright now. Mack took care of him."

"Um-hmm. Well, I'll go see about him in a little bit just to be sure." I eased over to the bed and sat down next to him. "And what about you? How are you doing?"

He looked up at me and a spark flashed through his eyes, and I knew right away he wasn't talking about his injury when he said, "Better now."

Even though he was wounded, bandaged and weak, he looked so damn good laying there in my bed. I found it difficult to keep my hormones in check. "Good. I'm glad to hear that."

"What about you?" He placed his hand on my upper thigh, and I felt a chill slip down my spine. "You feeling better after getting a shower and some sleep?"

"Yes. Much better, but I'm a little hungry."

"Hungry? Now, that's a problem that I can take care of." His blue eyes sparked as he smiled, making it difficult once again to remember that he was injured. He reached into his pocket and pulled out his phone. "What are you hungry for?"

My first inclination was to answer *you*, but instead, I simply replied, "Anything will do at this point. Cereal. Peanut butter and jelly. Grilled cheese … but only if they can make it as good as yours," I joked.

"Pfft … Nobody can make a grilled cheese as good as me, not even my mother, and that's saying something."

After he sent a text message, he put his phone on the bedside table. "They'll bring us something in a minute."

"Thanks."

He gave me a sexy wink. "Anything for you, wildcat."

As promised, a few moments later, there was a knock at the door. When I got up to open it, the cook from the diner came in with a tray of food. As he placed it on the table, he looked over to Sawyer and asked, "You feeling alright?"

"I'll be back at it by morning."

Horrified by what I'd heard, I fussed, "No you won't."

Amused, the man laughed and started walking towards the door. "You two let me know if you need anything else."

"Thanks, brother." Sawyer motioned his head towards the tray of food. "You said you were hungry."

"Please tell me you weren't being serious."

"About?"

"About being *back at it* by morning?"

His tone didn't waiver as he answered, "Yeah, I was being serious."

"But you aren't ready."

"I'm doing alright, and my brothers need me. That's all that matters."

"And if you bust your stitches or get an infection?"

"Then, I'll deal with it." He slipped his hand behind the nape of my neck, drawing me towards him. I knew he was about to kiss me. I'd seen that look in his eye many times before, and I should've tried to stop him, especially under the circumstances, but it was too late. He pressed his lips against mine, and I was putty in his hands. His tongue drifted over my bottom lip, and with a slight whimper, I

136

opened my mouth, giving him access to delve deeper. Unconscious of my own movement, I leaned towards him, and in a matter of seconds, we were both lost in the moment. It was like the world around us had just disappeared, and it was just him and me. My hands drifted up to his chest, and when my fingers grazed his bandage, I quickly pulled back from our embrace.

I bit down on my bottom lip as I scooted back away from him. "You've really got to stop doing that."

"Doing what?" he asked innocently.

"Distracting me with those kisses. That's not going to work for long."

His lips curled into a mischievous smile. "But it works for now."

"Yes. Yes, it does."

Sawyer Mathews had quickly become my weakness, and I wasn't so sure I hadn't become his.

BLAZE

I looked down at Kenadee curled up next to me in the bed, and I found myself reaching out to touch her, proving to myself that I wasn't dreaming. She was warm and soft, and just having her next to me set my mind at ease, letting me relax for the first time in weeks. As I lay there staring at her, I knew my feelings for her were growing stronger. After we had eaten, I'd managed to convince her to lie down next to me, and we spent the next hour or so talking. I couldn't deny that she had an effect on me, both mentally and physically. I also couldn't deny that I liked it. I liked it a lot. Kenadee was an amazing, beautiful woman, and as I lay there watching her sleep, I wished that we had more time alone before we were hit with the next round of mayhem. Unfortunately, that wasn't an option.

The club was at war. Members—my friends, my family, *my brothers*—had lost their lives. Unlike most of the battles we'd fought, we had no idea who we were up against, which meant we knew nothing about our enemy;

we had no idea how many of them there were, where they were coming from, or even the real reasons behind their attack. That no longer mattered. They'd made their move, and now, we'd make ours. We'd have our revenge, and we'd come at them with everything we had, showing them they'd made the biggest mistake of their lives by coming after Fury. We were the one club that no one fucked with and lived to tell about it, and we'd see to it that our reputation remained intact.

I was eager to hear any news the guys had uncovered, but first I needed to see about Kevin. I hadn't seen him since I'd brought him over to the clubhouse with my folks. When my dad came to check on me in the med-room, he mentioned that he'd been asking a bunch of questions. I couldn't blame him. With all the commotion, he had to know something was up. After losing his mother, Kevin tended to be a little overprotective, and since he hadn't actually laid eyes on me in a few hours, he was worried. I'd sent a few random text messages, hoping to buy a little time, but after I received his latest message, I knew he was ready to see his old man. Thankfully, he wouldn't have to wait long. With everyone stirring in the halls, doors slamming, and people talking, Kenadee started to wake up with a long, stretch and a sleepy groan.

"Good morning, beautiful."

She was lying on her stomach, and her face was planted in the pillow as she answered, "Um-hmm."

"Sleep well?"

"Um-hmm."

Clearly, she wasn't a morning person, so I asked, "Need some coffee?"

"Please."

I popped her on the backside before I eased out of bed. "Get dressed. I'll be back in ten. We'll head over to the kitchen for coffee and breakfast, and then I need to see about Kevin before I head out."

"Hold up!" She propped up on her elbows, and with her eyebrows furrowed, she snapped, "You're not going anywhere until I check those stitches and replace your bandages. And the same goes for Murphy."

"I think we can manage that."

"Coffee first."

I nodded. "I'll be back."

I started down the hall to my room to get changed. The first few steps were tough. While the shrapnel had only pierced the outer portion of my right thigh and wasn't nearly as bad as the wound on my chest, it had grown stiff overnight, making it slightly difficult to walk. When Kenadee warned me about exerting myself too soon, I dismissed her completely, thinking I was strong enough to handle a few fucking stitches, but when I started to put on my jeans, I had second thoughts. I sat down on the edge of the bed, and I was panting like a goddamn dog by the time I had them pulled up to my hips. I managed to slip into my boots, but when I looked at my shirts, I started rolling out curses that could be heard throughout the entire clubhouse. It wasn't long before I heard a knock at my door.

"Sawyer? Is everything okay?" Kenadee asked from outside my door.

"Everything's fine! I just need a goddamn minute!" I roared.

Knowing I was lying, she eased the door open and stepped inside. She could've rubbed it in my face and told me she was right, but she didn't. Instead, she looked through the clothes and picked up one of the oversized t-shirts. "Before I do this, I should probably check your bandage. Is that okay?"

I nodded.

She walked over and laid the shirt down on the bed, then went to the bathroom to wash her hands. Once she was done, she quickly came back over to me and lifted her hand up to my chest, gently easing the corner of the bandage back. "I really need to change this, and the one on your leg as well. It won't take long."

Knowing that it was only going to put me further behind, I grumbled under my breath.

"Come on, now. Don't get all out of sorts," she huffed. "Think of it this way. I won't have to hound you in an hour to do it then."

"Okay. Fine."

With a satisfied smile, she rushed out of the room and quickly returned with fresh bandages and ointment. "I'll be quick."

Once she was done with the bandage on my chest, she started working on the smaller one on my thigh. I tried to be patient while she worked, and after she finished, I pulled up my pants and asked, "Feel better now?"

"Much." She smiled as she reached for my shirt. "Now, let's start with the bad side first."

I grimaced as I lifted my right arm, letting her ease the sleeve up my hand and over my shoulder, and once she had it where I could manage, I finished putting it on and said, "Thanks for the help."

"No problem. You probably don't want me to say anything, but you're going to need to take your pain meds with breakfast. At least half of it," she suggested. "Today's pain is going to be much worse than yesterday."

"Got it."

"Okay. Now, how about that coffee?"

We started out the door, and as we got closer to the kitchen, I could hear voices barreling down the hall and knew we were going to be in store for a crowd. Before we walked in, I pulled her over to me for a quick, but heated kiss. She looked up at me with surprise and asked, "What was that for?"

"That one was for me." I teased her as I turned and headed into the kitchen.

I'd just started pouring me and Kenadee and myself a cup of coffee when Riggs came up behind us and said, "Hey there, sunshine. Good to see you back on your feet."

I glanced over my shoulder and grumbled, "Morning, Riggs."

"Kenadee, you're looking mighty fine this morning," he told her playfully.

He barely got the words out of his mouth when I jabbed him in the gut with my elbow, causing him to take a quick gasp for air. "Sorry about that, man. I was just trying to get the sugar."

"Yeah, I bet you were."

"Hey, Kenadee. You and Sawyer up for some bacon and eggs?" Sadie asked.

She and the other hang-arounds were busy making breakfast, and as usual, each of them were scantily dressed in low-cut tops and revealing mini-skirts as they went around serving each of the brothers. While we'd grown used to their seductive behavior, it was something new for Kenadee. I half-expected her to tell Sadie to fuck off, but she simply answered, "Sure, I'd love some. Thanks, Sadie."

As I handed her the cup of coffee, I asked, "So, you've met Sadie?"

"Yep," she answered as she started walking towards the table.

Riggs gave me a mischievous smirk as we followed her over and sat down next to Murphy. His left hand was bandaged from his wrist up to his elbow, covering his burns, but his other injuries, small lacerations and a slight concussion, were basically unnoticeable. I asked, "How's the hand?"

"Better." He nodded over to Kenadee as he continued, "Not sure I need all this shit, but Nurse Ratchet over here would give me hell if I tried to go without."

"Really?" Kenadee complained.

"Oh, come on, now. You know I'm just messing with ya."

Before Kenadee had a chance to respond, I asked, "Any word on Gunner?"

"Nah. He's still out. I guess no news is good news."

"Man, I hope you're right."

Before I got the chance, Riggs announced to the others, "Guys, this is Blaze's girl, Kenadee. The one Gus was telling you about earlier."

A light blush crept over her face as she brought her hand up and did a little wave of her hand. "Hi. Nice to meet all of you."

Riggs turned to her and said, "The big bald guy towards the end of the table is T-Bone, and over here ... this is Shadow." I wasn't surprised when Shadow made no attempt to even look in Kenadee's direction as Riggs introduced them. He wasn't one for meeting new folks, especially women, so he just kept eating as Riggs rambled on. "You'll find that he's not much of talker, but if you need anything, just let him know. He has a way of making things happen."

Kenadee chuckled at that remark. "Okay. I'll keep that in mind."

Without giving her time catch her breath, Riggs continued on down the table. "The big fella at the other end of the table … that would be our VP, Moose. He's not only one of the toughest guys you'll ever meet, there's nobody on the planet who can BBQ ribs like him. And next to him, that's his ol' lady, Louise. You might've seen her over at the diner." He motioned his hand to the teenagers beside them as he added, "Those are their grandkids, Kyleigh and Logan."

Moose smiled as he said, "Our daughter, Rayne is here, too, but she hasn't come down yet. I'm sure she'll be glad to know you're here."

Kenadee gave him a warm smile as she replied, "Great. I look forward to meeting her, and I'm really sorry to hear about the diner."

"That's alright, sweetheart. We'll have her fixed up in no time," Louise assured her.

Meeting so many of the brothers and their families all at once was a lot to take in, but she seemed to take it all in stride. Kenadee was taking a sip of her coffee when Sadie brought her over a plate full of food and sat it down on the table. "Can I get you anything else?"

She looked down at the plate and shook her head. "No, thank you. *This is plenty.*"

Just as she was starting to eat, Jasmine, another one of

the hang-arounds, came over with food. I felt her hand graze my shoulder as she leaned forward, thrusting her breasts in my face while she placed my plate on the table. She tossed her hair over her shoulder and purred, "There ya go, hot stuff. Need anything else?"

"No, darlin'," Kenadee answered in a tone that was firm and demanding, and it only became more so as she continued, "He's got *more than enough*."

Shocked by her reaction, I turned to her, and when I saw that fire in her eyes, my dick nearly broke through my fucking zipper. I knew that fire was misplaced jealousy over a broad I didn't give one single fuck about, but damn. Seeing her so worked up, got to me and I just couldn't seem to help myself. Jasmine rolled her eyes and sneered, "Hmph ... Alright, then."

Amused by the little display, T-bone leaned back in his chair and chuckled. "Well, we've got us a fiery one over there, don't we? I like it! We need some more of that around here."

Ignoring his comment and me, Kenadee turned her attention to her breakfast and started to eat. I could tell she wasn't happy. She made sure I knew that. Hell, I'd finished my entire plate, and she still hadn't even made eye contact. Thankfully, the tension started to break when my folks brought Kevin in for breakfast. The second he saw me, he started rushing towards me and shouted, "Dad!"

I tried to brace myself, fearing that he might try to jump into my lap, but just as he was about to reach me, my father shouted, "Kevin!"

My son stopped dead in his tracks. I extended my

good arm out to him and said, "Come here, kiddo, and give your old man a hug."

He eased over to me, hugging me cautiously as he said, "Is everything okay?"

"Yeah. Everything's fine." Once he let go, I looked down at him and said, "I had a little accident at the garage, and I've just gotten some stitches that I have to be careful with for a few days."

"Stitches? Why didn't you tell me you had to get stitches?"

"Cause it wasn't a big deal." I lied. "No sense in worrying you for nothing."

"You promise?"

Hoping to distract him from my injury, I motioned my hand next to me and said, "There's someone here you might like to see."

He glanced over his shoulder and his eyes lit up when he said, "Nurse Kenadee!"

"Hi, Kevin. How's that arm treating ya?"

He held up his cast and answered, "It itches like crazy. Sometimes, it feels like there's ants up in there, but I haven't stuck anything up in there to scratch it." He promised.

"Well, that's good. I'd hate for you to poke yourself. That would only make it worse."

"I don't know. Those ants seem pretty bad sometimes."

"Hey, bud. You hungry?" My father asked.

As soon as Kevin nodded, my father went over and told the girls what they'd like for breakfast. Then, they all sat down next to us. My mother sat next to Kenadee and immediately started in with her worrying. "Did you get settled in okay?"

"Yes, ma'am."

"Did the girls get you everything you needed?"

"They did." She nodded with a smile. "They've all been very nice."

"Oh, good. I'm glad to hear that. I don't know if you've had a chance to look around much, but there's a TV room and a library. I'll be glad to show you around later if you'd like," she offered.

"That'd be great. Thanks."

When the guys started clearing out, Riggs nudged me and said, "You ready?"

"Yeah. Just give me a minute."

I turned to Kevin and said, "I've got a few things I need to see about, but I'll be back in a couple of hours. We can hang out for a bit when I get done. You good with that?"

"Yeah. That'll be good. I can play video games with Logan or something."

I was relieved that Moose and Louise had decided to bring their grandkids in for the lockdown like they had before. Kevin had gotten used to hanging out with Logan, and it made it easier when I had to be away so much. Seeing that he was content, I smiled at him and said, "Sounds good. I'll have my phone with me, so just call me if you need me."

"Okay."

When I turned back to Kenadee, she smiled. "I'll be fine. Go do your thing. I'll hang out with your folks, and then, I'll go back to my room and watch TV."

"There are things you need to know ..." I started.

"I'll go over everything with her," my mother assured me. "Just don't overdo it today. You know how I worry."

I nodded as I stood up and followed Riggs out of the

kitchen. The time for pleasantries was over, and it was time to get down to the business of finding out exactly what the fuck was going on with our attackers. As he started down the hallway, he looked over his shoulder at me. "Gus is in the conference room with the others."

When we walked in, Gus and Moose were talking intently with Cyrus and several of the others about the destruction at the diner. "I put a call into Ronin last night. He sent some of his boys to board up everything at the diner, and they'll help us keep an eye on things until the lockdown's over."

"And the garage?" I asked.

"Son, there's not much left of the garage. We'll have to either rebuild or relocate."

"Fuck," I growled.

"Don't worry yourself about it. We'll get it sorted," Gus assured me, then he turned his attention to Riggs. "What's the latest on the police reports?"

"Not much, which isn't exactly a surprise," Riggs grumbled. "They've questioned twenty or more witnesses from the diner, and they all have the same story. Black Mercedes came to a screeching halt in front of the diner. Rolled down the windows. There were three or four men wearing white, devil-like masks. They were heavily armed, and in a matter of seconds, they'd killed six people and wounded nine. Cops got no idea who's behind it and doubt they ever will. They still got nothing on any of the other hits. Not even a single lead."

"Fuck," Murphy complained. "You'd think they'd have something by now."

"Hell, I was there myself, and I couldn't tell you much more." Cyrus got choked up as he continued, "It all happened so fucking fast. Glass and bullets were flying everywhere. Everyone was screaming and running. They were shooting innocent people. Mothers. Kids. People I see every fucking day ... It was fucked up."

"We'll get them, brother," I assured him.

"Damn straight, we will."

Gus turned to Riggs and said, "I know you've already looked, but I need you to go back over that security footage with a fine-tooth comb. There has to be something there that can lead us to these motherfuckers."

"You got it."

"I gotta hand it to 'em," Moose grumbled. "They cleaned their tracks at every turn. There's not a single soul who has been able to tell the cops a damn thing about the drive-by other than the guys were wearing masks. How the fuck did they manage that in broad fucking daylight?"

"I can see that much on the security footage, but with the congestion on the street, I can't see much else. There's no tags on the car and I can only make out three guys in the Mercedes, but I'll keep looking."

"And go over everything at the garage. There has to be something we've missed."

Riggs nodded.

A pained expression crossed his face as he said, "You all know we lost Runt and Lowball. I know times are tough right now, but we need to pay our respects. Neither of them had family, so we'll do it here. Arrangements have already been made." He ran his hand over his beard, and his voice was strained as he continued. "Losing a brother is hard. Lowball was a good kid ... smart and had real potential to make his place in the club. He was taken much too soon. As was Runt. He was a strong, loyal leader. One of the fucking best enforcers around." His eyes drifted to the ceiling. "We've got Gunner back there fighting for his life, and he's a hell of a road captain. We're praying he pulls through. He's gotta pull through."

Moose patted him on the shoulder, "He's a strong kid. He's gonna get through this. You'll see."

Gus nodded. "It's times like these when a man shows his strengths. Be watchful and think about the future as we move forward. We'll meet on the ground in half an hour." With a solemn look on his face, he stood and left the room.

Riggs gave me a light nudge. "Want to give me a hand with this security footage after the service? Maybe you'll pick up on something I've missed?"

"Absolutely."

As I followed my brother down the hall to his room, it hit me that as bad as things were, they were only going to get worse. In the end, we'd have to find our way through it. There was no other choice. One way or another, we'd have to find our way back to the good—because the good was definitely worth fighting for.

*a*fter we finished breakfast, Dan took Kevin to the play room to find his friend Logan, while Janice gave me a complete tour of the clubhouse. She took her time showing me all the places I could and couldn't go, and as we went from room to room, I was actually impressed by how they'd managed to turn something old and neglected into something so amazing. I loved its rustic charm, and it was clear she enjoyed sharing it with me. After we left the kitchen, we went down to the TV room where Kevin and a couple of the other children were playing video games. Along with the huge, flat-screen TV mounted on the wall, there were two pool tables, and I got a little excited when I noticed an air-hockey table in the back corner. I looked at the kids sprawled out on the oversized leather sofas and recliners, and I couldn't think of a better family room.

When we left there, Janice took me by the laundry room and the stock room, just in case I needed anything. From there, we headed towards the library. As we walked down a long hall, I found myself drawn over to the window.

With all that had been going on, I never had the chance to look outside, so it was the first time I'd noticed that the clubhouse was surrounded by a fence. It wasn't just *any fence*—it was a ten-foot high security fence that had barbed wire weaved at the top. I froze the second I saw it. I'd seen the tall gate when Riggs had brought me in, but in the dark, I'd totally missed the enormity of it. As I stood there staring out the window, the walls started closing in on me, and my heart pounded against my chest. Janice must've noticed that something was wrong and eased up beside me. As she looked out the window, she said softly, "I know it looks a little daunting, but it's for our protection, dear."

"Protection from what?"

"Well … I really don't know," she confessed and pulled her cardigan around her even though it wasn't actually cold. Janice was older, in her late fifties with blonde hair. When the sunlight hit her in just the right angle, I could see the gray starting to take hold, but she was still quite attractive. She pointed to the back corner of the grounds, and I saw that the guys were all dressed in black as they gathered around a large maple tree with two freshly dug graves. Gus stood in front of them, and it looked like he was reading from the Bible as the others stood with their heads bowed. "This is bad. I can't remember the last time a member was killed, much less two."

"They're burying them here?"

"For a lot of the boys, the club truly is the only family they have. It makes sense to bury them in the family cemetery."

The mere thought of being buried alone in an old pine box sent a cold chill down my spine. I looked back over to her and said, "There's a lot to this club stuff, isn't there?"

"Yes, dear. There really is, and I still don't know or understand a lot of it." She ran the tip of her finger over her brow, "I don't know if you realize this or not, but Dan and I aren't exactly members of Fury."

"You're not?"

"No, sweetie. Becoming a member of the club was Sawyer's dream, not ours."

"I had no idea. I just assumed your whole family was a part of Fury."

"I guess in some ways we are. They look after us because we're Sawyer's parents."

I sighed. "It's a lot to take in."

"Yes, it is. I'm still trying to get used to it, but when he came to us and told us that he was going to join a motor-cycle club, his father and I weren't exactly happy," she explained. "In the beginning, I had my reservations about the club ... *lots of them*. It pained me because I knew there were things that went on that I wouldn't want Sawyer to be a part of. I hated to even think about it, but as the years have passed, I've learned that it's not all bad. In fact, there's been a lot of good that's come from him joining Fury. These men have been like a second family to him ... and to us. When Kevin got sick, they were there for us in ways I can't begin to explain, and honestly, I don't know if Sawyer would've gotten through it without them." She shrugged. "So, I've learned to take the good with the bad and accept that this is the life that my son has chosen."

"And last night when he got hurt? You just have to accept that, too?"

"Yes. I just have to trust that Gus will do as he promised and take care of his boys." She cocked her eyebrow. "Because that's exactly what he did."

"Umm… There's a lot of trust going on in this place," I sighed.

"You're right, and there are times when it will seem like trust is all you've got." She turned to look down the hallway. "Are you ready to go see the library?"

"Sure." As we started walking, I asked, "So, you said there are things you don't know about the club. What do you know?"

She cut her eyes at me as she shook her head. "Not much. Sawyer has made it clear that club business isn't talked about. He says it's for our own safety, but I'm not so sure about all that." When we passed a hallway off to itself, she pointed to it and said, "That area is off limits."

"Why?"

"I don't know. It just is."

I sighed. "Umm. Okay."

Once we got to the library, it wasn't exactly what I would've called a library. It had several bookshelves of books and a quiet place to sit and read, but that was about it. After Janice showed me a couple of her favorite novels, we sat down on one of the sofas and started talking. It wasn't long before she started telling me about Kevin and everything he'd been through. There was no doubt that she and Dan were crazy about him. She was about to roll into her next story when she got a text message from Dan asking about lunch. As she stood up, she said, "I guess I better get back. The boys are ready for something to eat. Would you like to join us?"

"Thanks, but I think I'll just head back to my room for a little while."

"Okay. You know where we'll be if you change your mind."

I followed her out into the hall and said, "Yes, I do, and thank you for the tour and the talk."

"It was my pleasure, sweetie." She leaned towards me and gave me a quick hug. "Let me know if you need anything at all."

"I will."

I was just about to turn to leave when Janice said, "Kenadee?"

"Yes?"

"There's one more thing I should probably mention." She looked at me with concern in her eyes.

"*Okay.*"

"You don't talk about the club with anyone … No matter how insignificant it may seem, you just keep it to yourself," she warned. "It's really important that you remember that."

"I don't understand."

"Yeah, I think you do." She cocked her eyebrow. "There's a reason no one knows what goes on in the club. No one breathes a word about what they've seen or heard in the club."

While I wasn't crazy about the idea of keeping secrets, I nodded and said, "I get it."

"I knew you would." She smiled. "I better get going before my boys start wondering where I am."

"Okay, and thanks for all the advice."

"Anytime, sweetie."

After she left, I decided to make my way back to my

room. As I headed down the long hallway, I started thinking about everything Janice just told me and how hard it must've been for her to have a son who lived in a world with so many secrets, especially since there was so much danger involved. I was pulled from my thoughts when I thought I heard Sawyer's voice coming from one of the rooms across the hall. Feeling hopeful, I tiptoed over to the crack in the door, and after a few minutes of eavesdropping, I was certain that Riggs and Sawyer were the only ones in the room. Thinking they wouldn't mind if I popped in to say hello, I eased the door open and stepped inside.

The room was quite different from my own—like night and day kind of different. Where mine only had the bed, this also had a large sofa, a beautiful dresser, and not just one TV mounted on the wall, but three. There was a computer on the desk with a large flat-screen monitor, and Sawyer and Riggs were both staring at it as they talked back and forth. I walked up behind them, and as I looked over their shoulder, I saw an image of a man on the screen. There was something familiar about him, very familiar, and as I stood there staring at him, I noticed that he was wearing a jacket that I remembered seeing recently.

When curiosity got the best of me, I asked, "Who is that?"

Both of them seemed surprised by my presence as they whipped around with their eyebrows furrowed and scowls on their faces. Sawyer looked like he could spit nails as he barked, "What the hell are you doing in here?"

Confused by his reaction, I answered, "Um ... I was just walking by, and I heard your voice."

"Dammit, Kenadee!" he roared. "You can't just come barging in to places you don't fucking belong!"

"Are you being serious right now?" I shouted. "How was I supposed to know I couldn't come in here when it was just you and Riggs?"

"Because I told you I had shit I needed to do!" It was clear I'd fucked up, but I thought his reaction was a bit extreme and it pissed me off. "You should've listened!"

"Sorry for being so thick-headed, Sawyer." I snapped, and as I turned to leave, I caught one last glimpse of the man on the screen. "And just so you know, I know who that guy is, and he's a real jerk ... just like you're being right now!"

I slammed the door and charged down the hallway towards my room. I'd only taken a few steps when I heard Sawyer call, "Kenadee, wait!"

"Why? So, you can tell me that I'm breaking another rule." I stopped and threw up my hands. "What? Am I not supposed to walk down this hall?"

"Hey." His voice softened as he said, "You're right. I shouldn't have gone off like that."

While I was still mad, I knew I was wrong, too. "I'm sorry for going in there like I did, but I'm still figuring all this stuff out."

"We'll talk about that later." Then, the look on his face turned serious as he said, "For now, I need you to come back to the room and tell me everything you know about the guy on the computer screen."

"Hold up. So, now you *want me* to come into the room?" I asked, taunting him.

He stared at me for a moment, but then, as if he

couldn't help himself, his lips curled into a smile. "Yeah, I want you to come into the room."

"But, I thought I wasn't supposed to go in there."

"Kenadee." He sighed. "It'd really help me out if you would tell us what you know."

"Okay." I followed him back into the room and as soon as I sat down, I said, "He came into the hospital with his sister and her daughter a few weeks ago."

From there, I told him everything I knew. It took me a few minutes to remember that his name was Terry, but that was all Sawyer needed to put the pieces of the puzzle together. From everything I told them, they knew exactly who I was talking about—Terry Dillion.

Riggs turned to me with an excited look on his face and said, "We owe you one, Kenadee. We owe you big."

"If you say so. I'm glad I could help."

"We need to let Gus know. We gotta find this guy and bring him in."

Even though I knew they wouldn't tell me, I asked, "Why is this guy so important?"

Both of them looked at me, but neither of them answered.

"Is he behind the shootings or the explosion at the garage?"

Still nothing.

"Well, *if he is* … if he has anything to do with any of it, *anything at all* …" I could feel the anger building deep inside me as I looked at both of them and said, "Then, I hope you make this asshole pay for what he's done."

Sawyer leaned towards me and kissed me on the forehead. "We will baby."

I followed them out of the room, and as I watched

them head off to find their president, I almost felt sorry for Terry. While I didn't know for certain that he'd done anything wrong, I had no doubt that if he had, Gus and the brothers of Fury would make certain that he would pay dearly for his crimes against them. I figured it would be awhile before I'd see Sawyer again, so I headed to the med-room to check in with Mack and Gunner. When I walked in, Mack was sitting next to Gunner, and he looked exhausted. "How's he doing?"

"Still the same. I just don't know what else to do." It was clear to see that he was truly worried over his brother. "I can't lose him, too."

"He's young and strong. Give him time. He'll pull through this, Mack," I tried to assure him.

"I wish I could believe that, but Runt was as strong as a fucking ox. I would've thought he could've taken three times the bullets that he had, and we lost him in seconds. It just doesn't make any sense."

"How are his stats?"

"His heart rate is good. Blood pressure, too." He sighed as he ran his hand through his hair. "Got any ideas?"

Seeing how exhausted he looked, I knew he hadn't slept much in days, so I urged him, "You should go get some sleep."

"I will soon. I'm just gonna sit with him for a few more minutes." He lied.

"Okay." I glanced around the room, trying to see if I could find where I'd left my purse. "Have you seen a blue handbag anywhere?"

He pointed over in the corner. "I put it over there in the cabinet."

"Thanks." After I grabbed my purse, I walked towards the door. "Be sure to get some rest."

"I'll do my best."

Once I was back in my room, I reached inside my purse and grabbed my phone. When I tapped the screen, I had thirty-seven messages—twenty-two of them being from Robyn. I started reading them, one by one, and I'd only gotten through half of them when it was clear she was freaking out that I hadn't called. I knew I had to get in touch with her, but I hesitated. After talking to Janice, I didn't want to say something I shouldn't and wasn't sure what I should and shouldn't say to her. Knowing I couldn't keep putting her off, I dialed her number and prayed that I'd be able to come up with the right words to say. It had only rung once when she answered, "Kenadee? Is that you?"

"Yeah. It's me."

"Oh, my God. You had me scared to death!" She gasped. "I've been trying to get in touch with you!"

Overcome with guilt, I fell back on the bed and sighed. "I'm really sorry. I should've called sooner, but I was ... um ... *busy*."

"Busy? Are you fucking kidding me? I've been going out of my mind over here wondering where you are and if you're okay, and you've been busy?"

"Well, after you left for your date with that sales guy, Sawyer came by the apartment ..."

"Umm hmm," she grumbled.

"And I ended up going back to his place," I continued.

"Is that when he convinced you to run off to Vegas?" She snarled

"Vegas?"

Sarcasm dripped from her voice as she replied, "Umm, yeah. Riggs called me at the hospital and told me about your little trip to Vegas. I want to know why you didn't call to tell me?"

"Umm … it was so last minute. I had no idea we were going. It was a surprise, and Sawyer told him to call you so you wouldn't worry."

"Well, I did worry. He implied that you two might be eloping, but I knew you wouldn't do that without telling me." She paused for a minute, then asked, "Right?"

"Of course, I wouldn't! Don't be ridiculous."

"So, what's with this Sawyer guy?" Her voice was three octaves higher than normal, and she was almost ranting as she continued to fuss at me. "It's not like you to just take off on some trip with some guy you barely know. You're the one who's supposed to think things through."

"I'm really sorry, Robyn."

"When are you coming back?"

I braced myself when I replied, "Umm … I'm not sure yet."

"What do you mean, you're not sure?" she shrieked. "You have work tomorrow, and there's been this creepy guy who's been following me around."

"What creepy guy?"

"Some biker dude. He's been following me to work and sitting outside the apartment. I think he's a stalker. I should probably call the cops or something."

Remembering that Gus said he was going to have a prospect keep an eye on her, I said, "No. I don't think that's necessary. He's probably just a new neighbor. I wouldn't worry about it."

"It wouldn't be a big deal if you were home," she said. I

knew she was pouting.

"Robyn, I haven't had a vacation in three years, and I'm having a really good time." I lied, again. "Let me have this, okay. I'll call the hospital and let them know that I won't be in for a few days. It's not like I don't have the days off."

"You promise you aren't eloping?"

"Yes, Robyn. I promise," I assured her. "I'm a long way from anything like that."

"Okay, good. Will you please keep in touch a little better so I won't worry so much?" she pleaded.

"Absolutely, and hey. I'm really sorry I worried you."

"I'm not going to say it's okay because it isn't, and I'm not sure how long it will take me to get over it." She fussed. After a short pause, she sighed. "But, that doesn't mean I don't want to hear about what's going on with you and the Sexpot in Leather."

Giggling, I replied, "I can just imagine what he'd say if he heard you call him that."

"Pfft. Trust me. I've called him much worse," she teased. "Now, tell me. Are you falling for this guy or what?"

I stared up at the ceiling as I thought back over the time I'd spent with Sawyer, and if I could take the club and all its secrets and danger out of the equation, my answer would be easy. I would tell my best friend that my answer was yes, that I was falling for Sawyer Mathews. But the fact was, Sawyer and the club were a package deal, and I would have to decide if I could learn to accept them for what they were. And to know for sure, I would need more time.

Since I didn't have an answer, I simply said, "I guess time will tell."

BLAZE

*W*hen Riggs and I shared our news with Gus, he wasn't surprised, not in the least. After all the things he'd seen over the years, nothing shocked him anymore. I, on the other hand, couldn't believe it. Even after he'd seen Gus put a bullet in his buddy's head for stealing from the club, he still had the nerve to fuck with us. The guy was a fucking dumbass, and it was only a matter of time before he got what was coming to him. Gus called everyone into church, and after he'd given the update, he sent Riggs and me, along with T-Bone and Shadow, to hunt down Terry. We did some checking around, then loaded up in the SUV and headed to one of his known hangouts. I never would've dreamed he would've been there. I thought for sure the guy would have the sense to get out of town, but when we walked into High Pockets Pool Hall, there he sat, drinking a beer at the bar. To put the icing on the cake, the motherfucker was wearing the same damn gray hoodie that he wore in the surveillance video. Yeah. Terry Dillion was definitely a fucking dumbass.

When he noticed us walking in his direction, his eyes grew wide with panic, and he quickly stood up, hoping to find a quick exit. Unfortunately for him, there would be no way out. I reached out and grabbed him by the collar. "Going somewhere, Terry?"

"Nah, man. I was just gonna get me another beer." He lied.

"No time for another beer, asshole," T-Bone growled. "Gus wants a word with you at the clubhouse."

His voice was trembling when he asked, "Why would he want to see me?"

"I don't know, Terry." I jerked him forward as I asked, "Why would my Prez want to see a piece of shit like you?"

"I got no idea. I ain't done nothing."

"Get his ass in the truck, Blaze," Riggs barked. "We're wasting time listening to his bullshit."

With my fingers tightly wrapped around Terry's neck, I gave his throat a tight squeeze as I led him out of the bar and then out to the truck. He was gasping for breath as I shoved him in the backseat between me and T-Bone, and when he started to squirm, I shoved my elbow in his gut and said, "Stay put, asshole."

We sent word to Gus, letting him know that Terry had been found, and then headed back to the clubhouse. Once we were back, we took Terry to one of the holding rooms on the east side of the building, and he was a blubbering mess as we chained him to a chair and locked him inside. We stepped out in the hall and waited for Gus's arrival. Like us, he was eager to get information from Terry.

None of us truly believed that he was the one responsible for the attacks on the other clubs or ours, which ultimately resulted in Runt's and Lowball's death, but if Gus was right, he could give us information on the people who were. We hadn't been waiting long when Gus came charging towards us, and from the expression on his face, it was clear that he was ready to blow. "Is he in there?"

"Yeah," Riggs answered.

"Has he said anything?"

"Not yet."

Gus growled as he clenched his fists at his side. Seeing that he was fighting to maintain his control, I suggested, "Maybe one of us should go in there and talk to him."

"What the fuck's that supposed to mean?" Gus spat.

"This was always Runt's domain, Gus. You know he had a way of making a man talk … He was slow and meticulous about extracting information. If you go in there as hyped up as you are right now, you're liable to kill him in the first five minutes, and then we'll have nothing. Same for me, brother. I'm ready to end that motherfucker right here and now, but we need to find out everything he knows and that's going to take some … *creativity*."

Knowing I was right, Gus sighed as he considered our next move. He was still in deep thought when Shadow stepped forward. "I'll do it."

Surprised by his offer, we all turned and stared at him with this odd sense of wonder. We'd all known there was a dark side to Shadow—the man who fought his demons in silence. He'd been in the military, and while fighting in Afghanistan, he'd been captured and imprisoned for months. None of us knew what had happened to him when he was locked away in that prison, but we all knew it had fucked him up, giving him nightmares and a fierce edge. When I thought about him handling the situation with Terry, at first, I had my doubts. It wasn't that I didn't trust him, because I did. I trusted Shadow with my life, but I knew how his past haunted him. I worried a situation like this might set him back by bringing up old memories. But then there was always the slight chance that spending some time with Terry would be good therapy for him, letting him work out some old aggressions. In the end, it didn't matter what I thought. It would be up to Gus to decide if Shadow would go in that room with Terry. We all waited silently for his response, and after he studied Shadow for several moments, he finally asked, "You sure you're up for this?"

Shadow gave him a single nod.

"Do you want one of us to stay with you? Give you a hand or something?" Gus offered.

His dark eyes flashed with intensity as he answered, "*No.* I need to do this on my own."

"Alright. He's all yours, but you call me if you need anything."

Again, Shadow nodded.

"You let me know the second you get him talking," Gus ordered.

"Yes, sir," Shadow replied.

Gus turned to us and said, "Let's go, boys. Shadow needs some breathing room."

With that, we turned and started down the hall. We hadn't gotten very far when Gus turned and looked over his shoulder, watching Shadow as he entered the room. A proud smile crossed his face as he continued down the hall, and I knew then that Shadow had just made an impression on our president, an impression that might just have him as the front runner for the position as the club's new enforcer. It would all depend on how the next few hours played out, and how much information he was able to get out of Terry. Once we were at the end of the hallway, Gus looked over to us and said, "It's going to be a while before we hear anything from Shadow. Take a break, and when I hear something, I'll let you know."

With that, Gus turned and headed towards his office. Riggs looked over to me and asked, "You wanna grab something to eat?"

I was starving, but my bandages hadn't been checked since Kenadee had changed them earlier that morning. Knowing I'd hear three kinds of hell from her if I didn't at least get them looked at, I replied, "Nah, I'll get something later."

"Alright, man. I'll meet up with you later."

Since it was late, I figured Kenadee was already in bed, so I headed down to the med-room to find Mack. When I walked in, I found him sound asleep in a chair next to Gunner's bed. Even though he was clearly exhausted, he hadn't left his side since the night he'd been shot. We'd all tried to convince him that he needed to get a decent night's sleep, but he wouldn't listen, partly because he blamed himself for Gunner's condition. We all knew he wasn't being rational, but his dedication to his brothers was one of the reasons Mack was such an amazing doctor. There was no way in hell that I was going to wake him, so I turned to leave. Just as I was about to walk out the door, Jasmine came strolling in.

With a sexy smile, she whispered, "Hey there, handsome. What are you doing here?"

"I came to get Mack to change my bandage."

"I can do it for you," she offered.

I didn't see the harm in having her do it, so I nodded. "Okay, but be quick about it. I got shit to do."

I've been around Jasmine for years, and I've learned there was more to her than she let on. She liked to put on a show, acting like she was just an easy piece of ass, but she was alright. After she gathered up all the supplies, she motioned me over to one of the gurneys and said, "Sit."

"Bossy, much." I teased as I sat down on the edge of the bed.

"Um-hmm." The normally flirty Jasmine was gone, and she was quiet as she started to help me remove my shirt. I was actually surprised by her demeanor, until she asked, "So, is that Kenadee chick your new girl or something?"

"Yeah, I guess you could say that," I answered without really thinking it through. "It's not official or anything, but ..."

"She's here with you on a lockdown, so she means something to ya."

As she peeled back the bandage and started to clean the wound, I replied, "Yeah. I suppose you're right."

"I'm glad to see that you've found someone, Blaze." She looked up at me with sincerity in her eyes. "You're one of the good ones. You deserve to find someone who will make you happy."

I placed my hand on her hip and smiled as I said, "Thanks, doll."

I heard the door creak open and turned to find Kenadee standing in the doorway. She was wearing a pair of gray sleep pants that hung low on her hips with a tank top, and I could clearly see that she wasn't wearing a bra. Once I got past how beautiful she looked standing there, I noticed the blank expression on her face. Before I could even open my mouth, she'd turned and was gone. I looked down and saw that my hand was still resting on Jasmine's hip and grumbled curses under my breath. Jasmine also noticed Kenadee's quick exit and said, "I think she misread the situation."

"You think?"

"Come on, Blaze. You're a smart guy. You gotta know that this is a lot for someone like her to take in ... Look at you. You were almost killed. Then, you got all these men around here that she doesn't know, women she doesn't know ... women you've had sex with. The poor girl's just thrown right in the middle while you're off trying to fight some war that she doesn't know anything about. Can you imagine how hard that must be for her?"

"Yeah, but she's gotta be able to trust me or this thing's never gonna work."

As she replaced my bandage, she asked, "Do you trust her?"

I thought about it for a moment. "Yeah, I do. She hasn't given me any reason not to."

"Okay. Then, you have to do the same for her. Don't just tell her that she can trust you ... Prove to her that she can trust you."

Damn. I never expected Jasmine to be the voice of reason, but like it or not, she was right. After she helped me get my shirt back on, I thanked her for the help and for her advice, and then, I set out to find Kenadee. When I got down to her room, I knocked on her door. It took her several seconds to answer, and once she did, she feigned a smile and tried to act like nothing was bothering her when she said, "Hey. How's it going?"

"We need to talk." I walked past her, and when I entered the room, I was surprised to find a tray full of food sitting on her desk. "What's all this?"

"Riggs brought it by." She closed the door and came up behind me. "I guess he thought you'd be here."

"So, you came looking for me?" I didn't get a clear answer, just an irritated shrug, so I took a step towards her. "I went to the med-room to find Mack."

"Look, Sawyer. You don't owe me an explanation. Besides, it's pretty clear that when it comes to the club, you do whatever the hell you want, whenever the hell you want. I get it." Her voice remained calm and steady as she continued, "But you should know... I'm not one of those women who's going to chase after you. I'm not going to beg and plead with you to be with me. I'm not going to fight and be jealous about other women. I'm just not. Because the way I see it, you either want to be with me, or you don't. It's as simple as that."

I thought back to what Jasmine had said, and I knew this was one of those times when words just wouldn't be enough. My eyes never left hers as I took a step forward, closing the gap between us, and once I had her close, I brought my hand up to her face, gently running the pad of my thumb along her jaw. "There's no chase to be had, Kenadee. You're the only one I want. It's as simple as that."

I lowered my mouth to hers, kissing her with passion and hunger as I pulled her body close to mine. I closed my eyes, losing myself in the sensation of her touch. There was just something about Kenadee that made me forget about everything that was going on outside of that room, and it was just her and me as I felt her arms wrap around my neck, her fingers tangled in my hair. Kenadee's intoxicating scent teased my senses as I delved deeper into her mouth, and when she inched closer, pressing her warm body against mine, I could feel the blood rushing to my already throbbing erection. My need for her consumed me, and it was like she could read my mind as her hands slowly slipped down from my neck and found their way to my waist. Her fingers worked to unfasten my jeans, and she carefully lowered them down past my hips. Once she'd removed them, along with my boots and socks, she looked up at me and said, "I want you, too, Sawyer.

With her eyes locked on mine, she lowered herself to her knees, and a hiss slipped across my teeth when she took me in her hand and began teasing me with soft, easy strokes. A wicked smile spread across her lips as she watched my body grow more tense with every flick of her wrist. While I loved the feel of her hands on me, I was eager for something more, and a tortured moan echoed through the room when I felt the warmth of her tongue rake against me. I reached down, taking her hair in my hands, silently begging for more as she finally took me in her mouth, lowering her wet lips over my shaft. Damn. I couldn't imagine a better fucking feeling. Her mouth was soft, warm and wet, and I had to fight the urge to pull back on her hair and force her to take me deeper. Her tongue twirled around the head of my dick, and then her movements changed. Her strokes became firmer and quicker with a slight twist of her wrist, and she sucked harder as she took me deeper. The change was subtle, but damn near sent me over the edge. When I took a step back and pulled myself free from her grasp, she looked up at me with surprise.

I reached down, and as I lifted her to her feet, I said, "I love your mouth, wildcat, but I need to be inside you … now."

KENADEE

I could no longer deny it. I was falling in love with Sawyer Mathews. Our connection was like nothing I had ever known, and with each moment we spent together, I'd find another reason to love him. People would probably think I was crazy for falling for a man like Sawyer. They'd probably think I was naïve for thinking that things between us could ever work, especially when our lives were so vastly different.

I'd centered my entire life around trying to save lives, and now, here I am considering a lifestyle, Sawyer's way of life, one where death followed in Fury's wake. I was sure it had in the past and almost certain that it would again, but I knew there was more to Sawyer than just the cut he wore on his back. There was good in him. I'd seen it with my own eyes whenever he was with his son, his parents, and even his brothers. Most of all, I'd seen it when he was with me. He was loving and protective, and there was a tenderness in his touch that I'd never felt with any man. We might've been from two completely different worlds, but when we were together it was like two stars colliding in the night. Right or wrong, he was the man who held my heart in his hand, as I held his. He trailed kisses along my neck, sending chills throughout my entire body as he led me over to the bed. As much as I wanted him, I was worried that he wasn't physically ready, so I looked up at him and said, "I'm not sure this is a good idea."

"Oh, I think it's a good idea." He smirked. "In fact, I know it's a great idea."

"But what if we get carried away and you hurt yourself?"

"Oh, I plan on us getting carried away, wildcat, but I'll be letting you do most of the work." He winked.

There was nothing sexier than Sawyer's playful side, and without any further hesitations, I found myself reaching for the hem of his shirt, tugging unsuccessfully. "Um … This *has gotta go*."

"Gonna need a hand, beautiful."

I smiled as I held onto the fabric, making it easier for him slip his right arm out of the sleeve, and then he pulled it over his head. He winced as he lowered himself to the bed. Seeing how unbelievably hot he looked sitting there, my entire body hummed with anticipation. I eagerly removed my tank top, tossing it behind me, and his eyes followed my hands as they lowered my pants down my legs. I felt the heat of his stare as his eyes slowly roamed over me, and a needful ache burned inside of me when he growled, "Never seen a woman as beautiful as you."

"When you say it like that, I almost believe it." I stepped towards him but stopped when he reached for his jeans. Knowing he was about to get a condom, I told him, "I'm on the pill."

It was clear from the expression on his face that the news pleased him. I smiled as I continued towards him. I was careful not to touch the wound on his thigh as I eased myself down on top of him, straddling him as he pulled me in for another kiss. When I was in his arms, he made me feel beautiful and wanted, like I was the most desirable woman on the planet, and as his hand slid down my back, I became completely consumed with need. He took my breasts in his hands, gently caressing each with the pad of his thumb. My head fell back as he raised his mouth to my nipple and began nipping and sucking the sensitive flesh, sending jolts of pleasure down my spine. The warmth of his breath caressed my skin when he whispered, "You're the only one, Kenadee."

A low, agonizing growl vibrated through his chest when I rocked my hips forward, causing his erection to rake against my warm, wet center. I loved that I was having such an effect on him, and feeling like a powerful seductress, I rocked my hips back and forth, rubbing my clit against him.

"*Fuck*," he groaned as he dug his fingers into my flesh.

While I enjoyed seeing him respond to my touch, the anticipation of having him inside me had become too much to bear. I reached beneath me, taking his long, thick shaft in my hand, slowly stroking him up and down before positioning him at my entrance. With one swift thrust, he slammed deep inside me, giving me every inch of his rock-hard cock. I stilled for a moment, trying to adjust to him before I started to move my hips again. I gasped when he shifted forward, finding that spot that made every nerve in me tingle. He placed his hands on my hips as I slowly began to move, groaning at the jolts of pleasure that shot through me.

Consumed with lust and emotion, I looked at him and with my voice trembling, I whispered, "I've never wanted anyone like I want you."

"You've got me, baby. All of me."

I leaned forward, pressing my lips against his, and his hand instinctively reached towards the nape of my neck and grasped at the hair that fell around my shoulder, holding me in place as he deepened the kiss. I moved against him, and with each shift forward, I was getting closer to the edge. I pushed against him, forcing him further inside me, and inhaled a deep breath when I felt the tremors of my impending orgasm. His fingers dug into my hips as he guided me back and forth, over and over again, until I reached a demanding pace. I placed my hands on the headboard, trying to steady myself as I tried to maintain the relentless rhythm he'd set. My body trembled with anticipation when I felt my climax building, burning through my veins.

"Oh God, Sawyer. I'm coming."

"That's it, wildcat. Give it to me."

His breath quickened as I tightened around him, and I could see he was struggling to maintain his control. My muscles began to quiver when he put his hands under my ass and lifted me higher as he angled his position, finding the spot he knew would send me over the edge.

"Yes!" I cried out as my orgasm surged through my body. I was lost in my own sensuous pleasure when he finally found his own release. His brows furrowed as he thrust forcefully into me one last time.

After several moments, I slowly eased off him and lowered myself down onto the bed next to him. I laid my head on the pillow and listened to the sounds of our erratic breathing slow into a steady rhythm. Goosebumps rose on my skin when his lips brushed across my shoulder and along the curve of my neck. When he reached my ear, he whispered, *"Mine."*

When I heard those words, I was overcome with emotion. He was right. I was his, and I felt the exact same way about him. I turned towards him and placed the palm of my hand on his cheek as I whispered, *"Mine."*

He pressed his lips against mine, kissing me softly before he said, "I don't deserve you."

I smiled as I teased him. "Probably not, but you got me."

We settled back on the bed, and as I curled up next to him, he asked, "How did the tour go with Mom today?"

"Pretty good, I guess." I sighed. "This place is even bigger than I thought."

"It's easy to get turned around."

"Yeah or end up in rooms where you don't belong." I sassed. "But, I'll figure it out."

"I know you will."

"Oh, and she told me about not talking about anything that happens at the club and all that, which I get ... but it wasn't easy when I called Robyn this afternoon."

He glanced over at me with a concerned look. "You talked to Robyn?"

"She'd messaged me a million times, and I couldn't just keep her hanging like that. I had to tell her something, but it would've helped if I knew that Riggs had already told her that we went to Vegas. That one caught me by surprise."

"Vegas?" He chuckled. "Where the hell did he come up with that?"

"I have no idea, but he had her thinking we'd eloped or something. The poor thing was freaking out, but I managed to convince her that she had nothing to worry about. Then, I had to call my shift manager at work and do it all over again."

"How did that go?"

"Fine. I have lots of days built up, so she really couldn't say much. She was just ticked about the short notice."

"Sorry about that."

"It's not a big deal. I just wish I knew how long we were going to be here. I hated to tell her that I would need off indefinitely. It sounds so daunting."

"I'm thinking it might be sooner than later." My eyes widened when he said it, and I desperately wanted to ask him if something had happened. But I clenched my jaw and did everything in my power to keep my mouth shut. I just laid there and stared at the ceiling, trying to hide my agony. Like he knew exactly what I was thinking, he eased up on his elbow and looked down at me with a smirk. "You wanting to ask me something?"

"Nope. I'm good."

"You sure?"

"Yep."

"Umm-hmm."

He was clearly goading me, so I glared at him with a scowl. "I'm doing my best to follow the rules here, Sawyer. You're not helping matters."

"You're right, and since you brought it up, I've got one more."

"One more what?"

"Rule. No more walking around the clubhouse without any clothes on."

"You wanna tell me what the hell you are talking about because I'm pretty sure I've missed something."

"I'm talking about earlier ... when you came down to the med-room."

"Yeah. I was wearing a tank top and sleep pants."

"You weren't wearing a bra, Kenadee," he scolded. "I trust my brothers, but you're mine and what you've got under your clothes is for my eyes only."

"Okay. I think I can manage that. I'll add it to the list," I teased.

"Good." His stomach growled as he turned to the tray of food that Riggs had brought. "What do we got over there?"

"A couple of burgers, I think. Let me go check." I eased off the bed, and after I slipped on my clothes, I grabbed the tray of food, bringing it over to the edge of the bed. As I looked down at all it, I gasped. "There's enough here for ten people."

"Good." He grabbed one of the burgers and took a big bite. With his mouth full, he said, "I'm starving. Haven't eaten anything since breakfast."

Laughing, I reached for one of the burgers and took a small bite. Even though it was cold, it was still really good. "These are incredible."

"Cyrus must've made 'em." He grabbed one of the bottles of water and took a long drink, before finishing off his first burger. "He's gonna make someone a good husband one day."

"Yeah, it's hard to beat a man who can cook."

"Good thing I'm so good at it," he said playfully. "That's how I won you over, isn't it? That grilled cheese was the winning shot."

"Umm ... that, and you're a really good kisser."

"A good kisser, huh? Interesting." A sexy smirk crossed his handsome face as he asked, "What else do you think I'm good at?"

"Sawyer Mathews, are you fishing for compliments?" I asked playfully.

"Nope. Not at all. Just happen to think that there are things a man should know when going into a relationship with a woman."

"You're so full of it." When he just sat there staring at me, I knew he wasn't going to let it go, so I sighed. "Besides, it's hard to say. There just so happens to be lots of things that I like about you."

He cocked his eyebrow as he pushed, "Um-hmm. Such as?"

"Something tells me I'm going to regret this ... but, I like your walk ... I like the sound of your voice when you're tired. I love your eyes. It's like you can see right to my soul when you look at me, and I can see into yours. And ..." My eyes drifted to the ceiling as I quickly said, "And you have an incredible body and a great ass, but you already know that."

He sat there staring at me as he thought about everything I'd said. After several moments, his lips curled into a mischievous smile. "I do have a great ass."

"Yeah, I should've never told you any of that." I rolled

my eyes. "At least I didn't tell you what Robyn said about you earlier."

"And what did she have to say?"

"Oh, no way. I'm not going to tell you that. I don't think I could take it if your ego got any bigger."

"Seriously? You're not gonna tell me?"

"Nope. That one's staying a secret." I smiled. "At least for now."

After we finished eating, I cleared away our mess then crawled back in the bed with Sawyer. I snuggled up next to him, and as I trailed my finger along the lines of his tattoo, we continued to talk until we both eventually drifted off to sleep. I had no idea how long we'd been sleeping when I heard someone knocking on my door. Sawyer was sound asleep, so I got up to see who it was. As soon as I opened the door, Riggs asked, "Sawyer in here with you?"

"Yes."

Without invitation, he stepped into the room and walked over to the bed, nudging Sawyer. "Get up man. Gus wants us—*now*."

As he pulled himself out of bed, Sawyer huffed, "Give me a minute."

Knowing he'd need some help and guessing he wouldn't want Riggs to see, I turned to Riggs and said, "He'll be out in a second."

Sawyer seemed surprised as he watched Riggs walk out of the room. As soon as I heard the door close, I rushed around the room and collected all of his clothes off the floor. Sawyer looked at me with emotion in his eyes as I knelt down in front of him and helped him put on his jeans. Once we'd gotten them over his thighs, I turned and reached for his shirt. Like the time before, we worked together to put it on him. In a matter of a few seconds, he was dressed, boots and all. After he grabbed his cut, he turned to me, and as he kissed me on the forehead, he whispered, "You're the only one."

And then he was gone.

BLAZE

*R*iggs and I walked in utter silence as we made our way down the hall to meet Gus. Even though we were eager to see what Shadow had gotten out of Terry, neither of us were looking forward to going into that room. It wasn't that we felt sorry for Terry. Fuck that. He deserved everything Shadow dished out for playing his part in Runt and Lowball's death. For me, it was just the thought of the torture itself. While it astounded me just how much pain and cruelty that the human body could withstand, seeing the end results would often turn my stomach. Something told me that today would be no different. When we got down to the holding room, Gus and Murphy were waiting for us by the door, and as we approached, I was surprised to see that none of the other brothers were there with them.

"What's the word?" Riggs asked anxiously.

"Not sure yet. He asked for you three specifically, so I was waiting for you to get here before we went in.

When Gus reached for the doorknob, I took a deep

breath as I prepared to go in. It was the smell that hit us first, each of us nearly gagging as we stepped inside. It took us a minute to collect ourselves, and then, we spotted Terry. He was bound to a chair in the center of the room, wearing nothing but a pair of soiled boxers, and he was surrounded by his own excrement and vomit. When I looked at him, it was as if I was looking at a shell of the man we'd brought in earlier. He was beaten and bruised with blood oozing from his wounds, and even though he was still technically breathing, there was no life in his eyes, no sense of awareness whatsoever. As I stood there staring at him, I couldn't help but wonder what Shadow had done to him. When I glanced around the room, I first noticed the car battery and cables. I'd seen Runt's handy work with those, so it was easy to guess how they'd been used. It was the other tools, like plyers, switch blades, buckets, and old, wet rags that were scattered along the floor that sent an eerie shiver down my spine. There was no doubt in my mind that Terry had been put through hell and back. I just hoped that Shadow had been able to extract the information that we'd need to get the motherfucker who'd attacked the club.

Shadow was standing over in the corner smoking a cigarette when Gus walked over to him. "You okay?"

He nodded. "I'm fine."

Gus looked over his shoulder at Terry. "Looks like he's barely hanging on."

Shadow crossed his arms, making his muscles ripple as he snarled, "Yeah, but he's alive."

"Were you able to get anything out of him?" Gus pushed.

"I got plenty, but …" Shadow turned his attention

away from Gus and over to us, and there was an urgency in his voice when he said, "I need you to bring me his sister, Kate Dillion."

"His sister?" I asked with surprise. Suddenly worried that he was about to take things too far, I asked, "Why in the hell do you need his sister?"

His voice was low and threatening as he answered, "I need the sister. It's important, and *the baby, too.*"

"Oh, fuck, man. *The baby.* You gotta be kidding me. Why do you need the baby?" Murphy asked with horror.

Anger flashed through Shadow's eyes as he barked, "You want to know who's behind all this shit? Who killed our brothers?"

"Of course, I do!"

"Then, go get the goddamn girl!" he roared. He raked his hand through his hair as he took several deep, agonizing breaths. Once he regained his composure, Shadow turned towards Gus and said, "You've gotta trust me on this, Prez"

Gus nodded. "Okay, son. Take it easy. We'll get the girl, but we'll need to know where she is first. You think you can get Terry to tell us where we can find her?"

Shadow nodded, then walked over to Terry. After grabbing a fist full of his nappy hair, he jerked his head back and forced Terry to look at him. "Your sister. Where can we find her?"

Terry's eyes widened as he stuttered, "I ... uh ... at ... the apartment ... or the ... Rose's strip ... club. I don't ... know."

"We don't have time to run all over town looking for her," Gus complained. "Try having him call her."

Riggs stepped forward. "If we do that, I'll trace the call. Just to be sure."

"Good idea."

When Shadow started going through Terry's things, searching for his phone, Riggs rushed towards the door. "I'll go grab my laptop."

Just as Riggs walked out of the room, Shadow retrieved the cell phone and made his way back over to Terry. He knelt down in front of him, and in a low, domineering tone, he ordered, "You're gonna call your sister and find out where she is. If she starts asking questions, you tell her nothing. You got it?"

"I was ... supposed to ... watch the ... baby," Terry mumbled.

Murphy walked over to Terry and said, "Tell her you're laid up drunk with some chick from the bar."

Riggs walked back into the room, and once he had his laptop ready to go, Shadow reached down and released Terry from his constraints. As he handed him the phone, he growled, "Make the call and leave it on speaker."

"Okay."

Terry's hands trembled as he dialed the number. It was just after five in the morning, so we weren't surprised when it took her several moments to answer. "What the hell, Terry? *Why are you calling me?*"

"Where ... are you?"

"What's wrong with you?" Kate grumbled. "Why do you sound like that?"

"I had a few ... too many last night. Still kind of wasted."

"Of course, you are," she groaned. "You shouldn't be calling me. I heard about those Fury guys coming to the bar looking for you. I don't need that kind of trouble, Terry," she spat.

"That was … nothing"

"If Fury is looking for you, it's never nothing, Terry. Just stay the hell away from me and Lacie. You got that?" she ordered.

"Don't," he pleaded. When Shadow gave him a warning look, he asked her, "You at … the apartment?"

"No. When I heard about what happened, I packed our shit and left. I'm getting the hell out of town."

His voice was growing weaker as he asked, "Where you … going?"

"I'll figure that out when Lacie gets up. Look, I've got to go, but listen, Terry. You need to get the hell out of Memphis."

"But, where … can … I find you?"

"Dammit, Terry. Don't worry about finding me. You need to get out of town, now!"

The call ended, and after listening to that conversation, I started to think Shadow was right about Kate. There was a reason she was so eager to get out of town. Hoping that he'd been able to locate her, we all turned to Riggs. He gave us the nod, letting us know that he pinged the call. "We got her."

Gus went over to Riggs and asked, "Where is she?"

As he pointed to the screen, he said, "Here's the address. It's about three hours away in Paris, but if she's leaving, that doesn't give us much time."

"No, it doesn't." Gus pulled out his phone and said, "But I've got someone who might be able to help us out."

When Gus turned to make his call, Murphy glanced over at Shadow. As he watched Shadow put the restraints back on Terry, he whispered, "What's up with the girl?"

"Got no idea, but there's something," I answered.

"Shadow hasn't told us shit. I want to know what the fuck he found out from Terry," Murphy pushed.

I patted him on the shoulder and said, "We all do, brother, but we're just gonna have to trust Shadow on this."

Before he had a chance to respond, Gus came over to us and said, "Bishop runs a club up in Paris. He and Goliath are gonna see if they can get to Kate before she leaves. If they get her, they'll meet us for a drop off."

"Bishop?" I asked. "From the Devil Chasers?"

Gus nodded. "That'd be him."

There weren't many bikers around the area who didn't know about the DC's custom bike detailing. They were the best around. I shouldn't have been surprised that Gus had a connection with their president. There weren't many out there who Gus didn't know. "Good of him to help."

After Shadow was done dealing with Terry, he came over to Riggs and asked, "Did you find her?"

"Yeah. We found her."

"Then let's go get her!" he demanded.

"We're getting it handled now," Gus assured him. "You go get yourself a shower and something to eat. Try to get some shut eye, and we'll let you know when we have her."

"And you're getting the baby, too, right? It's important that you get the baby."

"Yes, Shadow. We'll get the baby," Gus promised.

"And you'll let me know as soon as they get back?" he asked, sounding hopeful.

"You know I will. Now, go," Gus ordered. "Get yourself some rest."

Once he was gone, we went to Gus's office to discuss our next move. None of us had any clear thought on what was going on with Kate, and we were all eager to hear something back from Gus's friend, Bishop. Thankfully, we didn't have to wait long. In less than an hour, Bishop called Gus back, letting him know that he and his brothers had retrieved Kate and her daughter, Lacie.

When he hung up the phone, Gus turned to us and said. "They'll meet you in Jackson. Figured it would be easier for everyone that way."

"Mighty good of him to help us out like this," Riggs told him.

"Bishop's a good man. Did some running with him back in the day, but that was a lifetime ago." Gus looked down at his watch. "You boys better load up. We don't want to keep him waiting."

We headed out to the truck, and after exiting the back gate, we took off to the main road. None of us spoke as we drove towards Jackson. Our minds were focused on the task at hand. As I stared out the window, I thought back to the conversation between Kate and Terry, and something about it just felt off. I just didn't know what. We were getting closer to Jackson, when Murphy looked over to me and said, "We're not going to let him hurt that baby, right? Like no matter what happens, that shit ain't gonna go down."

"No, Murphy. We won't let Shadow hurt the kid."

"Good. The sister … I'm not so sure about her," Murphy started. "You reckon he'll have to do all that shit to her?"

"Doubt it. Hell, all he'd have to do is show her Terry. One look at him, and I'd start talking." Riggs chuckled.

"You ain't lying. The joker looked like hell and smelled like fucking death," Murphy groaned. When he noticed that our exit was coming up, he pointed to the sign and said, "This is where we get off."

Riggs took the exit, and a few minutes later, we turned into the empty lot behind the airbase. It didn't take us long to find Bishop. There weren't many 1962 cherry-red Chevy pick-up trucks around, so when we saw it parked in the back of the lot, we pulled up next to it. A guy in his early fifties with salt and pepper hair and an athletic build stepped out of the truck with his Devil Chaser's cut, I knew without a doubt it was him. "Bishop?"

"You Gus's boys?"

"Yes, sir." We got out of the truck and walked over to him. "I'm Blaze. These are my brothers, Riggs and Murphy."

"Not every day I get a call to go chasing after a beautiful blonde so early in the morning." Bishop chuckled. "I'm guessing you're eager to get her back home."

"That we are," I replied.

"Goliath!" Bishop motioned his hand to the man sitting in the truck with Kate. "She wasn't exactly thrilled about the idea of coming with us, but I'm sure you already knew that."

"I imagine she wasn't, but I can assure you ... we wouldn't have gotten you involved if it wasn't important."

"Son, I've known Gus long enough to know that he doesn't ask favors unless ... *Fuck*. Gus, never asks favors." He chuckled as he waved us off. "I'm just glad I could help."

While Bishop walked around to the back of the truck and got the car off the trailer, his brother helped us get Kate in the SUV. He was right. She was far from happy about going with us, but she didn't try to put up a fight. Instead, the young blonde held the baby close to her chest and sat in the back seat of the SUV, never saying a word to any of us. Once I'd closed the door behind her, I looked back over to Bishop and Goliath. "Thank you both for your help."

As he got inside his truck and started the engine, Bishop replied, "Not a problem, and good luck with little Ms. Sunshine."

Once they had driven out of the lot, we messaged Gus to let him know we had the girl, then with Murphy driving Kate's car, we started back towards the clubhouse. As we started down I-40, I glanced over at the girl who Shadow was so adamant that we must find, and I just didn't get it. While she seemed pretty pissed as she sat there staring out the window, she looked like your typical stripper. I glanced down at her arms and was surprised to see no track marks. Her pupils weren't dilated or red, so it was doubtful that she was into drugs. The baby had bright, blue eyes and little, pink cheeks and looked perfectly healthy and happy. None of it made any sense. What was it about this woman and kid that Shadow thought was so damn important?

*A*fter Sawyer left with Riggs, I crawled back in bed and tried to go back to sleep. Unfortunately, that didn't happen. I couldn't stop wondering where the guys were going off to in such a rush. I knew it was one of the things I was going to have to get used to if I was going to be in Sawyer's life, but there was no way I'd ever be able to stop worrying—not after all the things I'd seen. I figured if I could find a way to keep myself busy that I might be able to distract myself from my thoughts. At least, that was what I was hoping when I pulled myself out of bed and got dressed. I thought a hot cup of coffee and some breakfast might help settle my nerves and take my mind off things, at least for a little while.

I headed down the hall, and when I walked by the med-room, I decided to check in on Mack and Gunner. I eased the door open, and to my surprise, Gunner was sitting up on his gurney. I'd only been around him when he was sleeping, so I wasn't sure how he'd react to me stopping by. I was relieved when he smiled and said, "You must be Kenadee."

"I am."

"Heard a lot about you."

"I could say the same about you." I teased. "I'm really glad to see that you're finally awake. You've given everyone quite a scare."

He was clearly still weak as he leaned his head back down on the pillow and sighed. "Don't guess you could tell me where the guys are."

"No. I just know that Sawyer left early this morning with Riggs." I shrugged. "You know they wouldn't tell me anything even if I asked."

"Mack told me we're on lockdown. I'm guessing that's why you're still here."

"Yeah, but hopefully it won't be for much longer."

His lips curled into a cute, little smirk. "Are the walls closing in on you already?"

"Maybe just a little."

"I'd like to tell ya it gets better, but it doesn't." His eyes drifted towards the ceiling. "I'm really ready to get out of this fucking bed."

I shook my head. "Easy there, killer. You just woke up from a coma. You're not getting out of that bed for a while, so you might as well just plan on hunkering down for a bit longer. That's an order."

"You sound like Mack."

"That's because Mack is a smart man. You need to listen to him."

"I will," he promised.

"Can I get you anything?"

"Nah. I'm good. Sadie just brought me some breakfast." He lifted his eyebrow as he continued, "She's coming back in a minute to give me a sponge bath."

"Oh. Well, I'm sure you're looking forward to that." I smiled. "I better get out of your hair, so you two can have some privacy."

As I started for the door, he called out to me. "Hey, Kenadee?"

"Yeah?"

"Thanks for everything you did that night to help Mack. I owe you."

"Glad I could help."

I left the room thinking I'd met yet another brother who I would consider a good guy. As I headed towards the kitchen, I was hit with the wonderful scent of bacon, eggs, and fresh biscuits, making my stomach growl with hunger. When I entered the kitchen, I expected it to be filled with the brothers, but it was eerily quiet. As I made my way over to the coffee pot, I started to think I'd missed something while I was sleeping. After I poured myself a cup, I leaned against the counter and looked around at the empty table and chairs. I was starting to get nervous that something was wrong when Shadow walked in. He didn't even glance in my direction as he walked over to make himself some coffee. Feeling awkward just standing there, I turned to him and said, "Morning."

His eyes skirted over to me as he replied, "Morning, Kenadee."

When Riggs introduced us, Shadow didn't seem to be all that interested, so I was surprised that he actually remembered my name. "It sure is quiet this morning. Did I miss something?"

Still not looking at me, he replied, "Tending to business."

"Oh, okay." Apparently, Riggs wasn't exaggerating when he said Shadow wasn't much of a talker. "I stopped by to see Gunner. Did you know that he was awake?"

"Hadn't heard. That's good news." He nodded. "Really good news."

"I thought so." Hoping to keep the conversation going, I asked, "Have you always lived in Memphis?"

"No." He finally looked over at me, and for the first time, I noticed just how handsome he really was. His dark hair was damp, like he'd just gotten out of the shower, and his hazel eyes seemed to shift between brown and green as he stared at me with a curious look. He was wearing a dark t-shirt with his cut and a pair of tattered jeans and biker boots. With his day-old beard, he had an edgy look about him that matched his enigmatic demeanor. After several seconds, he finally continued, "I moved here after I got out of the service."

"Oh. I didn't realize you were in the military." Wondering why he'd chosen to move to Memphis, I asked, "Do you have family that lives close by?"

Before he could answer, Kevin and Dan came into the kitchen, interrupting our little conversation. Kevin came over to me with a bright smile and said, "Morning, Kenadee!"

"Hey there, Kevin." I smiled. "How are you two doing this morning?"

"We're doing good, but Gammy isn't." Concern crossed his sweet, little face. "She had to stay in bed."

"Oh, I hate to hear that. What's wrong?"

Dan came over and poured himself a cup of coffee as

he answered, "She'll be okay. Just a headache. She gets them from time to time."

Out of the corner of my eye, I noticed that Shadow had grabbed himself a biscuit with a few slices of bacon and was making his way out the door. "Bye, Shadow. See ya later."

He looked back over his shoulder and gave me a quick nod before disappearing into the hall. I suddenly got a craving for one of those biscuits, so I went over to the stove, and as I started making myself a plate, I asked, "Can I get y'all something to eat?"

"Yes. That would be great. Thanks," Dan answered.

After I made each of them a plate, I carried it over to the table and sat down next to Kevin. So, what do you have planned for the day?"

"Logan and I are supposed to play Call of Duty later, but he has to finish some project for school first," Kevin explained.

"I heard him talking about that." Dan gave him a stern look. "What about you? Don't you have some homework you should be working on, too?"

"No, sir. I finished all mine. I even did the extra stuff that Mrs. Glenda sent Gammy for me to do."

"Good. I'm glad to hear that." Dan smiled. "I know it drives your grandmother crazy when you wait until the last minute to do it."

The guys started to quietly file into the kitchen. Without speaking, they each walked over and grabbed a plate of food, then sat down at the table and silently ate. With each brother who walked into the room, the tension grew heavier and heavier, until there was absolutely no doubt there was something going on. I glanced over at

Dan, and he was obviously feeling the same vibe as I was. He reached for Kevin's empty plate and said, "Come on, kiddo. Let's give the guys some breathing room."

He took their dishes over to the sink, and after I'd done the same, I followed them out into the hall. Dan looked down at Kevin and said, "I better go check on your grandmother."

"While you do that, can I take Kenadee up to the roof?"

"I don't know, Kevin. I'm not sure that's a good idea," he replied with concern.

"Come on, Pop. I'll be careful, and you know she'll like it up there," he begged.

Curious, I asked, "What's up on the roof?"

"There's a cool deck up there where you can look out over the Mississippi River and other cool stuff. There's a picnic table and everything."

"Kenadee may not even want to go," Dan told him.

"I would actually like to see it. It sounds kind of neat, but that's completely up to you."

Dan sighed. "Okay, but don't be up there too long."

"Awesome." Kevin started to rush down the hall. "Come on, Kenadee. It's this way."

Dan chuckled and said, "Good luck."

"Hold up! I'm not as fast as you!" I hurried to catch up with Kevin, and I just barely made it up to him when he opened a small door at the end of the hall. "I never even noticed this before."

"I don't think you're supposed to," he replied as started up the stairwell. I followed him up to the top, and when he got to the second door, he looked back at me with excitement. "You ready?"

"You bet."

When he opened the door, sunlight came flooding in, blinding me as I stepped out onto the deck, but after just a few seconds, I felt a warm breeze caress my face and the sound of birds chirping in the distance. Even before I opened my eyes, I inhaled a deep breath, taking in the fresh air, and it was absolutely wonderful. I was enjoying the moment, when I heard Kevin shout, "Hey, look! There's a barge coming."

I brought my hand up to my face, shielding my eyes as I walked over to Kevin. As I glanced out over the ledge, I could see that Kevin was right. There was a barge easing down the river, along with several other boats. "Wow. You can see for miles up here."

"Yeah. It's really cool up here." He smiled proudly. "It's one of my favorite spots at the clubhouse."

"I can see why."

We stood there quietly as we watched the boats travel down the river, and I couldn't believe how good it felt just to be outside. I looked up, letting the sun warm my face, and listened to the peaceful sounds of nature as Kevin tossed pebbles over the ledge. We'd been up there for almost a half an hour when I noticed a black SUV pulling through the back gate with a little, red Toyota following close behind. I peered over the side of the building and watched as they parked in the side lot. When the doors started to open, I took a step closer to the edge, trying to get a better look as the men got out of the vehicles. Seconds later, I spotted Sawyer with Riggs and Murphy, and they were leading a woman with a small child towards a part of the clubhouse I'd never been to before. As they got closer, I quickly realized that I recognized the woman and the child, and I couldn't help but wonder why they were bringing Kate Dillion here, and if her presence had anything to do with her brother, Terry.

BLAZE

*N*o man likes to admit he's wrong, but we doubted Shadow and we couldn't have been more wrong. We found just how wrong we really were when we brought Kate into the holding room. The minute she saw the condition that Terry was in, she completely lost it. Her blue eye filled with tears of anguish as she tried with all her might to break free from our grasp, but we held her there, forcing her to look at the pitiful state of her brother. Fearing that we'd do the same thing to her, she promised to tell us everything we wanted to know. Once Shadow gave the nod, we led her into another room and had one of the girls come get the kid so Gus could interrogate her without any distractions. We all sat down at the table, and Shadow leaned back in his chair with his arms crossed, glaring at Kate with a hatred like I'd never seen before. I didn't quite understand his repulsion for the timid, little blonde until she opened her fucking mouth. Then, it all finally started to come together.

"It started back when Johnny was selling for you." She rolled her eyes, obviously no longer feeling nervous for her life. "He was always coming up short with the week's payout or slacking off, so I took over. I'd sell his take at the strip club for twice the price that Johnny was charging, and I'd pocket the profit. I learned real quick that it was easy money. A whole lot easier than doing rounds."

"How did you get connected to the Culebras?" Gus pushed.

"That happened a few months ago when I made a sale to one of their guys. He liked how I handled myself and asked if I'd be interested in trying something that would make me twice the money in half the time." Her voice didn't waiver, didn't tremble, nor did it show any signs of her being the least bit rattled as she spoke. It was like she was almost proud of what she'd accomplished as she told us, "I took Eddie up on the offer, and after a few weeks, I got a couple of the other girls in on the action. We're making bank, and the club owner has no idea what's going on."

"Eddie?" Gus asked.

"Yeah. Eddie's my handler. I meet up with him at the paper mill over on Russel Street to drop off the money."

"The paper mill?"

"Yeah. That's where they do all their business. I think they even live upstairs or something. They're there all the time," she explained. "Anyway … after we sell everything he's given us, I go over to the mill to give Eddie the money. Once he counts it out and makes sure it's all there, he'll give me more drugs for the girls and me to sell," she explained. "Just like you used to do with Johnny at the warehouse."

"Damn. Johnny had a big fucking mouth," Gus grumbled.

"Yeah, he did. You really should've ended him a long time ago." She exhaled an aggravated breath as she shook her head. Once she was done with her little display, she looked over to Gus and said, "But it was nice of you to send that money over after you offed him. I wasn't expecting that."

"What about Terry and the cameras? Was that your way of thanking us for helping you out?" Riggs barked.

"I did what I had to do. When Rico asked if I knew somebody who could help them get close to Fury, I just kind of volunteered ... especially when I heard what kind of money he was offering. There was no way I could pass that up. I have my daughter to think about, you know." When she noticed the angry expressions on their faces, her tone softened. "Not that it really makes any differ-ence, but I didn't know they were going to do that to the diner or the garage, and neither did Terry. Actually, Terry didn't know anything about anything. He never does. He's an idiot who'll do anything I say for a hit."

The cute little blonde with the adorable baby wasn't some innocent victim. She was a total bitch who'd not only played Johnny, she'd played her own brother without even giving it a second thought. He'd spent hours being brutally tortured because she was a money hungry whore, pretending to give a shit about her kid when she'd ditched her all the time to grind a pole and sell fucking meth. Fuck. I hated the worthless bitch. Just looking at her made my rage surge through my veins, and it took every ounce of control I could muster to keep myself from reaching for her throat and squeezing the life right out of her.

Just when I thought the bitch had said all there was to say, she leaned forward with a confident smirk. "You know, they're coming here."

"What are you talking about?" Gus growled.

We all shifted in our seats as we listened to her say, "I heard Rico talking about it when I did my last drop off … I guess that was about two days ago."

Unable to hold back my response any longer, I barked, "What the fuck did he say?"

"I didn't get everything, just something about breaking through the fence and catching you off guard. I told Eddie it was a bad idea, and he agreed. He thought they should wait you out and kill y'all off one by one, but it didn't matter what he thought. Rico's the boss, and what he says goes."

"When?"

"He didn't say, but from the way they were talking, I'd say it's going to be soon."

Gus stood up with his fists clenched at his sides and ordered, "Outside, boys."

Knowing he was feeling enraged like the rest of us, we followed him out of the room, and once the door closed behind us, we watched as he took a long, cleansing breath. After he pulled himself together, he looked over to Shadow and said, "Fuck, brother. You couldn't have given us a heads up about this shit?"

"I knew she was the missing piece but wasn't sure just how far it would all play out."

"I never would've guessed that she'd be behind all this."

I looked over to Riggs as I said, "That bitch is fucking crazy."

"I hear ya, brother. She's definitely off her fucking rocker."

"You gotta wonder how she got so far gone."

With his eyebrow cocked high, Riggs replied, "While Shadow was dealing with Terry, I did a little digging into the Dillions."

"And?"

"I really didn't find much. Typical city kids. They weren't exactly well off growing up, but from what I could tell, their parents were decent folks. The dad worked two jobs, and the mom was a cashier at a local convenience store. They managed to keep a roof over their heads, food on the table, and stayed clean while they did it. They tried, but they didn't have a lot to show for it." Riggs shrugged.

"So, what happened?"

"I'm no shrink, but I'm thinking good ol' Kate was just a bad fucking seed. She skipped school more than she actually went, and she was just thirteen when she and Terry got caught shop lifting for the first time. A few years later, she was arrested for prostitution, and everything went downhill from there. The chick was always into something, and ended up moving out when she was seventeen.

"And good ol' Terry was just following her lead," I added.

"Yep. The guy is definitely not the sharpest tool in the shed," Riggs answered. "There's no real answer for why Kate was a money, grubbing, evil whore. Hell, none of us would've even suspected her if it wasn't for Shadow."

Gus turned to Shadow and said, "He's right, Shadow. You did good. You did *real good*."

Shadow nodded. "Glad I could help."

Without looking at anyone in particular, Gus announced, "I need eyes inside that paper mill. *Now*! I need to know how many men they've got, how much artillery they have, and every possible exit."

"With the kind of shit they're dealing, they've gotta be covered up with security cameras. I'll head over there now and hack into them, then we'll be able to see exactly what they have going on," Riggs replied.

"Take Sawyer and Murphy with you, but keep your distance. I don't want you taking any chances."

"Understood."

"This needs to happen *fast*," Gus ordered. "Time isn't on our side, boys. I'm calling church. By the time I've caught the others up, I expect to have eyes on that mill," Gus growled.

"Understood," we answered.

"What about the girl?" Murphy asked.

"Leave her. I'll send word to Jasmine, letting her know that the kid will be with her until we make further arrangements."

"Got it."

When we turned to leave, Gus called out to Riggs. "I'm counting on you, son."

"I won't let you down, Prez." Once Gus was gone, Riggs turned to Murphy and me and said, "I gotta grab my laptop. Meet me out at the SUV in two minutes."

Once we got over to the paper mill, Riggs parked across the street next to an abandoned warehouse. Even though the mill was still up and running, it was one of the few in the area. Most hadn't survived the low economy and had shut down, leaving most of the street desolate and quiet. The building itself looked pretty rundown, with bars on the windows and a broken-down metal fence surrounding the grounds. It looked like the perfect place for a meth lab. Once Riggs had pulled up his laptop, he looked over to us and said, "If their CCTV system is IP-connected, then we're set. I'll just need a few minutes to break the code."

Murphy and I kept watch while he hacked into the Culebras's security feed. The truck was completely silent except for the clinking sound of Riggs's fingers tapping the keys on his laptop. Over the years, we'd seen the incredible things he could do, and even though we were struggling with impatience, we all knew that he'd pull through for us in the end. Thirty minutes had passed when he finally said, "I'm in."

We all leaned forward as we studied the screen. When it scrolled down to the basement, Murphy snarled, "Holy shit. They've got twelve stations set up down there, and it looks like they're making this shit around the clock."

"Yeah, but they're doing it old school right now." Riggs pointed to three large stainless-steel containers in the back corner. "Look at that reaction vessel. These fuckers are about to move into a new phase of production, and this the perfect place for it, too. With the paper mill still running, they've got a great cover and the ventilation they need to conceal the smell. No one would suspect anything was going on."

"Damn," Murphy complained.

As I pointed to the bedrooms upstairs, I said, "Looks like Kate was right. They must be living there, too."

"We need to get back to the clubhouse and show this shit to Gus." As Riggs handed me the laptop, he said,

"Start doing a head count. We need to know just how many of these motherfuckers there are and see how many exits you can find. Most of the windows have bars, so we won't have to worry about those."

"Why do we need to know about the exits?" I asked.

"Because I just might have a plan that will end these motherfuckers once and for all."

Riggs was quiet on the way back to the clubhouse. It was clear that he was thinking over his plan, and from the intense look on his face, he had me curious as to what exactly his plan might be, especially knowing how slick he was. Not only was he our club hacker, Riggs was one of the smartest guys I'd ever come across. He was one of those guys who just knew shit—shit that normal guys like me just didn't think about. The things that would come out of his mouth used to surprise me, but over the years, I'd gotten used to the way his mind worked, and I looked forward to seeing how he'd use it against the Culebras.

By the time we made it back to the clubhouse, everyone was waiting for us in the meeting room. Riggs took his laptop with him into the room and placed it in front of Gus and Moose, showing them everything that we were able to pick up on the cameras. As Riggs stood behind them, he said, "Right now, there's only fifteen men on site, so if the girl is right, we've got some guys who aren't around."

Moose's eyebrows furrowed as he said, "They've got guards at every door."

"They do."

"We will have to work around that shit," Moose pointed out.

"Yeah, and we will. I'm not gonna lie … we've got some

obstacles here, but we do have some things that'll work in our favor."

Obviously on edge, Moose snarled, "Okay. Why don't you tell me what the hell those things are?"

"First and foremost, now we know they're planning to come here. We've got eyes on them, so they've lost their element of surprise," Riggs assured him.

T-Bone slammed his fist on the table as he snarled, "Let 'em come here. I'll be the first one standing in line to put a fucking bullet between their eyes."

"Yeah, we could do that … or … we can go on the offensive."

"How do you suppose we do that?"

"They're sitting on a ticking time bomb over there, brother. That meth lab is full of all kinds of volatile chemicals… the kind of chemicals that will blow sky fucking-high when they're met with the right reactant."

Just like I knew he would, Riggs had given us a plan I could get behind. I turned to him and asked, "What kind of reactant?"

"Depends on how creative you want to get, but a simple explosive would do the trick. If we can just get close enough to the lab."

"Why don't we use the girl?" I suggested. "We know she can get inside. We use her to get the explosive close enough to the lab, and then we burn these fuckers to the ground," I growled.

"It could work."

"Hell, yeah, it could work. Now, let's get over there and end this thing once and for all," I roared.

After several seconds, Gus leaned back in his chair and looked out at us with a cold expression. "I have to say … I think Blaze is right. They have it coming. These mother-fuckers killed our brothers. They blew up our garage, shot up our diner, and have the nerve to think they can make a move on our territory. It's time they paid the price for stepping up against Satan's Fury. And make no mistake, they'll pay with their fucking lives … every last one of them."

"You got that fucking right," Moose roared. "Let 'em burn."

Gus stood up and said, "Be ready to move out when I give the call. Blaze, you're with Shadow. You two get with Riggs and have the girl ready for the drop-off. Murphy, you're with me and Moose. We need to check all the artillery and make sure we're ready to roll out within the hour."

As soon as we were dismissed, everyone dispersed, and my head was practically spinning as I followed Shadow and Riggs down the hall. Everything was moving so fucking fast, and while I was eager for us to seek our revenge, I just wanted a minute to catch my breath. Unfortunately, that wasn't an option. There was too much shit that had to be done, including informing Kate that she would be paying a little visit to the Culebras tonight. When we walked into the room, Kate didn't look like she was exactly thrilled to see us. "What took so long? I've been sitting in here for hours!"

Ignoring her, Shadow slowly walked over and sat down in front of her. For several seconds, he didn't speak. He simply glared at her with a seething stare that would make the toughest of men shake in their fucking boots. "You know, when you helped the Culebras, you went against Fury?"

I was actually surprised to see that her unwavering confidence was quickly fading, and her voice trembled as she answered, "Yeah."

"You know you're not gonna get away without paying for that shit, right?" he growled.

"Yes. I know." Her eyes widened as she pleaded, "I'll do anything ... just don't hurt my Lacie. Please. I'm begging you."

"We won't hurt the kid. You have our word," he assured her.

Her head dropped, and for a moment I actually thought the bitch was going to cry. It was too late for tears. She'd already shown she had no heart. She was a selfish piece of shit, only caring about herself, and neither of us were buying any of her bullshit as she answered meekly, "Okay."

"This is what you're gonna do," he started. "You're going to the mill. You're gonna see Eddie ... and give him your payout for the past couple of days. While you're there, you're going to find out everything you can about their plans for striking the clubhouse."

Her eyes narrowed as she asked, "What makes you think they'll tell me anything?"

"You're a smart girl. I'm sure you can find a way to make them talk," Shadow answered. "We'll have a wire on you, so we can hear everything that's being said."

"But I don't have all the money. I'm a little short."

"How much more do you need?"

"Since I was leaving town, I spent some of it," she explained with a shrug. "I was actually planning to skip town with it and use that money to get me started. If I go there tonight and I'm five hundred short, they'll know something's up."

"We'll take care of it." Shadow glanced down at his watch. "What time are they expecting you?"

"I usually go by there around one in the morning when I get off of work."

"If she usually goes after work, then she'll need to change clothes," Riggs suggested.

"Agreed."

"That gives us just over three hours to get ready." Shadow looked over at us. "We'll need to get her something to eat and let her change clothes. Once she's ready, Riggs, you get her wired, and we'll need to get the bag of cash ready."

"Consider it done."

As we stood up to leave, Shadow glared over at Kate, and with a menacing tone, he said, "There are no second chances with this. You fuck up, even a little, and everything you care about will go up in flames. You got that?"

Completely terrified, she replied, "Yeah. I got it."

KENADEE

*A*fter Kevin and I left the rooftop, we went back downstairs, where he was thrilled to find that Logan had completed his school project and was free to play their video game. As soon as he walked into the playroom and left me alone, my mind started to wander. I started to think back to seeing Sawyer with Kate, and the expression on her face as he led her into the clubhouse. I cursed myself for even thinking about it. I'd already promised myself that I wasn't going to obsess over every little thing that happened here. It would simply drive me insane. But when I was walking down the hall and spotted Jasmine with Kate's daughter in her arms, that promise I'd made went flying right out the window.

Trying not to sound suspicious, I asked, "Hey, Jasmine. Who you got there?"

"This is Lacie." She smiled. "Isn't she the cutest thing you've ever seen?"

"Yes. She's adorable." Remembering that Kate had

brought her into the hospital less than a week ago with RSV, I ran my hand slowly over her precious, little head to see if she showed any signs of a fever. I was relieved when I found her skin to be cool to the touch. Hoping that she might know something, I asked, "Is she yours?"

"No. Gus just asked me to keep an eye on her for a little while."

"So, you don't have any idea who she belongs to?"

"He didn't really have time to give me the kid's full background information." She chuckled. "You know?"

"Of course." I smiled as I ran the tip of my finger across the bottom of Lacie's little foot. "I'm guessing you don't have any idea where her mother could be."

"No. I don't know that either." She got a worried look. "Is something wrong?"

"No. Not at all. I just thought I might've recognized Lacie, but I'm sure I've gotten her mixed up with some other cutie pa-tootie." I lied. "Anyway, have you seen any of the guys around?"

"No. If you ask me, I'd say they've got something going on."

"How can you tell?"

"Darlin', I've been around long enough that I can almost smell trouble a hundred miles away." Her expression grew serious as she continued, "Just hold tight, and it'll all pass before you know it. You'll see."

"Okay. I'll do my best."

"I'm going to take this little toot for a diaper change and a bottle."

"Alright. Maybe I'll catch up with you guys later."

When I got back to my room, I decided it was time to

check in with Robyn, but unfortunately, she was busy at work and couldn't talk until later. Once I hung up with her, I tried calling my mother, but got no answer. I couldn't remember the last time I actually picked up the phone to call my mother, and that's when it hit me. Thinking about work and all the things I was missing out on had made me homesick—really homesick. Hoping it might make me feel better, I checked my missed messages and emails, and after I'd gone through them all, I wasn't feeling much better. I turned on the TV and was relieved to find that one of my favorite movie series was on. I curled up on the bed and did my best to ignore the sounds of footsteps as they went charging past my door.

By the time I watched the last movie in the series, I could barely keep my eyes open. In hopes of seeing Sawyer, I'd tried my best to stay awake. I'd gone to the kitchen for a bite to eat, talked to Robyn for over an hour, and replied to my mother's text messages. It was getting late, so I decided to just go on to bed. I'd just pulled the covers over me, when I heard someone knocking. Seconds later, my door eased open and Sawyer stepped inside. "You asleep?"

"No. Not yet," I told him as I turned on the bedside lamp.

"Gonna be heading out in a bit, and I wanted to stop by to tell you goodnight."

"You're leaving?"

"Sorry, wildcat." He dropped down on the edge of the bed. "I've got some things I've gotta tend to with the brothers."

I didn't try to hide my disappointment, when I replied, "Oh."

"You doing alright?"

"I'm fine. Just missing you a little."

"Just a little?" he asked playfully.

"I wouldn't have to miss you at all if you didn't have to go running off again, but I know you have things you need to take care of."

"That I do." His tone changed as he said, "But before I go, I wanted to talk to you about something."

"What about?"

Like it was no big deal at all, he answered, "When the lockdown is over, I'm thinking that I'll get some of the guys to help move the stuff from your apartment over to my place."

"What?" I gasped.

"Well, I didn't figure you'd want to stay here."

"You're right about that," I retorted in a rather negative tone. "But that doesn't mean I'm just going to drop everything and move in with you."

His eyebrows furrowed. "And why not?"

"Seriously, Sawyer. We've been on two dates."

"So?"

"We're just getting to know each other. We can't just move in together on some whim."

"We know each other well enough." I could hear the aggravation in his voice when he said, "I've already told you ... *you're the one*, Kenadee. I wasn't just blowing smoke when I said that shit to you."

"I know that, Sawyer." I placed the palm of my hand on his chest. "I meant what I said to you, too. We've got a good thing here. A really good thing, and I don't want to mess it up by moving too fast."

"I want you in my house and in my bed. What's so wrong with that?" he growled.

"For one, it's not all about *you*." His back stiffened, and I could see that he wasn't really hearing what I was saying. I leaned towards him as I continued, "I'm falling for you Sawyer Mathews. I'm falling hard, and I'm falling fast. And that scares me. This world that you live in is different from anything I've ever known. There are things that go on here that I just don't understand, and I'm still trying to make sense of it all."

"Like what?"

"Like the fact that Kate Dillion and her baby are here, and I can't figure out why."

"How the fuck do you know about that?"

"Because I was up on the roof with Kevin when you and the guys dragged her in here. At first, I thought you were protecting her and she was going to be under lock-down with us, but since I haven't seen her, I can only assume that she's here for a different reason ... maybe because of her brother, Terry."

"Fuck," he grumbled under his breath. "You aren't going to make this easy, are you?"

"No, I'm probably not, Sawyer. Maybe you should think about that before you start throwing around ideas like moving in together!" I snapped. "I won't apologize for having questions and worrying about someone I care about. That's who I am."

"I don't have time for this shit," he grumbled. "I've gotta go."

He stood up and as he started for the door, I called out to him softly, "*Sawyer.*"

"I need to go, Kenadee."

I walked over to him. "I know you have to go, but you can't leave here mad, not when you're heading out into danger."

"I'm not mad."

"Yes, you are." I smiled as I stepped closer to him. "I have one more thing to say ... Just because you have all this crazy stuff going on and just because I don't want to move in with you right at this very moment doesn't mean that I don't want you or that I don't want a future with you. Cause I do. I really, really do."

"So, what are you saying?"

"I'm saying that I just need a little time. That's all." I wound my arms around his neck as I added, "It'll also give Kevin a chance to get used to the idea of us being together, too. It wouldn't be fair to just throw all this on him."

"You seriously gonna use my kid against me?"

"You know I'm right."

His expression softened as he said, "Maybe, but that doesn't mean I like it."

I eased up on my tiptoes and pressed my lips against his, kissing him softly. His hands slipped around my waist, quickly pulling me closer as he took over the kiss. Just as things were about to get heated, there was a pounding on my door and Riggs shouted, "I got it done. It's time to roll out, brother."

Sawyer took a step back, and after kissing me on the forehead, he said, "I'll see you tomorrow."

"Okay." As I watched him walk out of the room, I had to fight the urge to ask him to stay. Needing to see him one more time, I rushed to the doorway and called out to him, "Sawyer?"

He and Riggs turned to look at me as he answered, "Yeah?"

"You two be careful."

"Always, wildcat. Always."

BLAZE

*T*he plan was in motion. As he was putting on her wire, Shadow had gone over the plan with her one last time, making sure Kate knew exactly what was expected of her when she went inside that mill. While he was busy working with her, Murphy was out in the artillery room with Gus and Moose, checking all our weapons and ammo. Riggs also had them searching for a specific piece of equipment, one that we'd need to put our plan into effect. We left nothing to chance as we each prepared to leave the clubhouse, and after we had everything together, Gus called us back together to go over all the final details, leaving no stone unturned. Once we were set to go, we all headed out to the parking lot to load up. It had already been decided that Murphy would ride with Kate in her car, at least until we got closer to the mill, so he could ensure that she didn't try anything stupid. They'd just gotten inside and buckled up when Riggs took the duffle-bag of money over to them.

"She'll need this," Riggs told him as he offered him the bag.

As he reached for the handle, Murphy raised his eyebrow and asked, "Is everything here?"

"Yep. *Everything's* there," he assured him.

Murphy nodded as he placed the bag in the back seat. "Then, it looks like we're ready to roll."

"That we are."

After checking their security cameras to make sure the Culebras were all in place, Gus gave the signal, and with Kate and Murphy in the lead, we pulled out of the gate. As we started to get closer to Russel Street, Kate pulled her car over to the shoulder, just long enough for Murphy to get out, and then she continued towards the mill. Hoping to get as close as possible without getting noticed, we all started to disperse and approached the building from various intersections. Once we were as close as we could get, Riggs pulled up his laptop. With the cameras and the hidden microphone, we were able to watch as Kate pulled up to the back parking lot and got out of her car. With the duffle-bag in tow, she started towards the back door, and one of the guards motioned her inside. After he patted her down, he reached for the bag, examining it for a minute before he led her through the entrance.

"Looks like we're in," Riggs announced proudly.

When he turned up the sound on her microphone, we heard one of the men say, "Eddie's downstairs. Stay put, and I'll let him know you're here."

"Why do I have to wait? He busy or something?" she asked nervously.

I wanted to reach through the screen and shake her,

warning her not to act so fucking suspicious, but there was nothing any of us could do. We could only sit there and watch as the guy answered, "Just do as you're told, puta."

As Kate stood there waiting, fidgeting with her fingernails, we could see the men and women working feverishly in the basement. Every station was up and running while guards walked back and forth, monitoring their every move. As each mixed the different chemicals into various containers, it was clear that none of them were new to the game. Like a line of factory workers, they'd all been making this shit long enough to know exactly what they were doing. It was easy to get caught up in the insanity of it all, but my attention was pulled away when I noticed two men talking in the corner of the room. Their hand movements were erratic like they were arguing, and when one of them took a charging step towards the other, I said, "Damn. That doesn't look good."

"What the fuck is that all about?"

"No idea, but we need Kate downstairs. Now!" Riggs growled.

"Just give it a minute," Moose told him. "She hasn't been waiting up there long."

Patience had never been any of our strong suits. We were men who lived by the seat of our pants, acted first and asked questions later, and sitting like a duck wasn't something any of us were very fond of. Just when we were all about to lose it, the guard turned to Kate and said, "He's ready for you."

"It's about fucking time," she huffed as she turned and started towards the stairs, cursing under her breath all the way down. We watched as she walked over to a short, stubby man at the back of the assembly line. As she handed him the duffle-bag, we heard her say, "Eddie! How ya doing, sweetheart?"

"Where the fuck have you been?"

"I know I'm a little late, but my daughter was in the hospital. It put me a little behind."

"How many times do you expect me to believe that shit?" Eddie sneered.

"You know I wouldn't lie to you about something like that. She's been really sick."

"I don't give a fuck," he snarled, jerking the bag from her hand.

When Eddie started to pull the money out of the bag, we knew it was time to move. Riggs reached for his head lights, flashing them three times to signal the others that it was time to put the second stage of the plan in motion. We waited several minutes and once everyone was in position, Gus gave Riggs the nod, giving him the go ahead to proceed. Riggs took out the detonator, and then looked back at the screen. We watched as Kate stepped closer to Eddie and whispered, "So … has there been any more talk about Satan's Fury?"

He gave her a suspicious look as he asked, "Why you asking?"

With just those words, she'd secured her daughter's safety. It was unfortunate that it was too late to do anything about her own. Riggs pressed the button on the detonator, triggering the small IED hidden in the handle of the duffle bag. It was just a small explosive, barely enough to blow up a car, but when its contents ignited with all the other chemicals in the lab, it was a sight to behold. A rush of blue flames skirted across the room, before a second, larger blast sent flames and mortar soaring through the entire building. The discharge was so intense that we felt the truck vibrate a hundred yards away. We needed to ensure that no one was able to exit the building, so as soon as the fire had taken hold, Gus turned to us and ordered, "Let's move."

We were about to get out of the SUV when I remembered that Riggs had mentioned killing the power so the fire wouldn't set off their fire alarms. I wasn't sure if he remembered, so I turned to him and said, "Don't forget to kill the power."

"Already, got it."

Once he was out of the truck, we rushed to meet up with the others. I could feel the heat of the flames as we inched closer, and the smell nearly choked me as we came up next to Cyrus. Riggs warned, "We need to make this fast. This shit is

toxic."

Through the haze of smoke, I noticed some suspicious movement on the second floor. Moments later, glass sprayed out as a chair crashed through the window. With fire blazing behind him, a man started waving his hands as he shouted, "Hey! Over here!"

Without a moment's hesitation, I aimed my gun at the guy's head and squeezed the trigger, sending him flailing back into the flames before he could make another sound. Cyrus came up behind me and said, "Good catch, brother. Keep an eye on that back door. We had a couple who tried to escape a few minutes ago, but Gauge got to them before they got out."

"On it."

When T-Bone came walking up, none of us were surprised when he said, "Damn. I forgot to bring the fucking marshmallows."

"How are things looking from the back?" Gus asked.

"One made it out, but we put a bullet in him and loaded him up in the back of the truck."

As we stood there watching, one explosion erupted after the next, making it look like the Fourth of July as the building was consumed with fire and smoke. We continued to monitor every exit, making sure there was no sign of any movement whatsoever. Once we were certain there were no survivors, we headed back to our vehicles and made our getaway just before the police and firemen started to arrive. We left there knowing that we'd gotten our revenge, but our job wasn't done—not even close. We all knew we'd just won a small battle in a never-ending war, so there would be no grand celebration. No party or hurrah. It was time for us to lick our wounds, mourn our losses, and start rebuilding what had been destroyed.

When we pulled up to the clubhouse, it was nearly three in the morning. We were all exhausted and ready to call it a day. Before we went inside, Gus called us all over to him and said, "You boys did good tonight. I wish Runt and Lowball would've been here to see it, but I know they were here in spirit. Tomorrow starts a new day. Lock-down is over, but we're not out of the woods just yet. Stay alert. I want you to keep your eyes and ears open in case there is blowback from all of this. As of now, we don't know much about these Culebra motherfuckers, and there could be more of them ... *lots more.*"

My blood ran cold at the thought. With everything happening so fast, we hadn't had the time to gather the intel that we normally would. Concerned, I asked, "And if there are?"

"Then, we'll need to be ready for them to retaliate. Before we worry about that, we'll need Riggs to do some digging—lots of digging. For now, take the next few hours to re-coup, and then, I want us working to get the garage and diner back open, and we'll need to plan a memorial run and cookout for our boys this weekend."

"Ready whenever you are, Prez. Just say the word," T-Bone assured him.

"Get some rest, boys."

As the others started to disperse, I heard Riggs ask Gus, "What are we gonna do about the kid?"

"I'm sure we can find someone to take her in," Gus grumbled.

Moose shook his head as he said, "Louise has someone that'll take her."

"Who?"

"One of the waitresses at the diner. A real sweet girl. She and her husband have been trying to have kids for years and haven't had any luck. Poor thing's been working double shifts for months just so she can cover the costs of adoption. They'll take good care of the baby."

"You think she'll keep quiet?"

"No doubt. Besides, we've got Riggs. He can make anything look legit."

"Then make it happen, and tell Louise that we'll do whatever we can to help them out."

"Got it."

I hated to bring it up, but it was a question that needed to be asked. "And Terry?"

Riggs looked at me with a grimace. "Shadow put that dude through hell. Maybe we should consider giving him a second chance."

"Fuck no. He was there the night we took out Johnny. He knew the consequences for fucking with the club," Gus growled. "There'll be no more chances for Terry Dillion. I'll have T-Bone and a couple of the prospects take care of him in the morning. Too fucking tired to deal with that shit tonight."

"Understood."

Once we were done talking, I followed Riggs inside and then headed straight to my room for a hot shower. After I threw on a pair of sweats, I started to get in my bed, but stopped. The thought of climbing into it alone just didn't appeal to me—not when Kenadee was just down the hall. Without a second thought, I headed towards her room. I was so intent on lying in the bed next to her that I didn't even feel guilty when I picked the lock and slipped into her room without knocking. Just being in the same room with her set my entire body at ease, and the tension I'd been carrying with me through the night quickly started to fade. I carefully lowered myself onto her bed, trying my best not to wake her as I lay down next to her, inhaling her scent as I draped my arm across her waist.

I lay there for several moments, just listening to the soothing sound of her breathing, and I thought she was still asleep until I heard her whisper, "Sawyer?"

I kissed her lightly on the shoulder. "It's late. Go back to sleep."

"Is everything okay?"

"More than okay." I paused for a moment, then told her, "Looks like you'll get to sleep in your own bed tomorrow night."

"What?"

"The lockdown's over. You get to go home."

I didn't miss the hint of disappointment in her voice, when she muttered, "Oh."

"You can always change your mind about coming back to my place."

"I know."

Wishing she would, I ran my hand along her hip. "Now, get some sleep."

She slowly inched her hips back, gently pressing her ass against my cock as she whispered seductively, "What if I don't want to go back to sleep?"

"You're not tired, wildcat?" I asked as my hand trailed down her abdomen and slipped beneath her lace panties.

"No. I'm not tired at all," she whimpered as my fingers slipped between her legs. Her ass slid back against my growing erection, and I groaned in response. With one simple move, she'd made me want her even more. There were no limits to my desire for her. She was everything I'd ever wanted, and I didn't even realize it until she was in my arms. I slid my fingertips inside her, and the blood rushed to my cock when I found she was already soaked. I'd just begun to stroke her when she moaned, "Oh god, Sawyer!"

The sound of my name from her lips spurred me on, and I couldn't wait a moment longer to be inside her. Before she could protest, I withdrew my fingers and quickly lowered her panties down her long, lean legs.

Once I'd removed my sweats, I dropped my hands to her hips, pulling her ass against me. Instinctively, her legs spread wide for me, giving me complete access as I placed myself at her center. A sense of contentment washed over me when her back arched against me as I drove inside her. She was so fucking tight, and just being inside her made me forget about the craziness of the night. Like all the times before, when she was in my arms, there was no one else. *Just her.*

"You drive me crazy, wildcat. Never wanted anything like I want you," I growled as my fingers dug into her hips.

I drove into her again and again, fucking her deep and hard. A fevered moan vibrated through her as she started to grind against me, taking more of me with every shift of her hips. Knowing what she needed, I slid my hand from her hip down between her legs, and her breath quickened when I reached her clit. Pleasured cries echoed through the room when I began to stroke her with a tormenting rhythm, and it wasn't long before I could feel her muscles contracting all around me as she pleaded, "Don't stop!"

She felt so damn good, so fucking perfect, and she was mine. Her body started to tremble around me, urging me on as I relentlessly drove inside, over and over, until at last, she let out a tortured groan and clamped down around me. There was no better feeling in the world, and I felt my release building as the muscles in my abdomen and legs grew taut. With one final thrust, I pulled her to me and came deep inside her, growling with complete and utter gratification.

Neither of us moved. We just lay there nestled close together as our breaths started to slow. She reached for my hand, and as she laced her fingers through mine, she tucked my arm under her in a tender embrace. "Sawyer?"

"Um-hmm?"

"Don't let me go."

"You want to tell me what you're talking about?"

"When I go home, don't let that be the end of this," she replied softly.

"Again, you could change your mind about coming back to my place." I teased.

"I'm being serious, Sawyer." She sighed. "I want this, and I'm just afraid that you'll give up on me or something."

"No way that's gonna happen, baby." I trailed kisses along her shoulder. "I probably shouldn't tell you this … but I've got this plan. I'm not going to tell you all the details of this *said plan*, but I will say, I'm thinking this plan might just help me reach my goal."

"You must be really sleepy, because you're not making any sense."

"Let me put it like this … the sooner I get you in my house and in my bed, the better."

"I like the sound of that."

"Good. So, you want to move in tomorrow?" I poked.

"*Sawyer.*"

"I know. I know." I chucked. "Since you're heading home, there's something I need to tell you about Robyn."

"Robyn?" she asked with surprise.

"Yeah. You know she and Runt had a bit of a thing going."

"There wasn't that much to it. They went out that one night after they met at the diner, and she drank way too much. Nothing really happened."

"Yeah, well. It didn't exactly end there."

"What are you talking about?" she shrieked as she broke our embrace and rolled over to face me.

The news obviously took her by surprise and I didn't want to create a rift between them, but considering the situation, Kenadee needed to know. "It didn't end that night. They'd been calling and texting, and he even went over to your apartment a couple of times while you were sleeping or when you were out with me."

"Why didn't Robyn tell me that?"

"Hell, if I know. Runt didn't get it either. Actually, it kind of bothered him that they were sneaking around." I snickered. "Especially after our night out."

With her back flat on the mattress, she looked up at the ceiling and mumbled, "That little hooker!"

"The only reason I'm even bringing it up is she might ask about him or something. You can't tell her he was killed at the diner. His death wasn't reported to the cops, and she'd ask questions about why he hadn't gone to the hospital, just like you did. We don't need those kinds of questions. You can say he got called away on a job or you can tell her he was killed in an accident when he was on a run for the club. That's your call."

"Neither one of those are exactly great options."

"Nope, but they're all you've got."

Her head rolled to the side as she turned to look at me with tired eyes. "Gee, thanks."

"Just doing what I can to help." I slipped my arm around her waist and pulled her back over to me, snuggling her close. "Got a big day tomorrow. You're gonna need your sleep."

"Okay." Her body grew still for a moment, and then she whispered, "Sawyer?"

"Yeah?"

"Goodnight."

I had a feeling she was going to say something else, but since it was late, I didn't push. Instead, I kissed her shoulder. "Goodnight, wildcat."

J just wanted to spend the morning wrapped in Sawyer's arms, revel in the warmth of his body next to mine, but that just wasn't an option. He needed to help Kevin and his parents get packed up, and I needed to get back to work. Neither of us were exactly thrilled about getting out of that bed. We both knew it would be a while before we had a moment alone together, so we made use of the time we had and made love one last time before he headed out to find his folks. Once he was gone, I took a shower, and after I'd gotten dressed, I started to gather up what few belongings I had that were actually mine. I put everything Sadie had given me in a basket, including the clothes, and placed it on the dresser. I wrote her a quick note and thanked her for letting me borrow them and left it on top of the stack. Once I was done, I went to see if Sawyer was ready to run me over to my apartment.

When I started down to his room, I ran into Riggs. "Hey, doll. You looking for Blaze?"

"Yeah. Have you seen him?"

"He's just down the hall with his folks. I think he's helping them load their car."

"Okay. Thanks, Riggs."

When I turned to leave, he said, "Hey, Kenadee?"

"Yes?"

"Just wanted to thank you for all you did to help us out. If you ever need anything, and I mean anything, you just let me know," he told me with sincerity in his voice.

"Thanks, Riggs. I appreciate that."

"You take care of my boy, Blaze," he teased. "He's a good one. He deserves a good woman like you."

As he started walking away, I called, "Bye, Riggs. You take care of yourself."

"Plan on it."

When I got down to Sawyer's parents' room, the door was wide open, so I stuck my head in to see if anyone was around. I was surprised to see that the room was empty, and all of their things were already packed and gone. I'd just turned to leave when I heard Janice call out my name. "Kenadee?"

I turned around and found her coming out of the bathroom with a small cosmetics bag. "Hey. I was starting to think you'd already gone."

"Not just yet, but we're getting close," she replied with a twinge of excitement. "Are you looking for Sawyer?"

"Yes, ma'am."

"He just took some of our things out to the car with Dan and Kevin. They'll be right back." A strange look crossed her face as she started to walk over to me and said, "I wanted to tell you how much I enjoyed our morning together the other day. I think you're a very special young lady."

I smiled as I replied, "Thank you, Mrs. Mathews. I enjoyed it, too. Hopefully, we can do it again sometime."

"I really hope you mean that." She placed her hand on my shoulder. "Sawyer is very fond of you."

"And I'm very fond of him."

"I've always said it was going to take a strong woman to show him what it is to really love someone. I think he found that with you." A hopeful expression crossed her face as she continued, "I hope you found the same in him."

Just as I was about to respond, Sawyer came up behind us and asked, "What's the hold up, ladies? We need to get moving."

"I was just telling Kenadee that I hoped that I would be seeing her again soon." She stepped over and gave me a quick hug. *"Real soon."*

"I'm sure it won't be too long," I assured her. "Be sure to tell Dan and Kevin that I said goodbye."

"I sure will." As she started walking towards the door, she looked over to Sawyer and said, "I'll see you back at the house later tonight."

Once she was gone, I helped Sawyer gather up the last of his things, and then we headed out to his bike. The ride to my apartment was bitter-sweet. While I was thrilled to have my freedom back, I wasn't looking forward to saying goodbye to Sawyer. I knew it wasn't going to be forever. I knew in my heart that my future was with him. I'd just have to be patient and make sure we were both ready before jumping in with both feet. If our love was as strong as I truly believed it was, then spending a little time getting to know one another better would only make what we shared even better.

When he pulled up to the curb, he turned off the engine and helped me off the bike. As I handed him my helmet, he said, "I'll be here at seven thirty to pick you up for dinner."

"For what?"

"You said we needed to date, so that's what we're gonna do." He smirked. "Dinner tonight at seven thirty."

"Oh, okay."

"Need your mouth, wildcat," he growled as he pulled me over to him and pressed his lips against mine. There was no better feeling than being kissed by the incredibly sexy, Sawyer Mathews. In a matter of seconds, he had every hormone in my body raging, and I was practically panting as his hand drifted down past my hip. He gave my ass a firm squeeze before releasing me from our embrace. "I'll see you at seven-thirty."

"Looking forward to it."

I was practically skipping as I headed upstairs, and when I walked into the apartment, I was surprised to find Robyn sound asleep on the sofa. Trying my best not to wake her, I stepped inside, carefully closing the door behind me, and just as I was about to turn to go to my room, I tripped over several boxes that were scattered on the floor. The commotion startled Robyn, causing her to shoot up off the sofa with a shriek. "Shit, Kenadee! You scared the crap out of me."

"Sorry about that. I was trying not to wake you." I used my foot to scoot the takeout boxes out of the way as I asked, "What is all this?"

"They're mine. I just haven't gotten around to picking

them up." She dropped back down on the sofa with a pitiful looking pout. "How was your trip?"

"My trip was fine." Clearly something was up with her, so I walked over and sat down next to her on the sofa. "What's going on with you?"

"I'm just in a funk. It'll pass."

To say that she was in a funk was the understatement of the year. The apartment was a total wreck and smelled like dirty socks. Her greasy hair was on top of her head, and there were stains on her shirt, making her look like she hadn't showered in days, and from the dark circles under her eyes, it looked like she hadn't been sleeping. There was definitely something wrong, which made me wonder if Sawyer had been right about her relationship with Runt. Maybe she really had been seeing him, and the fact that he had suddenly disappeared was making her a little off balance. "This seems like it's more than just a funk, Robyn. Are you okay?"

"Yeah. I've just had a rough couple of days." She feigned a smile. "Now that you're home, I'll be back to my old self in no time."

For reasons I didn't understand, she simply wouldn't open up to me. There was no way for me to know for certain if Runt truly was her reason for being so upset or if it was something else altogether. Either way, I couldn't keep his death a secret from her, so I said, "I've got some news I need to tell you."

"Oh, man. I don't like the sound of that."

"You're right. It's not exactly good news." I let out a deep breath before I asked, "You remember Runt, the guy from…"

"Yes, Dee. I remember Runt. What about him?"

"He died the other night." I waited for a moment, giving her a chance to comprehend what I'd just said, and my heart ached for her when I noticed the tears trickling down her cheek. I hated lying to her, but like Sawyer told me, I didn't have a choice. "He had an accident on his bike when he was heading back to the clubhouse."

"What are you talking about?" her voice trembled.

"Honey, he's gone."

She dropped her head into her hands and started to weep. Through the muffle of her sobbing, she muttered, "I couldn't figure out what happened to him."

"What do you mean?"

With tears steadily streaming down her face, she looked up at me and said, "He called me at work and said that he was coming to get me. He said there was something going on with the club, and he wanted me to stay with him at the clubhouse until the dust settled."

"When was this?"

"The night of my mystery date," she confessed. "I was actually planning to go meet him."

As much as I didn't want to believe it, Sawyer had been right about Robyn and Runt, and I was shocked to hear that he was planning to bring her in for the lockdown. I tried not to let it hurt my feelings that she hadn't told me about their relationship as I asked, "So, you and Runt were still seeing each other?"

"Yeah … I don't know why I didn't just tell you about it. I felt bad, especially with everything that was going on with you and Sawyer. You were so upset that he hadn't called, and I didn't want you to think that I was rubbing it in your face that I was running off with one of his brothers."

"You know I would never think that," I scolded.

"I guess none of that matters now." She wiped the tears from her cheek as she said, "At least now I know what happened to him."

"I'm really sorry, honey."

"I'm sorry, too. I shouldn't have kept any of this from you."

Knowing I hadn't been exactly honest with her about my situation, I couldn't hold it against her that she hadn't been completely forthcoming with me. "It's really okay. I understand."

As I looked at her curled up into a ball on the sofa, I wanted to help take her heart ache away, but I knew time was the only cure for the pain she was enduring. I reached over and gave her hand a gentle squeeze as I asked, "Are you going to be okay?"

"Yeah. I'll be fine. I just need a day to wallow in my self-pity."

"So, I take it you aren't going to work today?"

"Nope. I took the day off, but I'll go in with you tomorrow," she assured me.

As I stood up, I told her, "Good. We can have a veg out day together, but first, I'm going to pick up some of this mess."

"Leave it. I'll get to it tomorrow," she whined.

"I've got it. You rest and watch TV for a bit. We'll figure out something for lunch when I'm done."

"Okay. Thanks, Dee."

Once she'd turned on the TV, I went into the kitchen for a garbage bag, and just as I started to pick up some of the trash, I heard a news anchor talking about an explosion at a Peterson Paper Mill on Russel Street. The woman went on to say that there was a meth lab located in the basement of the building, and police officers believed that it was the cause of the explosion. Several bodies had been uncovered, including one of the ring leaders in the notorious Culebras gang. As I stood there staring at the television screen, I couldn't help but think that it was an odd coincidence that this terrible gang was killed in a horrific explosion on the same night that the club was released from their lockdown. Noting my odd interest in the news report, Robyn asked, "Something wrong?"

When I thought about the gang and what they'd been doing, it was difficult to feel sorry for them, regardless of who was to blame for the death. "No. Nothing's wrong."

I went back to picking up the apartment, and after I spent the entire day lying around with Robyn, watching movies and eating junk food, it was time for my date with Sawyer. Just like he'd promised, he arrived promptly at seven thirty and took me downtown to eat ribs at one of my favorite BBQ restaurants. Once we were done eating, he took me for a ride on his bike, and we spent several hours just talking at one of the local parks. It was a wonderful date, and it was the first of many. Over the next few weeks, we went on one outing after the next, going to baseball games, to movies, and even a couple of concerts. But there was a catch. On these wonderful little excursions he took me on, there was no sex—none. Not even a little heavy petting. While he was still Sawyer, alpha through and through, he was a perfect gentleman. The man was killing me. While I pretended not to know what he was up to, his plan was working. With each night I spent with him, I found myself wanting him even more than I dreamed possible, and I was becoming pathetically desperate for his touch.

When he called to tell me that he had a special night planned, I decided it was time to step up my game. It was time to show Sawyer Mathews exactly who he was messing with, so I got dressed up in one of my favorite little black dresses, the one that hugged my curves in just the right way. Then, I curled my hair just the way he liked it and wore his favorite perfume, hoping to persuade him to drop this "no sex" notion of his, even if it was for just one night. I took one last glimpse in the mirror and smiled at my reflection. My girls were propped up high with lots of cleavage showing, my makeup was flawless, and my ass looked incredible in the form fitting dress and heels. I thought I had him exactly where I wanted him, but I couldn't have been more wrong.

When he knocked on the door, I gave my hair one last toss and adjusted my lipstick. With my mind set on blowing him away, I opened the door, and my mouth dropped open the second I saw him. He looked absolutely incredible standing there in an all-black suit with a black shirt and matching tie. I'd never seen him look sexier than he did at that moment, and I knew I'd just been played. That sneaky bastard had just beaten me at my own game. I stood there gripping the door handle, trying to keep myself from pouncing on him like a rabid dog, and said, "You win."

His lips curled into a sexy smile. "I win?"

"Yep. You win … fair and square. I'm done."

"Whatcha saying, wildcat?"

"I'm saying … *I'm moving in.*"

BLAZE

*S*he was everything I'd always wanted and more, so I agreed to do the dating thing like she wished, but I was going to do it my way. I would "wine her and dine her, but there'd be no sixty-nining her'. I made it clear from our first night out that there was only one way she would get my cock, and that was when she'd moved into my house and she was in my bed. Simple as that. But it wasn't so simple. It had taken every ounce of restraint I had to keep my hands off her, especially at the end of each date. I didn't want her to go, and I certainly didn't want to spend another night with a raging hard-on. But I had to stick to the plan and remember that with each date I was one step closer to making her mine. I was doing pretty good with this plan of mine, until I'd gone to pick her up for our date and she opened the door wearing that little black dress. The moment I saw her, I knew I was in trouble. I'd never seen her look so beautiful, so fucking sexy, and as I stood there looking into her lust-filled eyes, I could feel my resolve starting to crumble around me. There was no way in hell I would be able to keep my hands off her, not when that dress was hugging her curves in all the right places.

I was so overcome with need that I almost missed it when she said, "You win."

A smile spread across my face as I stepped towards her and asked, "I win?"

"Yep. You win... fair and square." Her eyes slowly drifted over me, appraising me like a prize she'd just claimed, and with a defeated sigh, she announced, "I'm done."

"Whatcha saying, wildcat?"

Finally, after weeks of absolute torture, she finally said the words I'd longed to hear. "I'm saying ... I'm moving in."

"You sure about that?"

She moved towards me, and as she wound her arms around my neck, she whispered, "Absolutely."

My mouth crashed down on hers as my hands dropped to her waist, inching her closer as I kissed her passionately. I hungered for her. It was the only thought that was going through my mind as my tongue delved deeper in her mouth. Our tender moment quickly grew heated. Our hands became frantic and full of need as we stumbled into the apartment. She quickly closed the door, and her mouth never left mine as she started to remove my jacket. I knew I should stop. I was giving into her without completely fulfilling my plan, but I was too far gone. There was no way I could stop, but thankfully, Robyn came to my rescue when she walked up behind us and said, "How about that. The Sexpot in Leather also looks pretty damn good in a suit. Well played biker boy. Well played."

Startled, Kenadee broke from our embrace and said, "Robyn! I thought you were still in the shower."

"Hold up ... Did you just call me *Sexpot in Leather?*"

Ignoring me completely, she smiled as she said, "I thought you two were going on one of your dates."

"Well ... we were, but ..."

"We were actually just about to leave," I interrupted. "The show starts in an hour."

"But I thought ..."

"Not until you're moved in, wildcat."

"I just told you that I was gonna move in."

I shook my head. "Saying and doing are two different things, darlin'."

"Oh, good grief. You're killing me here."

"Let me make this easy for the both of you," Robyn interjected. "Kenadee go grab some of your stuff now and I can help you get the rest of it moved tomorrow."

"Works for me," I told her with a smile.

"Okay." As she rushed down the hallway, she shouted, "Give me ten minutes."

As she sat down on the sofa, Robyn asked, "Where are you taking her tonight?"

"I got us tickets to see *Rent* at the Orpheum."

"Wow. Impressive. She's going to love that."

"I hoped she would."

Her expression turned serious as she said, "I'm just going to throw out this little warning ... As a nurse, I've seen a lot of things, and I've learned a lot of things. I know *pretty interesting* ways to remove a man's testicles, so if you want to keep yours intact, *don't fuck with my girl.*"

"I'll keep that in mind."

"Let's hope that you do." She brought her fingers up and crossed them like a pair of scissors. "Otherwise *snip... snip.*"

Just as I was starting to feel a little anxious about my balls, Kenadee came back into the room carrying her bag. A worried look crossed her face as she turned to Robyn and asked, "Are you sure you're okay with this?"

"Kenadee, we've already talked about this. I told you, I'm going to be fine. I have no problem living alone, and we'll see each other at the hospital." She paused for a moment, then continued, "Trust me. If I were in your shoes and had a chance to be with the man I loved, I wouldn't hesitate."

"Love you, chick."

"I love you, too. Now, y'all go have a good time, and I'll see you sometime tomorrow."

After taking the duffle-bag from Kenadee's hand, I led her out to the truck and helped her inside. As we pulled away from the curb, I was tempted to take her straight to the house and spend the entire night making love to her, but I fought the temptation and headed over to the Orpheum. I even managed to make it through the entire Broadway show without ripping her clothes off, but when we got home, that was a different matter altogether.

As soon as we walked into the house, I reached for her hand and led her into the bedroom. "Do you have any idea what you put me through tonight? You knew what that dress would do to me ... and now, you're going to get exactly what you were asking for."

"Promise?"

"Just wait and see, baby. Just wait and see."

I put one of my hands behind her neck and pressed my mouth against hers. Her lips parted in surprise as I pulled her body close to mine. The kiss was possessive and demanding, leaving no question as to what I had in mind for her. My mouth roamed over the curve of her neck as I whispered, "I've been thinking about this night for weeks, wildcat."

"*Sawyer...*" she breathed.

My hands greedily moved to her shoulders, easing the straps of her dress down her arms as I caressed her breast. In almost a whisper, I heard her say, "I missed you."

"I missed you, too, baby. More than you know."

"Sawyer?"

"Yeah?"

"*I love you.*"

I'd known from the start that Kenadee Brooks was going to change my life. I just had no idea how much. She was my missing piece, and now that I had her, I wasn't letting her go. "I love you, too."

My words seemed to stir something in her as she reached for my suit jacket and pulled it from my body, tossing it onto the bed. When my hands dropped to my belt buckle, she bit her bottom lip as she lowered her dress to the floor, revealing that she was wearing nothing underneath. Fuck. She was even more beautiful than I remembered, and I grew even harder as I imagined all the wicked things I wanted to do to her. My fingertips roamed over her bare skin, only stopping when I reached her breasts. A low growl rumbled in my throat as I lowered my head to her breast, flicking my tongue across her sensitive flesh. Her breath quickened as I moved to her other breast, and she gasped as I continued teasing and tormenting her with my mouth.

Unable to wait a moment longer, I lifted her into my arms and carried her over to the bed, carefully lowering her down onto the mattress. She looked so damn perfect sprawled out on my bed, every glorious inch of her was mine, and I intended to cherish her in ways she couldn't begin to imagine. Her eyes locked on mine as I stood before her and slowly removed my clothes. My entire body was on fire, burning to touch her, to taste her, and seeing the way she was writhing on the bed with anticipation, only made my hunger for her more intense. I lowered myself onto the bed, and goosebumps prickled against her skin as I settled my head between her legs. With my beard tickling her inner thigh, I whispered, "It's about fucking time."

I spent the rest of the night making love to her, showing her exactly how much I'd missed having her in my arms, and just as we were about to drift off to sleep, I turned to her and said, "There are no words to express what you mean to me, wildcat."

As she nestled into the crook of my arm, she whispered, "You don't have to say the words, Sawyer. I feel it every time you touch me."

I kissed her softly on the forehead as I said, "The only one."

"The only one," she repeated.

Everything had fallen into place. I had my woman, and things at the club were finally coming together. After weeks of busting our asses, both the diner and the new garage were finally up and running. After seeing what was left of the old garage, we all agreed that it was best to just buy a new one. It wasn't an easy decision, especially since so much time and energy had gone into building the first one, but time wasn't on our side. We had the club's finances to consider, and we needed to get orders in as soon as possible. Luckily, we were able to find an old garage that met all our needs, and after some minor renovations, we were ready to get to work. Unfortunately, things hadn't gone as smoothly with the diner. While the damage wasn't nearly as extensive, we quickly learned that the drive-by had some lasting repercussions. People in the area were still holding on to the memories of what had happened that day and were hesitant to return to their favorite local eating spot. It took some time, but thankfully, the diner's reputation of having the best burgers in town was enough to eventually bring folks back in.

The club was going to be okay—more than okay. Our prospects were continuing to show progress, and after proving himself with Terry and Kate, Shadow had been voted in as our new Enforcer. It was a position he'd earned, and I had no doubt that he would make us proud. While we'd taken a hit and no one's future is set in stone, there was one thing I knew for certain— when it comes to the brothers of Satan's Fury, it's going to take one hell of a fight to take us down.

EPILOGUE

Three months later

KEVIN'S BIRTHDAY had always been a special time for us, but this year was even more so. After going through another long round of testing, the doctors informed us that he was officially in his fourth year of remission. That in itself was enough to warrant a celebration, so I wanted to make this particular birthday party something he would remember. I called all the brothers and Kevin's buddies from school and football to invite them over to the house for a cookout. Just as I'd hoped, the minute I mentioned Kevin's party to Moose, he volunteered to grill some of his famous BBQ ribs and a pork shoulder, and Louise promised to bring one of her famous cakes. It would be a grand time for everyone, especially Kevin. Not only had I planned what I hoped would be a great party, I had a surprise coming for him that would make his day extra special.

On the morning of the party, we all worked together to get everything set up. While Kenadee and Mom worked to get things organized inside, Dad helped me in the backyard. We were putting the table cloths on the picnic tables when he asked, "Did ya get her?"

"Yeah. Riggs has her and is bringing her over when he comes."

"You think Kevin has any idea?"

I'd done my best to keep my gift a secret from Kevin and Kenadee. They'd both been hounding me for weeks about getting a Mastiff puppy, promising that they'd work together to make sure it was taken care of, but I'd told them both that there was no way in hell that I was going to get a dog—especially one the size of a fucking horse. I'd meant what I said, but after considering everything Kevin had been through over the past few years, I decided he deserved something special. There were times when I thought they knew what I was up to, but after seeing the way Kevin had been pouting for the past few days, I knew I had him fooled. "Nope. Not a chance."

"Good." My father smiled. "I can't wait to see the look on his face when he finally sees her."

"You and me both."

When we finished setting things up, I went over to the smoker to check on Moose. He'd been there for hours, tending to the coals and making sure everything was just right. I'd offered to keep an eye on things for him, but he turned me down, refusing to budge from his post. He was coating his ribs with another layer of his special sauce when I asked, "You need a hand?"

"Nah. I got it."

Some might say that Moose was a man who liked to tend to things himself and that's why he always refused to accept anyone's help, but I knew the real reason he didn't want a hand. He was scared I might figure out his recipe for his secret sauce and share it with the brothers. Since I didn't want to look a gift horse in the mouth, I just smiled and said, "Alright then. I'll leave you to it, but if you need anything, just let me know."

"You know I will."

When I walked back into the house, I found Kenadee in the kitchen with Kevin. They were both talking quietly at the counter, and for the first time in days, I actually saw my son smiling. He was crazy about Kenadee, and she was just as crazy about him. Over the past few months of living together, I'd learned lots of things about the woman I loved. Not only was she beautiful, smart, and sexy as hell, she was also incredible with my son. She absolutely adored him, and there wasn't anything she wouldn't do for him—which only made me love her even more. She looked up at me with one of her bright smiles as she said, "Hey there, handsome. How's it going out there?"

I went over and kissed her on the temple as I said, "We're all set. What about you? Need any help in here?"

"I think we got it. All the food is in the oven, and Louise just called to say she was headed this way with the cake."

"Awesome." I grabbed a bottle of water from the fridge as I asked, "Is Robyn still coming?"

"Yeah." Her face lit up at the sound of her best friend's name. Kenadee was worried that she and Robyn would drift apart after she moved out, but she'd worried for nothing; they were just as close as ever. With an excited look, she continued, "She should be here any minute, and she's bringing her new fella along with her."

"New fella?"

"Yeah. She hasn't been able to stop talking about him for the past few days, and I finally convinced her to bring him along."

"Good. I look forward to meeting this new fella of hers."

"Me, too." She looked down at her clothes, and as she started towards the bedroom, she said, "I'm going to get changed."

As soon as she left the room, Kevin leaned forward and whispered, "Did you get it?"

"Yeah. I got it."

"You think she's got any idea?"

Kevin wasn't the only one getting a surprise today. I also had something special planned for Kenadee as well. Kevin and my folks had made it clear that they were crazy about her, so they couldn't have been more excited when I shared my plans with them, especially Kevin. Seeing the concerned look on his face, I smiled and said, "No, buddy. I don't think she has a clue."

"Good."

When I noticed several trucks and bikes pulling into the drive, I looked out the window to see if Riggs had made it. When I spotted his truck, I looked over to Kevin and said, "Riggs just got here."

With an uninterested sigh, he replied, "So?"

"He's got something in his truck you might wanna go check out."

He perked up a little as he asked, "What's he got?"

"Why don't you go out there and see for yourself?"

When he got up and started for the door, I motioned for Kenadee to follow. When we stepped outside, the guys were all circling the grill like a bunch of vultures, but they all stopped to watch as Kevin walked over to Riggs. "Happy Birthday, buddy."

As he stood up on his tiptoes and tried to peek in the windows, Kevin said, "Dad said you've got something in your truck."

Riggs looked over to me and smiled. "Yeah, I do. You wanna see?"

"Yeah."

As he opened the door, he said, "Go check it out."

Kevin crawled inside the truck, and when he looked inside the box, he shouted, "Holy Toledo, Dad! You gotta come see this!"

I walked over and watched as my son lifted the small puppy into his arms. "Whatcha got there, buddy?"

His eyes lit up as he announced, "It's a puppy!"

"I see that."

"Isn't it cool? It's a Mastiff, Dad ... just like I told you I wanted."

"Yeah, it sure is. She's a real beauty, Kevin."

His eyes widened as he looked at me with surprise. "Wait ... *Is she for me?*"

"Yep. She's all yours."

"You're freaking kidding me!" With the puppy cradled in his arms, he jumped down out of the truck and gave me a big hug as he said, "Thank you, Dad!"

"You're welcome. I'm glad you like her."

"I more than like her, Dad. I love her!"

"Then you'll have to come up with a good name for her."

He turned to Kenadee, and showing that he valued her opinion, he asked, "What do you think we should name her?"

"Honey, that's something you'll have to decide. She's going to be your dog."

"Okay. I'll think of something."

With the puppy in tow, he rushed over to my folks to show them the new addition to the family. I couldn't help but smile as I watched him hug and kiss on her, like she was a prized treasure. I'd done good. My boy was happier than I'd seen him in years.

"You're a sneaky one, Sawyer Mathews. After all that stuff you said, I can't believe you actually went and got him that puppy."

"I know, but I just couldn't help myself. I guess I'm just a glutton for punishment."

"Pfft. The dog is going to be fine. You wait and see. You'll end up loving that crazy dog just as much as he does."

"Maybe, but I'll always love you more," I teased.

"Um-hmm. Either way, I think it was a wonderful gift. I don't think I've ever seen a happier kid."

I looked around the yard at my brothers and watched as they gathered around my son, sharing the special moment with him, and I realized just how lucky I really was. I was a man who had it all. Brothers who always had my back, a family who stood by me through thick and thin, a son who I adored, and a beautiful woman who I loved more than I ever dreamed possible. I had it all, and I wanted the world to know it. I reached in my pocket and pulled out an engagement ring. As I slipped it on her finger, I told her, "I think it's time we made this thing official."

Her mouth dropped open as she looked down at her hand and asked, "Did you just ask me to *marry you?*"

"I thought the ring was a dead giveaway, but yeah, I'm asking you to marry me." I placed my hands on her hips and pulled her close and said, "I want you to be my wife. You okay with that?"

Tears filled her eyes as she wrapped her arms around me and kissed me. "Yes, Sawyer. I'm definitely good with that."

"Good. 'Cause I wasn't taking no for an answer." After I turned and gave Kevin a thumbs up, letting him know she'd accepted my proposal, I leaned towards her and lowered my mouth to hers, giving her another kiss. "You're the only one, Kenadee. Now and forever."

The End

Shadow: Satan's Fury MC Memphis will release in July
A short excerpt of Diesel: Satan's Fury Book 8 will begin after the acknowledgments.

ACKNOWLEDGMENTS

Natalie Weston – I can't begin to thank you for all that you do for me. From the late night phone calls, last minute changes, and all my insecurities, you handle it all like a champ. Thanks for being awesome. Love ya, chick.

Ena and Amanda from Enticing Journey Book Promotions- Thank you for being such an amazing promotional company. You guys rock!

Lisa Cullinan – Yet again, you have managed to blow me away. Thank you for all your help with Blaze. You are the best, and it hasn't gone unnoticed. (I am still trying to get used to sharing you.)

Tempting Illustrations – Gel- thank you for your amazing teasers. I love them all! If you're looking for some amazing teasers, be sure to check them out. http://www.temptingillustrations.com

Neringa Neringiukas – I can't begin to thank you enough for all that you do. You are truly a blessing in my life, and I will be forever grateful for all the wonderful things you do.

Rose Holub- Thanks for being such an awesome proofer. You were such a big help this time.

Sue Banner- Thanks for being the final set of eyes on Blaze. I truly appreciate you help.

Terra Oenning, Amy Jones, and Daverba Ortiz- Thank you for continuing to post my books and teasers. You guys are awesome. It truly means so much to me that you take the time out of your busy day to sharing my work.

Tanya Skaggs and Charolette Smith- Thank you for reading Blaze early and giving me feedback. Thanks to you, he's even better. Your support means so very much to me.

Wilder's Women – I am always amazed at how much you do to help promote my books and show your support. Thank you for being a part of this journey with me. I read all of your reviews and see all of your posts, and they mean so much to me. Love you big!

A Special Thanks to Mom – I want to thank you for always being there and giving me your complete support. You are such an amazing person, and I am honored to call you my mom.

EXCERPT FROM DIESEL: SATAN'S FURY MC

PROLOGUE

Scotty

As a kid, I never knew much about my father—in fact, not a damn thing. I figured that my mother would've, at least, given me some small pieces of information about him if she thought he was even the slightest bit worth it. Instead, I convinced myself that he was just some deadbeat dad who'd left her in the lurch. A real man would've taken care of his kid regardless of what kind of relationship he had with his mother, so I decided he was better off kept in the shadows. He remained there the entire time I was growing up as I tried to pretend that neither his identity nor his actual existence bothered me. When I was three, Mom married Carl, and the pretending became a little easier. Carl was a good guy: kind-hearted and easygoing. He was older and already had kids from a previous marriage, so he had no problem adding one more.

Together, they worked their asses off to make sure that I had everything I could possibly need, and I don't mean by putting a roof over my head and clothes on my back, they loved me and made damn well sure I knew it.

Overall, I had it pretty good growing up. I was happy, but thoughts of my father were always in the back of my mind. Every time I looked in the mirror, I wondered if I had his eyes, his build, or if I looked *anything* like him at all. It was the nature of the beast to be curious about the man who had something to do with bringing me into this world. I often wondered if he would've been proud of how I'd turned out. By the time I had turned twenty-four, I figured I'd never find out, but that all changed when my mom got sick. She'd given her fight with cancer everything she had, but in the end, it got to be too much for her.

Things were looking bleak, and we all knew we could lose her at any time. After a long night at the shop, I came home and found Carl sitting on the front step with a beer in his hand. He wasn't one to drink, so I knew it had been a bad night. "She's been asking for you."

I patted him on the back and started towards her room. When I walked in, it was completely silent as the nurse hovered over her; suddenly, I worried that I'd gotten there too late. "Is she …"

"No, sweetheart. She's still holding on," she warmly replied as she made her way over to me. "She's been waiting for you to get home."

Dread washed over me as I looked towards her bed. Seeing my mother's frail, ashen body made my heart ache in a way that made it hard to breathe. I walked over to the edge of the bed and took her hand in mine; she was just skin and bones. I leaned towards her and whispered, "Hey, Momma. It's me, Scotty."

Her eyes slowly flickered opened as she turned to look at me. Her voice was weak and strained as she mumbled, "I need you to go … over to my jewelry box … Bring it to me."

"What for?"

"Just … bring it to me, Scotty."

"Okay, Momma." I walked over to her dresser, retrieved the small wooden box, and brought it back to her. "Here. I've got it."

"Open … the bottom drawer"—she watched me intently then took a deep breath—"and look under the fabric."

I did as she asked and found an old photograph hidden beneath the bottom layer of red velvet fabric. Carefully, I picked it up and studied the picture of a man who was standing next to a motorcycle. He looked to be about my age with shaggy, blond hair, and he was wearing a leather vest and jeans. The photograph was faded and yellow and looked like it was at least twenty years old. As I sat there staring at it, it quickly dawned on me that it was a picture of my father. I flipped it over and noticed a name and address written on the back and then looked over to Mom. "Is this really him?"

"Yes, sweetheart. That's your father." She sighed. "You should know … he doesn't know about you, Scotty."

"What?"

She placed her hand on mine as she continued, "I was young and naïve. He never loved me the way I loved him, Scotty. When he met Melinda … he fell head over heels for her … and forgot all about me. I was embarrassed ... I couldn't bring myself to tell him that I was pregnant."

"So, he never had *any* idea about me?"

"No, sweetheart. I left town ... as soon as I started showing." A tear trickled down her cheek. Listening to her say that he had no idea I was his son felt like the rug had been pulled out from under me.

"Why are you telling me this now?"

"I was wrong to keep you from him ... It wasn't fair to either of you. I was selfish, and I regret that now." She gave my arm a squeeze. "You should go to him ... and tell him who you are ... Tell him you're my son."

"It's too late, now. Too much time has gone by."

"It's never too late to meet your father, Scotty." Her voice trailed off as she turned and looked up at the ceiling. "I'm sorry I never told you sooner."

"You did now. That's all that matters," I assured her and then leaned over to place a kiss on her forehead. "Now, get some rest. It's been a long day."

Just as I was about to walk out of the room, I barely heard her soft voice, "You're a wonderful boy, Scotty. He'll be proud to know you're his."

I wasn't so sure she was right about that. I doubted any man would be exactly thrilled to know that he had a son he never knew about, only to have him show up at his door twenty-one years later. I didn't have a response for her, not one that she'd want to hear, so I just nodded with a half-hearted smile.

"I love you, Scotty."

"Love you, too, Mom."

When I left her room that night, I had no idea that it would be the last time I'd actually speak to her. The next morning, Mom had slipped into a coma and she died two days later. I did my best to be there for Carl, helping him with the funeral arrangements and everything in between, but once the dust had settled, I couldn't handle being in that house—not with all the memories. After I said my goodbyes, I packed a bag and got on my bike, hoping some time on the road would clear my head. A few days later, I found myself in Seattle. In the back of my mind, I think I always knew where I was going. I needed to see him—even if it was just from a distance. It was almost dark by the time I finally found the little brick house with a car and a Harley parked out by the garage. Relieved to see that the lights were on inside, I parked my bike across the street and waited, hoping that someone would eventually come out. Since I hadn't taken the time to search his name or even call the phone number listed on the back of the photograph, I had no idea if he still lived there.

After about an hour of sitting and waiting, the front door finally opened, and a man and a beautiful, young woman stepped outside. The woman rushed to her car, and with a big smile, waved to him and pulled out of the driveway. When I glanced back over to the man, I could tell he was older, much older, but there was no doubt he was the man in the photograph. As he got on his bike, I noticed he was wearing the same leather vest that he'd worn in the photograph. Curious to see where he might be going, I followed him out onto the main drag; after a twenty-minute drive, he turned down an old country road.

When he approached the entrance to an old warehouse, I held back and pulled over on the side of the road and watched as he drove through the gate. I killed my headlight and got off my bike, moving closer to get a better look. There were a bunch of bikes parked by the front door, and every time it opened, I heard loud music blaring from inside. Several guys were standing outside talking with beers in their hand and scantily dressed women at their side. It was right then when I realized my old man was part of a biker club.

One day, after following *my father* for almost two weeks, I went over to the diner across from their garage for a cup of coffee. I was staring out the window, watching the brothers wander in and out of the shop, and never noticed that the front door of the diner had opened. Seconds later, the seat across from me shifted, and I quickly turned to see why, only to get the shock of my life when I found my father staring back at me. "You wanna tell me why the fuck you've been tailing me?"

"What?"

"You don't think I've seen you?" he scoffed. "I know you've been watching me. I just wanna know why."

"I ... uh ... I," I stuttered, not having a clue what to tell him.

"You got a problem with me, kid?"

"No, sir. I got no problem with you." I certainly didn't want to piss him off. I knew what kind of man he was. Over the past few weeks of stalking him, I'd learned that he wasn't just *part of a club*, he was the fucking president. He'd actually been the one who founded the Chosen Knights. He and a group of his friends started riding together, but it quickly turned into something more. They lived by the motto "Chosen by Fate. Bound by Honor," and it was clear that my old man was pleased with his life and his club.

"You in some kind of trouble with the cops or something?"

I shook my head, "No, sir."

"Then, what the fuck is your deal?"

I didn't want to tell him I was his son, not until he had a chance to get to know me. I wanted to prove myself and show him that I was someone he could be proud of before I told him, so I decided to keep my true identity a secret, at least for the time being. "I was hoping I might be able to prospect for the club."

His eyebrows furrowed. "What makes you think I would let you prospect?"

"I don't know. I guess I was hoping you'd take a chance on me. I've heard a lot of good things about the Chosen and would really like to contribute."

"What the fuck have you got to contribute? The way I see it, you got nothing. I know you ain't got nobody you know around here. No job. No decent place to stay."

"How'd you know that?"

He tugged at his long, unruly beard and chuckled. "Hell, I've had eyes on you since that first night out at the house, boy. You been staying out at the old Weston place, which ain't exactly the nicest dive around"—he glanced down at my cup of coffee and plain piece of toast—"*and* you're running low on cash."

Most of the Chosen's brothers worked blue-collar jobs like mechanics, welders, and line workers. Eventually, they decided to pool their resources and open a shop of their own. Thinking I might be able to use that to my advantage, I said, "Yeah, but I've gotta lot of experience with engines. Almost eight years. There's not a motor I can't fix. New and old. I'm a hard worker, and I think I could be a real asset in your garage."

He sat there listening and studying me as I spoke. I wondered if he might've seen himself when he looked into my eyes. It was doubtful, but maybe, by some kind of intuition, he already knew I was his son. I'm not sure what he saw, but I could definitely tell the wheels were turning inside his head. A man like him wouldn't trust easily, not with the men he's dealt with, but for some reason he seemed to take stock in me. Otherwise, he wouldn't have asked, "You got a name, kid?"

"It's Scotty."

"Okay, Scotty. Are you good at doing what you're told?"

"Yes, sir."

"You know, prospecting isn't for everyone. It's grunt work at its best."

"Yes, sir. I'm good with that. I just need a chance."

He hesitated for a moment, then said, "I'm not making you any promises, but come over to the clubhouse tonight and we'll talk." He stood up and as he gave me a disapproving look, he said, "I'm guessing you still know where it is."

"Yes, sir."

"And kid?"

"Yeah?"

"Stop calling me sir. You're making me feel old as shit." He scowled at me and added, "Just call me Lucky."

I nodded. "Yes, sir."

Shaking his head, he walked towards the door. "See you tonight, kid."

That conversation changed the direction of my life in

ways I couldn't begin to imagine. I got to prospect for my old man and learned that not only was he a good man, loyal and hard-working, but I also discovered that he had a daughter—my half-sister, Zoe. I'd found what I was looking for, and I busted my ass to prove myself to the brothers and to my father. Almost a year had passed, and I'd yet to reveal my identity to my father. I tried to tell him, but the timing was never right. And with each new day, it became harder to come clean about who I really was to him. Now, I'd never get that chance. A few weeks before I was to be patched in, my father wrecked his bike, killing him on impact.

Nothing haunts a person more than the words we'd never get a chance to say. They fester and grow into something they weren't intended to be—lies and untold truths.

Zoe was devastated. Hell, I was, too. It seemed everything I'd worked for was in vain. Without my old man around, things quickly started going to shit in the club; I was actually relieved that no one knew who I was. I considered leaving, but deep down I knew I couldn't walk away from Zoe. Whether she realized it or not, she was family, and it was up to me to protect her. I had no idea how bad things would get after I'd made my decision to stick around, but I saw things that made my blood run cold and knew I had to get Zoe the hell out of there, especially when one of the brothers started making claims to her. Slider was a member of the Chosen with nothing but greed running through his veins—a piece of shit through and through. There was little I could do since I hadn't been patched in yet, but I couldn't have been more relieved after finding out she'd gotten herself tangled up with one of the brothers from Satan's Fury.

When they caught wind of what the Chosen were up to, and that Zoe was in danger, the Fury took them down. By the time they were done, there wasn't a trace of their club or any of their shit left behind. Zoe was finally free, and for that matter, so was I. Once the dust settled, I laid it all out there and told Zoe everything, and when it was all said and done, we'd both found ourselves at the footsteps of the Satan's Fury clubhouse.

DIESEL

One Year Later

LOYALTY. Code. Brotherhood. For the longest time, those were all just words to me. When I made the mistake of prospecting for the Chosen, I threw myself into a world of treachery, betrayal, and death, just so I could try and prove myself to a man who didn't even know I was his son. It wasn't until I spent a year prospecting for the brothers of Satan's Fury when I started to understand what it meant to belong to something that was bigger than yourself. It wasn't easy. Hell, it was one of the hardest things I'd ever done, draining me emotionally, physically, and mentally. I was always on the road, going on runs and following orders, but in doing so, I got to know each and every one of them on a different level. They weren't just members of some club; they were brothers. With them, I gained a sense of family, and by the time I got my patch, there wasn't a single one of them who I wouldn't lay my life on the line for, and there was no doubt they'd do the same for me.

I sat in the truck next to Clutch and groaned while I stretched out my legs, knocking them against the side door. "Damn. I hate a fucking cage."

"You and me both, brother, but with this weather, we don't have a choice," Clutch grumbled and kicked up the windshield wipers, trying to clear the snow and ice from the windshield.

We'd just left Topeka, Kansas and were headed down to Memphis, Tennessee; it was a drive we'd taken many times before. A couple of years back, Cotton, the club's president, had worked out a deal with several of the other Satan's Fury's affiliate chapters to broaden the club's distribution. Together, they'd created a pipeline for transporting illegal weapons, which had grown bigger than any of them had expected. As road captain, it was Clutch's job to ensure the safety of the route from Washington to Memphis. In doing so, he had to change up the exchange points with our affiliate chapters in Salt Lake, Denver, Topeka, Oklahoma City and Memphis. Each location had to be off the radar with obscure entrance and exit points, and it was up to Clutch to find them and make sure the pipeline stayed intact.

I had no idea how long we'd been driving when I asked, "How long until we get to Norman?"

"We'll hit the Oklahoma border in about an hour and a half; it's another two hours from there." He looked over to me, and when he noticed the look of agony on my face, he mocked, "I'm guessing with that peanut-sized bladder of yours, you need a break."

"Peanut-sized bladder? Cut me some slack, man. We've been in this damn truck for seven hours, and my fucking ass is killing me."

"I hear ya. Mine, too." Over the past year, Clutch and I have spent a lot of time together. As a prospect, I did lots of traveling with him, and while all the guys were great, there was something about Clutch that was just easy. I enjoyed my new role as his right-hand man. He was level-headed and rarely let anything get to him, which was a good thing when you were dealing with the brothers of Satan's Fury, where opinions were dished out whether you wanted to hear them or not. His ol' lady, Liv, was pregnant and expecting in the next couple of months, so I knew he was eager to get back—meaning we weren't going to make many stops. I was relieved when he looked over at me and said, "We'll pull off at the next exit."

I nodded and stared out the window, praying for an exit to be close. "You wanna grab a bite to eat while we're there."

"Might as well. Then, maybe we can make it to the Wellington exit before we stop for the night."

After a quick pit stop, we stretched our legs and grabbed some food for the road. It started to snow again as soon as we got back on the road, but we still managed to make good time and pulled into Wellington a few hours later. Clutch had a few locations to check, and once he'd found a place he felt would suit our needs for the pipeline, we pulled into the parking lot of a small pizza place right next to our motel. After ordering our food and drinks, I asked Clutch, "You met Liv down in Memphis, right?"

"Yep." He nodded with a proud smile. "Met her at Daisy Mae's."

"Daisy Mae's? Is that a strip club or something?"

He shook his head. "Fuck, no. It's a diner. The club owns it and the apartment upstairs. While I was there, I stayed in the apartment next to hers, and one thing led to another."

"Did you ever consider staying in Memphis?"

"Hell, no. It's a great place to visit, but I wouldn't live there for shit. I know where home is, and it sure as hell ain't in Tennessee."

Even though I've only been a member of the club for a short time, I knew exactly what he meant. I'd found my home, and there was no other place I'd rather be. Turning to look out the window, I noticed that it had finally stopped snowing. We still had a long drive, so I was hoping that it would finally clear up for good. As soon as we finished eating, we walked over to the motel and grabbed a room. After a few hours of sleep, Clutch was up and ready to roll. Relieved I wouldn't be the one driving, I pulled myself out of bed, used the bathroom, threw some clothes on, and started out to the truck.

It was still dark outside when he started up the engine, but it was clear that Clutch was eager to get going. "Do you need anything before we get out on the road?"

"Is this your way of saying that we're not stopping until we get to Memphis?"

He gave me a small shrug. "It's only six hours, brother. No sense in wasting time."

"Just need a cup of coffee, and I'll be set."

"You can grab one when we hit the gas station up the road."

The minute Clutch pulled up to the gas pump, I jumped out and went inside to get us both some much-needed coffee and a bite to eat; by the time I walked out the door, he was back inside the truck waiting for me. As soon as I got settled, he pulled out onto the main road, and we were on our way to Memphis. Clutch was one of those quiet drivers, spending his time focusing on the road or inside his own head, so I spent the first two hours dozing in and out. By the time we hit Arkansas, I was getting pretty restless; my thoughts turned to meeting the brothers from the Memphis chapter, when I realized I didn't know a lot about them. Hoping to get a better insight to the men I was about to meet, I turned to Clutch and asked, "So, Gus ... he's the president, right?"

"Yeah. He's a good guy. Reminds me of Cotton. Runs his club with honor, even with all the bullshit that goes on in that town. I also got to know Blaze pretty well when I was working at the shop. The guy works his ass off to keep the place running right. He's got a kid named Kevin, who he's raising on his own. His wife died a few years ago, which makes it hard, since his kid's been sick."

"What's wrong with him?"

"He had some kind of cancer, but he's been in remission for a while now. I think Blaze is worried that it might come back," he explained.

"That's gotta be tough."

"No doubt, but he's doing the best he can. I've kept in touch with him, and the last I heard, they were doing alright." I could hear the concern in his voice as he spoke, which made me wonder if he was worried about him getting sick again.

"And the others?"

"I really didn't get to spend a lot of time with many of them." He thought for a moment, then continued, "There's Cyrus. He runs the diner, and he helped me and Liv out when that asshole, Daniel Perry, came looking for them. I'm not sure if you heard about that nightmare. Perry's father and Olivia's were real estate business partners. In order to fuck up a huge development project, that greedy douchebag, Daniel, killed her folks and was planning on doing the same to Liv and her younger brother and sister, thinking he'd get rid of any witnesses. That didn't work out too well for him." He sighed with a disgusted look on his face. "So, I owe Cyrus a lot."

"I see that, and I'm looking forward to meeting them. So, what's the plan when we get there?"

"I'll meet with Gus and go over the changes with the route. I figure we'll crash there tonight. I want to check in with Blaze and Sam and see how they're doing. We can head back in the morning."

"Sam?"

"Sam ... well, that's a long story," he scoffed.

"All I've got is time, brother. Let's hear it." Clutch spent the next half hour telling me how Liv met Sam at the diner. At the time, he was a homeless vet, and she had a soft spot for the old guy. Turned out that he had one for her, too, and he'd been keeping an eye on her and the kids, helping them stay safe during that whole fiasco. Not too long afterwards, the club took him in as a prospect, and now he's a patched member. "Damn. It's a good thing he was around when that asshole came looking for them."

"Yeah, there's no telling what would've happened if he hadn't been there."

We continued talking for the next few hours, which

made the long ride much more bearable. By the time we pulled up to the clubhouse gate, Clutch had told me everything about his time in Memphis, and I felt more prepared to meet the brothers. He rolled down his window when he saw one of the prospects heading over to us. "Clutch and Diesel. We're here to see Gus."

He gave us a quick nod and motioned us on through. Clutch pulled up to the front door and parked the truck. I followed him inside, and as soon as we stepped through the door, someone called out, "Clutch! How's it going, man?"

"Hey, Murph," Clutch answered as he started walking towards one of the brothers with long, shaggy hair and a scruffy beard. Clutch gave him a quick side hug and a slap on the back as he said, "Good to see ya, brother."

"We weren't expecting you until later this afternoon."

"Made good time." Clutch smiled proudly. "I don't reckon you've met Diesel. He's one of our newest members."

Murph extended his hand as he replied, "Good to meet, Diesel. Did you have a good trip?"

"It was alright, but damn, the snow was really coming down at times."

"Heard it's pretty bad up north."

"Yeah. It's a hell of a mess, but it cleared up once we got out of Oklahoma," Clutch replied.

"Hope that shit doesn't make its way down here. People around here lose their mind with just an inch. I can't imagine what they'd do with a foot of snow."

"I think you're safe for now." Clutch chuckled. "Hey, is Gus around?"

"Yeah. He's in his office." Murph turned and called out

to one of the guys at the bar. "Hey, Runt. Clutch is here to see Gus. You mind taking him back?"

He stood up and started walking over to us. "Clutch. Good to see ya, brother."

"You, too, Runt." After he shook hands with him, Clutch turned towards me and said, "I shouldn't be long."

"Take your time," Murph told him. "We'll be waiting for you in the bar."

Clutch nodded, then followed Runt down the hall. Once he was gone, Murph led me into the bar. When we walked in, the place was deserted, so I assumed most of their guys were like us and worked during the day. Murph grabbed us a couple of beers, and as he offered me one, he sat down behind the counter. He didn't look like your typical Sergeant of Arms, but there was a fierceness behind his eyes that let me know he wasn't a man you'd want to get tangled up with. He ran his hand over his beard as he said, "Clutch mentioned that you were new to the club."

"I am." I took a drink of my beer before I said, "Got my patch about a month ago."

"I've only been around him a couple of times, but from what I could tell, Cotton is one of the good ones."

"He is. Proud to be a part of his club," I told him truthfully. "Some of the best men I know."

We spent the next hour talking about anything from reconstructing engines to football playoffs, and just as we were finishing our beer, a hot little number came up behind Murph and slipped her arm around his waist. She leaned towards him, whispering something in his ear, and as he listened, a smirk crossed his face. Once she was done, he looked back at her and said, "Not now, darlin'. We've got company."

After his rejection, she turned her attention to me. As her eyes slowly roamed over my cut, a sexy smile spread across her face. "And who is this handsome fella?"

"This here is Diesel. One of our boys from up North."

"Hi there, Diesel. I'm Jasmine." In a seductive tone, she continued, "It's really nice to meet you."

"Nice to meet you, too."

"Can I get you both another beer?"

"Get us a couple out of the back cooler. Need to restock the one behind the bar," Murph answered.

"Sure thing, babe."

Once she was gone, I looked over to Murph and asked, "She your ol' lady?"

"Hell, no. Jasmine is one of the hang-arounds. Sweet girl, but just like all the chicks around here, she's too young and naïve for me."

Surprised by his response, I said, "So, I take it you don't have an ol' lady."

He shrugged. "Hard to find a woman strong enough to tame the beast."

"Gotcha." I laughed. "It can be a struggle."

Before he could respond, Clutch walked in with an older guy sporting a thick, gray beard following behind. Murph looked over to them and asked, "What about it, Prez? Did y'all get the new drop-off points worked out?"

"We did."

Clutch added, "A couple are a little out of the way, but it's better to be safe than sorry."

"You got that right," Gus answered. "You chose well. Cotton was right to put it in your hands."

"Thanks, Gus. Appreciate that," Clutch replied.

"When's the next run?"

"In just over two weeks. If we ..."

His voice trailed off when Jasmine walked back into the bar. As she placed our beers on the counter, she looked over to me and asked, "Will you be staying at the club tonight?"

"Sorry, darlin'," a man's voice replied. "They've decided to stay over at Daisy Mae's tonight."

Clutch looked over to Gus, and with his hand extended out to him, he said, "Thanks for giving us a place to crash, Gus. I could use a decent meal and a good night's sleep."

"I'm sure you can after that long-assed drive. I'll give Cyrus a call and let him know you'll be heading over."

"Tell him it'll be a bit. I thought I'd run by the garage and see Blaze before we head over."

Gus nodded. "I'm sure he'd be glad to see you, and Sam, too. He's been helping out, and turns out, he's a damn good mechanic."

"Glad to hear that," Clutch replied. "It'll be good to catch up."

"Be careful heading back tomorrow, and let Cotton know I'll be calling him."

As we started towards the door, Jasmine came over to me and said, "Bye, handsome. If you're ever back in town, be sure to come by. I'd love the chance to get to know you better."

"I'll keep that in mind," I told her with a smile.

I followed Clutch outside, and my stomach started to growl as we headed towards the truck. "You said Daisy Mae's had good burgers, right?"

"Best around," he answered as he got inside the truck and closed the door.

"Any chance we'll be going by there any time soon?"

"Soon enough," he mocked. "Trust me. It will be worth the wait."

ELLIE

I had two choices. I could face my fear and risk losing everything, including my life, or I could run. Maybe if I'd had more time to think about the consequences, I would've chosen differently, but instead, I did the only thing I thought I could. With only the clothes on my back and a few bucks in my wallet, I ran. Consumed with panic, my legs didn't feel like my own as I rushed out to my car and got inside, locking the doors behind me. It was as if I was watching a horror movie play out in slow motion, and as much as I wanted to make it all stop, I couldn't. With my hand trembling, I placed the keys in the ignition and started the car. In my entire life, I couldn't remember ever being so scared, and the thought that it was just the beginning on

Made in the USA
Monee, IL
19 February 2020

22028557R00157